Children's books by
Michael LaLumiere and Kim Messinger

Princess Caitlin's Tiara
Birthday Snow

WHY IS CRATER LAKE SO BLUE?

A Novel by Michael LaLumiere

Stagger Lee Books
Peoria, Arizona

LCCN: 2007901466
ISBN: 978-0-9791006-2-8

Cover photograph by Quang-Tuan Luong
Cover and book design by 1106 Design
Maps by Carol Zuber-Mallison

www.whyiscraterlakesoblue.com

Published by Stagger Lee Books
P.O. Box 442
7558 W. Thunderbird Rd Suite 1
Peoria, Arizona 85381

Dedication

For my father, who deserved a more forgiving son.

"*The national park is the best idea America ever had.*"
— JAMES BRYCE, BRITISH AMBASSADOR TO THE U.S., 1912

"*If future generations are to remember us with gratitude rather than contempt, we must leave them more than the miracles of technology. We must leave them a glimpse of the world as it was in the beginning, not just after we got through with it.*"
— PRESIDENT LYNDON B JOHNSON
ON SIGNING THE WILDERNESS ACT, 1964

Acknowledgements

I cannot describe how important my wife, Gail, has been to me in the writing of this book, and in every other meaningful project I've ever undertaken. She found me years ago, nervous about the future and unsure if I could ever accomplish anything good. Her unwavering support has made all the good things in my life possible. As my mother tells me, I am a very lucky man, because Gail is one of a kind.

Kim Messinger was my personal editor on the book. The book would never have been started or finished without her extraordinary effort to see me through it. Poor Kim. She constantly poked, prodded and pulled me through this project. She agonized over every sentence and phrase; her words and ideas are sprinkled throughout the text. If the book has any success at all it will be because of her dedication.

Rosanne Catalano came along at just the right time. A professional editor, she stood fast against my childish rejection of correct punctuation and capitalization. More importantly, her enthusiasm for the story and characters lifted my spirits and helped me believe that I had accomplished something good.

When I first considered this project, I ran across an unofficial log of events at Crater Lake during the time of the water crisis. The log had been kept by the Smith brothers — Larry and Lloyd. The brothers served as seasonal rangers at Crater Lake National Park for many, many years. The log in Chapter 10 is largely based on their recollections. Their unofficial written history was invaluable in creating timeframes. I would have been lost without it.

Several of the details in this book regarding the water crisis at Crater Lake National Park in 1975 are true, but many are not, and serve only to provide fodder for the fictional story. All characters, other incidents and dialogue are drawn from the author's imagination and are not to be construed as factual.

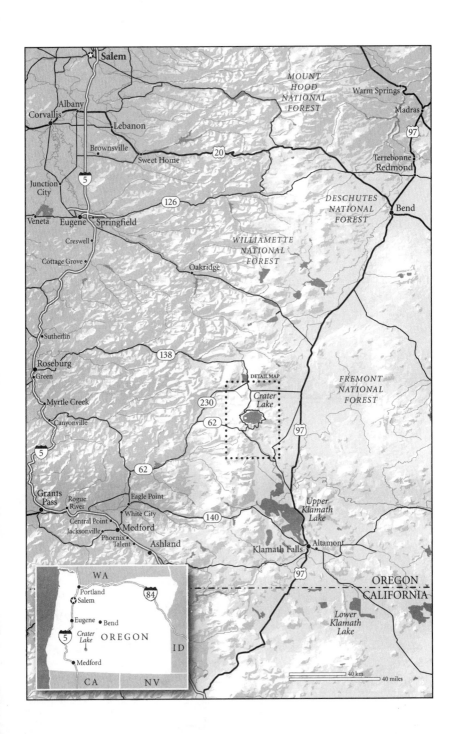

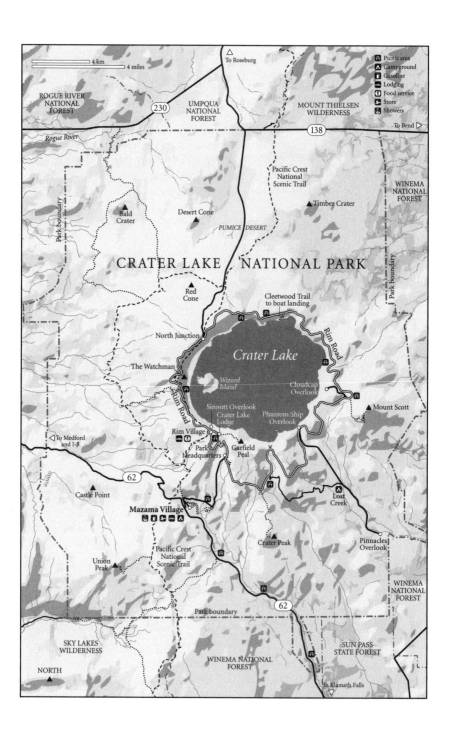

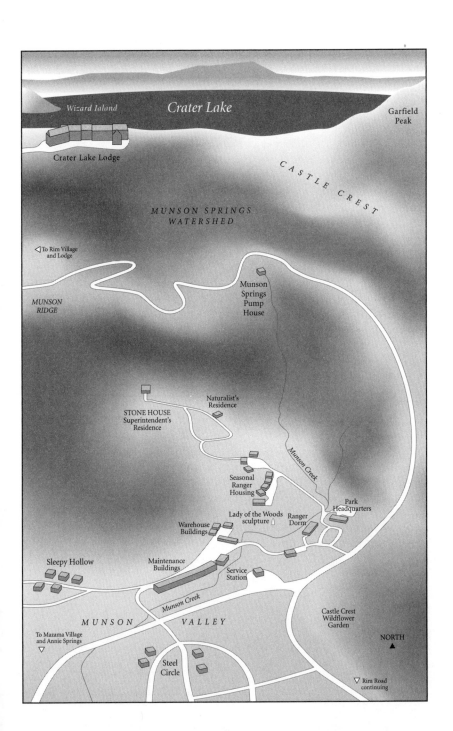

Wizard Island

Crater Lake

Garfield Peak

Crater Lake Lodge

CASTLE CREST

MUNSON SPRINGS WATERSHED

◁ To Rim Village and Lodge

MUNSON RIDGE

Munson Springs Pump House

Naturalist's Residence

STONE HOUSE Superintendent's Residence

Munson Creek

Seasonal Ranger Housing

Park Headquarters

Lady of the Woods sculpture

Ranger Dorm

Warehouse Buildings

Sleepy Hollow

Maintenance Buildings

Service Station

Munson Creek

Castle Crest Wildflower Garden

MUNSON VALLEY

To Mazama Village and Annie Springs ▽

NORTH ▲

Steel Circle

▽ Rim Road continuing

CHAPTER 1

June 4, 1975

THE GREEN ROAD SIGN SAID fifty-three miles to Crater Lake. Hard rain splattered against the windshield. Trucks carrying King Kong–sized trees threw off blankets of water as they roared past me, going the opposite way toward the lumber mills in Klamath Falls. Not much traffic going my way—Northwest on Highway 97—on a Monday morning in June. Even with the monsoon, I was making good time.

The summer of 1975 was going to change my life. Tomorrow I started work at Crater Lake National Park and I couldn't wait to start punching that government-wage, going-to-pay-for-college time clock.

This job paid more than I had ever made. My dad would laugh at that. "What job have you ever had, son?" I tried not to think about my father. Nothing was going to ruin my summer. All I needed to know was the job paid five-fifty an hour and I got free room and board at a national park. Actually, it wasn't free room and board. I'd be charged a dollar a week for a room in a cabin and I had to buy and cook my own food. But that was close enough for me.

Yes, it was just a maintenance job. Not even that, really. Flunky first class under some grizzled old plumber guy, probably. I might be digging ditches or raking leaves or cleaning bathrooms. I didn't care. Bring on the port-o-potty! I didn't get the job because the Park Service wanted me to run Crater Lake National Park. This summer would be all about hunkering down in my cabin, saving every penny I could.

Next fall, I'd be a junior in college—University of Oregon. By my calculations I could make enough money this summer to pay my way through an entire year of school. That would be like pulling a giant hatchet out of my neck. Yeah, my father was real cavalier about giving me the money, but the second I got it, it was, "You know I had to borrow that," or "You better be hitting the books, I didn't give you that money to screw around," or "What do you mean you're an English major, where is that going to take you?" Drop dead. I had to take the money for tuition, but I ate greasy hamburgers every night and washed dishes in the steaming back room of a cafeteria so I didn't have to ask for money for anything else. My senior year in high school he had said money was no problem, I didn't have to worry about it. RIGHT.

On my way to financial freedom, I drove along the part of Highway 97 that hugged the hills that bumped up against Klamath Lake. If Crater Lake was supposed to be the deepest, purest lake in the United States, then Klamath Lake had to be the shallowest and most dingy.

I'd driven by Klamath Lake thousands of times. My parents lived just east of Klamath Falls, so this was the way to college in Eugene, to Portland, to all points north—almost anywhere else in Oregon, really. The lake always seemed to stretch on forever. I kept glancing over, through the raindrops on my side window. Like everything else today, the lake was gray. Even on bright sunny days, it reminded me of dishwater. I spent a couple summers waterskiing on Klamath Lake. It wasn't so bad, except for all the dead fish. About every other year, there'd be a huge fish kill because of the pesticides and other nasty cattle by-products washing into the lake. Sometimes you had to be real nimble on those water skis, like a boxer, bobbing and weaving as the boat kicked up fish that flew at your head. Nothing worse than a dead fish sandwich. And you'd better keep your knees bent when you hit a school of dead perch or you'd skid into a nasty wipeout.

Klamath Lake was about twenty-eight miles long and several miles across. With all that water, you would never guess that, in many parts of the lake, you could get out of your boat, stand on the bottom and only have water come up to your chest. Of course, you wouldn't do that because the lake was thick with algae. You couldn't tell what was down there. And on the protected, pretty side of the lake, only first-timers stopped for leisurely wading because swarms of mosquitoes would descend like a buzzing, biting rainstorm.

I turned left off Highway 97 onto Highway 62, also called the Crater Lake Highway, and drove around Upper

Klamath Lake. Upper Klamath isn't actually part of the lake anymore. The water was pumped out long ago and it's all hayfields now. In the days when Indians still called the shots, Klamath Lake was probably at least three times as big. But much of the reclaimed lake is now used to graze cattle or for farming. Houses are sprinkled around the fields.

I had taken this two-lane country road once before—the only time I'd ever been to Crater Lake. The rain poured down that day too. My dad drove. Whenever he got mad at someone, he drove somewhere. He must not have been mad at me that time, because I was with him when we got to Rim Village, overlooking Crater Lake. After that day, I could say I'd been to Crater Lake, but I hadn't actually seen Crater Lake because, on that day, the crater where the lake resides was socked in. The lake lies at the bottom of the crater, one thousand feet, straight down. Apparently, spring mornings are about the worst time to try to see the lake.

So my dad and I had stood at a lake lookout, solitary figures about fifteen yards apart, staring into the impenetrable white fog. I must have been about seventeen, so we had lived in Oregon for about a year. My dad was stationed at Kingsley Field in Klamath Falls then and I went to Henley High School out in hay-growing country.

Because snow blocked the road around the lake until midsummer, the only thing left to do was go to the gift shop and buy potato chips for the ride back. We walked across the parking lot, the evaporating ice and snow floating above the warming black top like steam.

Then I did get to see Crater Lake—or, at least, pictures of it—because its likeness was plastered on everything sold in the store. Postcards, t-shirts, salt and pepper shakers, spoons. Even toothbrushes. Apparently, awestruck tourists will buy just about anything. The only other thing I remembered about that trip was that my father and I drove all the way home without speaking a word. On the drive up, we'd had a typical verbal exchange. Like always, he'd asked a question in his sergeant's tone.

"How are your grades going to be this time?"

It always felt like an interrogation. I usually answered in less than five syllables. "Fine."

"Do you think your sister needs help with her math?"

"Yes."

"Will you help her?"

"Sure."

Dad's body language made it clear that my interpersonal skills were unsatisfactory. I think the only reason he said anything to me at all was because silence made him uncomfortable. That was no problem for me. Silence was a friend of mine. I could always escape by losing myself in what I saw out the window. It took my parents years to figure out that sending me to my room was a reward, not a punishment. During our silent journey home I glanced over at my poor dad. His lips moved fast in a silent rant about something or somebody.

On this second visit to Crater Lake, I was on my own. At Fort Klamath Junction, I took another left.

In southern Oregon you have about four different kinds of terrain—rolling ranch land, Douglas Fir forests, high plains and mountains. Now it felt like I had entered a transition area. I had left the rolling ranch land of the Klamath

Basin and entered a high plains valley. The pine forests crept in on both sides and the mountains rose in front of me. Klamath Lake was in the rearview mirror. I wasn't going to miss that lake. Up ahead looked much more interesting.

I'd never been this lucky before. A week ago I was set to work the food line at a lodge near Mount Shasta. Minimum wage. Had to pay a lot more than a dollar a week for a room. I wasn't going to accumulate much money for school and it was all my fault. I was awful at finding summer work. Most summers I didn't work at all. I couldn't bring myself to ask anybody for a job. Sad, but true. All the other kids worked. I slept. My dad steamed. Thank God when school started again. I wasn't a lazy kid. I was just too petrified to walk into some business and ask someone I didn't know for a job. It was like asking a girl for a date. I couldn't do that, either. Nobody got that, especially my dad. How could a father live with a son for twenty years and not get that? Shouldn't a father study his son? Shouldn't he be able to see past any disappointment he feels? I'm sure I missed important signs about him, but I was the kid and he was the adult.

I remembered being at baseball practice in junior high. I played catcher and the ball bounced past me to the backstop. I heard someone yell, "Chase that ball, fat boy." It was my dear dad. What an idiot. Just one of many scars I'll have the rest of my life. He deserves the son he's got.

But those were the bad old days, right, Sam? A bona fide miracle had rocked my underachieving world. Out of the blue, my mother found me a great job. She had a friend at the Klamath Falls office of the National Park Service and she put in a word for me. I didn't even know she'd done it.

A summer maintenance position opened up at the very last minute and she got a call. I hit the lottery.

It was like mom to come through for me when I needed it. She was always secretly in my corner, even when I'd battled her and my father over almost everything since I can remember. In the middle of some skirmish over how long my sideburns were or why didn't I take shop class in school, she'd ask if she could fix me a plate because I had missed dinner. Didn't matter if missing dinner had started the fight. That was mom. It drove my dad up the wall.

While he laid down some law, the last thing he needed was his wife being nice to his disrespectful-slacker-thinks-he's-smarter-than-me kid. If I kept from laughing, I won. I got a plate of food. If I listened till he was ranted out, I could just stare at him like, "Is that it?" Odds were he wouldn't hit me. If I laughed, well, who knows? Don't laugh. Eventually, he'd go on a tilt and storm off toward the backyard. Game over.

Actually, Dad only ever hit me once, after I smarted off to my mother when I was in the fifth grade. He hit me hard. I deserved it.

My mother didn't understand me any better than my dad, but at least she had normal parental instincts—not everything she said or did crushed my floundering confidence. She had a fierce temper except when it came to me. She and my father would yell and scream at each other for days on end up to about my fourteenth birthday. Then it stopped. It was like mom suddenly decided life was fine just the way it was. And my dad decided he didn't always have to be right. They became teammates of a sort. But I honestly don't remember either of them hugging me or being affectionate with me until the day I left for college. That day mom cried and hugged me goodbye before I squeezed into the loaded car. A few miles down the road, dad said I shouldn't hold it against her that she had stayed home. Saying goodbye in Eugene would just be more than she could manage, he said. I guess I didn't really understand my mom any more than she understood me.

Up ahead, I saw a row of buildings on each side of the road. A large, fading sign said, "Welcome to Fort Klamath, Population 126." This was definitely a one-street town: no stoplight, no stop sign, a general store, a small restaurant and a few houses, with more houses scattered back off the main road. The most interesting thing about Fort Klamath was the Wood River. Slow-moving mountain streams like the Wood come down to the high plains thick and flush with water. The still-pristine stream ducked under the road midway through town and reluctantly headed for its fate in Klamath Lake.

Just on the other side of Fort Klamath, another sign told me I had six miles to the south entrance of Crater Lake National Park. I could see a pine forest ahead and off to one side, but the mountains that had loomed over me earlier had disappeared as the gray sky hung heavier and darker. The rain grew more hostile. There might have been a little ice in the mix now. I guessed I was at about forty-two hundred feet of elevation. Could it really snow in June?

Ahead, a hole opened in the pine forest; I drove toward it and then into it. "Welcome to Crater Lake National Park," the sign said. Hmm. I was expecting a gate or a ranger or something, but instead I was simply sucked into the dark forest. And yes, it was starting to snow. The map said eight miles to Annie Springs where I was supposed to turn right. Then another couple miles to park headquarters.

The drive to Annie Springs was beautiful, but you had to like pine trees because that's all there was to see—except for the tall orange snow poles on both sides of the road. The patches of snow by the road grew into full-fledged snowbanks by the time I drove past the boarded-up ranger station and over the Annie Springs Bridge.

As my tired, blue Volkswagen bug chugged up toward park headquarters, the gentle snow turned into a legitimate and annoying blizzard. Crater Lake averages 531 inches of snow a year. But at 11:00 on the morning of June 4th, 1975, I didn't expect to be driving in near-whiteout conditions. I hadn't really expected to see any snow. What in the world was going on? I could see the headline:

Maintenance Flunky Killed in Freak Summer Snow Blizzard, Park Service Mourns

A hole in the six-foot wall of snow on the left side of the road turned out to be the driveway to the park headquarters parking lot. I'd made it. As I later found out, the road around the rim of Crater Lake doesn't even open until after the Fourth of July. The way the snow came down that day, I would have guessed maybe September.

CHAPTER 2

I CHECKED IN AT PARK HEADQUARTERS, a big building made of rock and wood. Very historic-like. A noisy fire blasted heat from an enormous fireplace. The grayish woman behind the front desk looked over her bifocals and told me I could wait outside. She would call my boss on the radio. Her tone told me that I had no other option. I took a seat on the rock steps out front. Apparently, early June wasn't a time many tourists visited the park—there were no cars in the parking lot. The blizzard was still going strong.

A green park service pickup skidded to a stop in front of me. The man behind the steering wheel waved me over.

"Get in, I'm Dan Jenkins, I'm the Buildings and Utility foreman. We've got a little problem with your cabin, but we should be able to get you in there today. You're Hunter, right?"

I nodded. It would be nice to have accommodations for the night. It would be a long commute from Klamath Falls. "So what's the problem with the cabin?"

"It's under a snowbank. And the chimney's a little wobbly."

How do you know the chimney's wobbly if the cabin is under a snowbank? I asked myself.

"The 'cat we use to dig out the cabins snagged the top of the chimney. Like I said, it's a little wobbly. But don't worry, happens all the time."

As we drove, Dan explained that all seasonal maintenance workers lived in Sleepy Hollow, which turned out to be a meandering circle of cabins located on the far side of the maintenance yard. When the seasonals left at the end of the each summer, the cabins were boarded up and left unattended until they were dug out from under tons of snow in June.

I now saw how a snowplow could collide with a chimney sitting on top of a two-story cabin. I assumed there were cabins under all that, but the snowbanks were taller than most roofs. Monster-sized metal culverts reached out from under the white mounds. I guessed the culverts must be attached to cabins. Before this, the only place I'd seen a culvert was planted under a road so water could flow.

Then Dan pulled up in front of my home-sweet-home. I recognized it by the chimney bricks scattered out front and in the road. Redwood paneling peeked out from behind the drifts. I could hear the snowcat working out back.

"That chimney problem isn't going to asphyxiate me, is it, Dan?"

"No problem, we'll have that fixed up in a jiffy. Why don't you just wait here? You won't be able to get your car in yet anyway. I need to go back to the maintenance shed and get some tools to get this place opened up."

Out I got. *Welcome to Crater Lake National Park, Sam—cold, dark, blowing snow and twenty-five degrees at a little past noon on June 4th.* Even for someone who likes weather, this seemed bleak. Back at park headquarters I had pulled my old parka out of the backseat of the bug and put it on. My father thought I was nuts for bringing it and I hadn't been sure about it myself. But they said to bring warm clothes and that was the warmest thing I owned.

Whap! The 'cat driver had hit the cabin again.

Two hours later Dan still hadn't made it back. Charlie, the snowcat driver, had given me a shovel to dig out the front porch while he dug out the rest of the cabin—only denting the wood paneling here and there. A snowcat is basically a small tractor with a scoop. It can push snow around in tight places. But Charlie clearly wasn't into precision plowing. I leaned on my shovel and looked back down the road. Who were those two?

Two people in large coats with hoods had appeared from a door in the long maintenance building and now trudged slowly toward the cabin. Really, really slowly. I turned back to shoveling. Those boys weren't going to arrive anytime soon.

The snowstorm eased up a little. Looking back toward the maintenance yard, I stared at the cliffs that dominated the horizon. The giant rock wall must be a thousand feet high. From where I stood, the cliffs rose up behind the maintenance building. The storm clouds poured over the top and swept down into the valley. The gray clouds moved so fast that they looked like a waterfall.

There were about twelve cabins in Sleepy Hollow. A street of packed snow ran in a circle through the carved-out housing space. A stream cut across the middle. I couldn't see where the water came from or where it went because of the snowdrifts. And thousands of mature, majestic, forest-green Hemlocks grew south and east, as far as I could see.

I heard Dan's truck and looked up from my shoveling. He had stopped to pick up the two slow walkers.

Charlie roared around from the other side of the cabin with a scoop full of snow. He pulled up next to me. He waved and yelled something. I couldn't hear what he said over the engine noise and the blowing wind, but reading his lips it looked like, "All done. I'm outta here. See you later." And then he gunned the engine and off he went. The icy conditions didn't slow him down even a little bit.

Dan gave Charlie a wide berth as he drove by. I guess he didn't want any dents in his truck. After Charlie was safely past and heading back to maintenance, Dan drove up to the cabin with his two passengers.

Everybody got out of the truck and joined me on the almost-clear porch.

"Sam, these are your two new roommates." I nodded. Obviously, these guys had been here before. They weren't surprised by their surroundings. They also knew enough to be wearing parkas in June. Dan pulled out a key ring with about two hundred keys. He tried one. Nope. Tried another. Tried another. "Finally—okay, let's get inside and see if we can get this place set up for you guys."

While Dan walked around the cabin, checking to see what worked and what didn't I introduced myself to my new roommates. It was a tough room.

Sarge looked to be about sixty-five, sixty-six, somewhere in there. He had a pipe that was perpetually in need of a light. He was a worn-down old Army non-com, should-be-sitting on-a-porch-in-a-rocking-chair-telling-war-stories kind of guy. Sarge talked a lot. Sarge kept talking even when someone was answering his questions. The words came out with a nasty little laugh attached. I think I heard him say that he lived in Medford in a trailer, he'd worked here ten summers and this was going to be his last year. The pipe clenched in his teeth didn't make for a clear exchange of ideas.

Johnny Sukraw was a Klamath Indian, an Army vet and a high school football player. And that was pretty much all I would learn about him during our stay together in that cabin. He was about five feet, seven inches tall and three hundred pounds. He didn't strike me as fat. He was more like a large boulder that you didn't want to roll over you. Johnny was not friendly or sociable with people he didn't know. That was clear. He talked in monosyllables.

"Sarge, what do you think we'll be doing tomorrow?" I asked.

"I expect it will be pulling up snow poles," said Sarge. He stopped to light his pipe. "It's the hardest thing all summer, heh-heh. Especially if it's still snowing." Puff, puff. He put his lighter away. "But I won't be doing it. They know I'm too old for that crap, so I'll probably be somewhere emptying trash cans, heh-heh."

"Johnny, is this your first summer here?"

"No."

"What job do you usually do?"

"Drivin.'"

Dan shouted out from the kitchen that he was ready to pronounce the cabin livable. The water was running. The electricity was on. The gas stove in the middle of the small living room was blowing heat.

I had a bad feeling about that gas stove. And then there was the chimney problem. All the first-floor windows were below the snowbank.

"Dan, have you ever lost anybody from gas explosions or, you know, waking up dead because of the gas?" Sarge found that pretty darn funny. He laughed while trying to light that damn pipe. "Heh-heh, heh-heh."

About the size of a large, one-bedroom apartment, the cabin had one small bedroom, a small living area, a kitchen and a bathroom. In the bathroom, a set of stairs led to a roughed-out attic with two bedrooms separated by a sheet of plywood. Thankfully, a door at the top of the stairs kept the privacy of the bathroom intact. I had the downstairs bedroom. I had no complaints about the cabin except for that nasty smelling furnace with the black pipe stuck into the ceiling.

Dan drove me back to park headquarters for my car. When I got back to the cabin, I unloaded my provisions. A case of Beanie Weenies, cans of chili, cans of cream of chicken soup, a loaf of white bread, pecan cookies, Twinkies, a box of Cocoa Puffs, Hamburger Helper , but no hamburger just yet, milk, Dr. Pepper and orange juice.

I hurt my mom's feelings when I told her I had survived two years of living at college and would get my own groceries on the way out of town. Really, I just didn't want her to see what I'd grown accustomed to eating at school. She always lectured me about all the junk I ate. She didn't realize that simplicity and ease were the rules I lived by. On my way out the door, she gave me a plastic container of chocolate chip cookies, a hug and a big sigh. She told me she'd be available for dinner consultations when I came back for the weekend.

Apart from the food, I had an alarm clock, a tinny-sounding cassette player, a bunch of tapes—Crosby, Stills & Nash, Jesse Colin Young, Fleetwood Mac, stuff like that—a box of books, two pairs of boots, blue work shirts, jeans, underwear and socks, a clothes bag, sweatshirts, and a windbreaker. I had a military-issue green sleeping bag, a couple blankets, Puma tennis shoes, a writing tablet, and a pen.

Inside my bedroom a single mattress rested on a metal frame bed. Whoops, I didn't bring sheets. The sleeping bag was going to come in handy right away. There was a wooden night table and a short, squat chest of drawers with three drawers, a chair that looked like it came from a teacher's desk and some pegs on the wall.

I bounced on the bed. Not bad. I could hear my roommates walking around in the attic. The most interesting thing to me at the moment was the view out my window—the insides of a block of ice.

My roommates left to get their trucks from the maintenance yard. They stopped back in the cabin for a few minutes, then headed out for Fort Klamath to buy more supplies. Sarge said they'd get back around dark. That was fine with me. I needed to catch up with my surroundings—get a feel for life buried in a snow bank.

* * *

I woke up the next morning and I wasn't dead. That was a relief. But I heard dripping. *What was that?* It wasn't drip, drip, drip like an annoying faucet. It was more like a crackling sound with the occasional drip, drip chiming in. *Where the hell was I?* The alarm had gone off. *Oh, that's right, Crater Lake National Park.* In a cabin buried in a snowbank in June. With two new roommates—a senior citizen named Sarge and a large, scary boulder person. The crackling and dripping sound was snow and ice melting from the warmth of the cabin.

It wasn't exactly the Twilight Zone, but I wasn't getting a warm and fuzzy feeling early on in this adventure. *Concentrate on the money, Sam. You have a summer job and you're making good money.* Well, technically, I hadn't made any money yet and I wasn't sure how close to death I had come on my first night with that killing machine Dan called a furnace.

"Seven thirty-five, Sam, get out of bed. Shouldn't be late on your first day." I could hear some bumping around and the muffled words outside my door. The boys sounded like they were making their lunches. Wow. To a college slacker like me that seemed very impressive and adult. I was pretty sure that the summer would pass without me making a single lunch before it was actually time to eat it.

Dan had told me that I would be able to walk home for lunch because that's what the permanent maintenance people preferred. And because I'd been assigned to Buildings and Utilities, I'd never be too far from home.

Knock, knock, knock. "Better get ready to go, Sam. Heh-heh." I noticed last night that when Sarge wanted to be understood, his voice got louder and went up an octave or two. In normal conversation, his words were so scrunched together they were often undecipherable. But when he cranked up the volume, the words got drawn out and it was almost like you could understand exactly what he was saying. If the pipe wasn't in his mouth.

I was going to have to explain to my roommates that I would never be opening my bedroom door before 7:35 a.m. I could wake up at 7:30, put on my clothes and boots, go to the bathroom, wash up, grab a handful of Twinkies and easily walk to the maintenance office by 8:00.

Knock, knock, knock. "Thanks, Sarge. I'm getting ready. Thanks." Sarge said something that I couldn't understand. The front door opened and then closed. The window rattled as the door shut tight.

The weather had improved to windy and cold, but no snow or rain. As I walked to the maintenance office, I got a better look at the cliffs that hovered over our little valley. I think yesterday's estimate of one thousand feet was way off. The cliff wall had to be at least two thousand feet straight up. The clouds just dribbled over the top this morning. Those cliffs, man. I expected I'd see a lot of impressive nature here once the weather stopped being ridiculous. *I wondered when I'd actually see Crater Lake.*

Okay, the moment had arrived. Open the door, walk into the maintenance office and punch that government clock. How bad could it really be?

CHAPTER 3

JOHNNY DROVE US THE TWO MINUTES it took to get to park headquarters from maintenance in a bruised-up, pale green, park service pickup. There had been no question that he was going to drive. Dan dangled the keys and Johnny gave me and Sarge a look, a split-second stare down like you might get from a bully in the school yard.

The three of us had been given the critical task of dumping wastebaskets at headquarters. "And, while you're there, check the paper in the bathroom," said Dan as he shooed us out the door. "Have the lady at the desk tell you where all the offices are."

It seemed like busywork to me. Who had dumped the wastebaskets before today? I'm sure it wasn't Dan. *Sam, Sam, Sam, remember why you're here. The paycheck, remember.* I knew I was going to have to keep telling myself that.

The three of us wandered up the rock steps to the front door of the park headquarters building. Sarge said, "Let's make this last, boys, heh-heh. We don't want to go back to the maintenance office too soon. They're just going to find some other crap for us to do." Johnny nodded. We all stopped on the top step while Sarge lit his pipe. Then in we went, heads held high, the professionals from Buildings and Utilities.

"Put out that pipe, Sarge," barked a voice from the back office. "There is absolutely no smoking in here. You should know better than that."

An older woman walked up to the office side of the front counter. She was the lady who had dismissed me to the steps outside when I first arrived at the park yesterday. Her words were icy daggers, shot across the room so fast that they were through you before you could get your hands up to ward them off. *Zip. Phumpf.* Dead. Very effective, except Sarge was talking to the air around him and never heard a single word.

I felt insulted even though she wasn't talking to me. Her tone was demeaning. I had a feeling that downright rude lurked right around the corner.

"You put that pipe out right now. This is the Visitors' Center for Crater Lake National Park. The superintendent works right in there. What are you thinking?"

She asked the wrong person that last part. But Sarge did get the message this time. He did an about-face and went right back out the door he had just come through, mumbling some expletives as he went. Johnny didn't blink. He stared back at the lady behind the counter. He didn't move. He didn't say a word. Johnny was using the illegal alien act. He wasn't going to understand English unless it clearly benefited him to do so.

A man peered out from a doorway down the hall. He had a brown, wide-brimmed park ranger hat on. He took a few steps toward us, looked at the lady behind the counter, looked at me and Johnny, judged that he wasn't needed and hurried back through his doorway. An office worker popped out of a cubicle to offer backup for the counter lady. It was obvious the counter lady didn't need any help with the likes of us, so she ducked back into her cubicle.

Looking out over her glasses, the counter lady now turned her stare on Johnny. Johnny blank stared her right back. She saw nothing responsive in those eyes and slowly aimed her evil gaze at me.

"Can I help you with something?" she asked. It wasn't in a friendly tone.

"We were told to come here and dump the wastebaskets and check the paper in the bathroom," I said, keeping my voice low and docile. "Could you show us where to dump the wastebaskets?"

"I thought you were supposed to vacuum, too," she said, launching an icy dart my way.

"We weren't told that," I said nicely. "Maybe you should call Dan Jenkins."

"Well it's too late in the day anyway. You can't be vacuuming when visitors are here. There's a cleaning room down the hall on the right. Dump the wastebaskets there. And tell Dan I want to talk with him about what the regular cleaning schedule will be."

As I walked by her, I could see "Elizabeth" on the name tag. She looked about sixty. She wore her thin gray hair wound tightly around her head and a chain of green sparkly beads hung from her bifocals. She was a cross between a librarian and my tenth-grade English teacher. And obviously mean as a snake. I guessed she was the office manager. An air of superiority hovered around her.

Sarge had rejoined us, his pipe safely stowed in his parka. Ol' Liz didn't want to make any more eye contact with us, but she gave Sarge a little side glance to check for any sign of lit tobacco coming from him. She sniffed a couple times to make sure we knew she could still smell it.

The three of us meandered down the hall. I brought up the rear. I assume Elizabeth thought we were out of earshot when she turned to the woman in the cubicle and said, "Every year the people they get for seasonals gets worse and worse. Did you see those three? My God, they have to be the dregs."

I stopped. What? She can't be talking about me, can she? *Of course she was talking about you, stupid, you and your two partners.* Anger boiled up. Who in the hell does she think she is? I wanted to storm right back there and get in her face. "What was your S.A.T. score, lady? You want to go head-to-head on American Literature? Let's go. C'mon, you old bat." I didn't know quite what to do next. I was mad, humiliated. I stood frozen in the hall.

Sarge was trying to get my attention. "Sam, over here. We found the toilet paper."

Great. I'm getting insulted by some school-teaching-retirement-home-wicked-witch-of-the-west-office-manager and, for my next trick, I'm cleaning johns. Let's hear it for three guys in parkas, wearing bright yellow safety helmets, stumbling around the building trying to successfully empty wastepaper baskets.

"All right, Sarge, I'll get the trash can in this room."
Damn.

After we rescued park headquarters from the cata-
strophic effects of crumpled eight-and-a-half-by-eleven paper
and plastic coffee cups run amok, Sarge called for a smoke
break in the parking lot out back. Sarge, his pipe and Johnny
with a cigarette, sat inside the pickup. I waited on the side-
walk with my hands in my parka, contemplating the battle
that had just taken place inside.

Liz was the clear victor. Most of the bombs she unleashed
had gone unanswered. I did get off a couple potshots by dropping a wastepaper basket not once, but three times, in hopes
it would get her out from behind the counter. Yup, there she
was, peering around the corner. I happily gave her a clenched-
teeth, no-comprende kind of smile. I was a pitiful, sheepish
dreg. She didn't feel sorry enough for me to hold back her
"you idiot" look. I got a little solace out of making her do what
I wanted, but I clearly wasn't ready for the main event.

Sarge's prediction came true after lunch. I was assigned
snow pole removal on the Crater Lake Highway, down near
the entrance to the park, along with Johnny and one of the
permanent park service truck drivers, Wes Brown. Sarge
was also right that his services weren't required for that
task, and he stayed in the maintenance office while we got
in the truck.

The bright orange plastic snow poles come in different
lengths. At the lower elevations, they used ten-foot poles
because the snow didn't get as deep. They used twenty-
footers up above. The poles had been planted on both sides
of the road at roughly fifty-yard intervals. When the serious

snow arrived, the poles had to be sticking high out of the ground or the snowplows wouldn't know where to plow. The road to the rim had to stay open all year-round so tourists could get to the lake, and so the park concessionaire could sell film and shiny trinkets to the tourists. It's in the contract.

The good news about pulling snow poles is that each pole sits in a pole hole that's been there for years. When the ground thaws, the poles come out without too much trouble. The bad news is there were hundreds of poles, they got heavy, it was wet out, we were at elevation, and I didn't exactly work out in my spare time at college.

Wes wore the dark green park service uniform with matching cap. He looked about fifty, was trim, and seemed quite knowledgeable on the ways of the world. Johnny and I basked in his wisdom during our frequent breaks. We couldn't hear him the rest of the time because, while we pulled poles, he sat in the cab of the flatbed, smoking cigarettes and drinking coffee from an enormous gray and green thermos. He encouraged us through the back window because there was no chance he was going to pull a single snow pole this day or any other day. He was a permanent park service truck and snowplow driver. It would break a federal law or worse if he got out of that cab to pull a pole even once.

Of course, that didn't mean he never got out of the truck. Whenever another permanent park service truck driver drove by, they invariably held a meeting that seasonals were not invited to. Wes would get out of the truck and walk to his contemporary's driver's side window and proceed to shoot the shit for at least fifteen minutes. Cars occasionally whizzed by, but, no worries. I could see life was grand if you wore one of those dark green uniforms.

It wasn't as cold as yesterday, maybe about forty-five degrees, no snow. It wasn't raining either, more of a hard mist. But after the first hour of enthusiastic pole pulling, Johnny and I were pretty much spent. By midafternoon we fell into a rhythm: pull a pole, slide it into the back of the truck, break, pull a pole, slide it into the back of the truck, break.

To my great surprise, Wes didn't care one little bit how many poles we pulled or how fast we pulled them. When we were ready, we pounded on the back of the flatbed and he pulled fifty yards up the road so we could get the next couple poles loaded. And if we decided to take a break in the cab with him, all the better, because he had lots to tell us about his many exploits and life at the lake and there are just so many hours in the day.

"Boys, no matter how many poles you pull today, goin' to be plenty to pull tomorrow and the next day and the day after that. Don't want to go crazy. Got to pace yourself."

At about 3:30, Wes got out of the truck and announced that he had run out of coffee and it was time to get back to the maintenance office. That wasn't possible. I mean, there was no way he could have drunk three gallons of coffee or whatever that gigantic thermos held. I stared at him in awe. Johnny bumped me and said, "Let's go." Then he enthusiastically walked to the front of the truck and opened the door. He looked back at me fiercely. "C'mon, let's go."

Okay. No problem. Let's go. I'm all for it. I got in the truck and we headed out. Slooooowly, we drove up the

Crater Lake Highway to Annie Springs. Wes drove really, really, slooooowly. Wes apparently hoped to time our arrival back at maintenance with the approaching end of the workday. No way he could make it take forty-five minutes to drive six miles or whatever it was. *What a rookie, Sam.* Wes pulled into the snowbound Mazama campground, where no one could see us from the road, and—just like that—time was no factor at all.

"Wes, when do the rest of the seasonals start getting here?" I asked.

"I expect most all of 'em will start getting here next week. But then they'll have the crud for a few days, so they won't be worth much."

"What's the crud?" I asked.

"Oh, you seasonals can't seem to handle the water here, or maybe it's the food up at the rim. But people get pretty sick right after they get here every summer. It's like the flu. Some get it real bad and it starts coming out both ends and then you got problems. Some guys get it every damn year, but us permanents seem immune to it. After a few weeks, everyone is fine."

"Does that mean I'm going to get sick, Wes? When I was hired nobody said one word about stuff coming out both ends. No, I can't remember that coming up once."

"Well, there should be plenty coming up really soon, Sam."

Johnny laughed out loud. I gave him a hard look. He punched me in the chest with the heel of his hand. I struggled not to cough. I guess Johnny didn't believe in hard looks unless he was giving them—he was staring me down right now. Great, how was I going to get out of this? How many battles could I lose on my first day of work at Crater Lake National Park?

The three of us sat in the cab of the flatbed truck, Johnny in the middle. I was sure the worst course of action was to punch him back. So I threw up my hands, "Sorry, Johnny, just got a little heated, I didn't mean anything."

Johnny just stared. I wondered if there were a lock on my bedroom door at the cabin.

"Hey, calm down, you two," said Wes. "If you fight here, you're breaking federal law and they just don't kid around about that stuff. The rangers wake up every morning hoping that this will be the day they get to arrest a maintenance worker. Remember that."

I'm sure I could remember that. But someone needed to talk to Johnny. I think the real reason Johnny didn't find an excuse to pound me was Wes. During one of our many breaks that day, Wes had talked about his colorful past growing up in Bakersfield, California. At one point he told us that twenty-five years ago he was the Golden Gloves champ of Central California. Johnny nodded. I gave Wes a look.

"Get out of the truck," Wes demanded. "You don't believe me? I'm going to give you a demonstration. Show you some boxing moves. C'mon."

"I believe you, Wes, you don't have to show me anything. Really. I believe you."

Johnny wanted out, so I opened the door and reluctantly stepped toward Wes, who already had his hands up, ready to demonstrate. Johnny was smiling. That couldn't be good. But how much faster could a fifty-plus-year-old man be than me? Short answer: a lot faster. As soon as I raised my hands, I felt a punch in my stomach and then, immediately after, a slap on the side of my head.

"Wait a minute, Wes. If you're going to beat me up at least let me get ready, okay?

Wes stepped back, smiled, put his hands on his hips, and said, "Ready now, bubba?"

"Fine. I'm ready."

Punch. Smack. I saw his arms start to move, but I couldn't get a single muscle to react before he punched me again. Wow. If I weren't getting beat up, I'd think that was pretty cool. I'd never seen anything like Wes's hand speed before. It would be nice if he'd pulled his punches a little more, but that wouldn't be a manly thing for me to bring up. In school yard brawls you could always see the punches. This was like a nightmare, where you couldn't move to stop some impending disaster.

Then I did something really stupid. I took a playful swing. Before my fist got halfway to its target Wes had pivoted and punched me in the stomach. He didn't even bother to block my useless blow.

I bent over, trying hard not to rub the spot where I had just been hit.

"Sam, don't ever take a swing at me. My instincts are likely to take over and someone might get hurt."

"Well, then what am I doing here, Wes, if you didn't want me to spar with you?"

You're doing an impression of a punching bag," said Johnny, without changing expression. "That's what's happening here."

I straightened up and stared at Johnny. He stared back, a lot meaner.

"That's it. I'm going to pull some poles. Anybody ELSE want to do some actual work around here?"

They both laughed.

Walking back to the cabin after work I added up the wins and losses of my first day at Crater Lake National Park. I got humiliated and browbeaten by a librarian/school teacher. I had been pushed around by my new roommate. I was beat up by an old park service truck driver. How did that all happen? I planned to fly under the radar, hunker down, not be noticed, stuff paychecks in the bank. How's it going so far? I'll be on life support by the middle of July.

Instead of going into the cabin, I kept walking straight for my car. It was time to find out if there was a damn lake up there at all. The way things had been going today, I thought it possible that when I got to the rim I'd find some dinky little pond with a sorry-ass concession stand next to it. All this talk about a national park was a hoax to get me here to be pounded into submission by everyone that happened by. Actually, I did know there was a gift shop because of that trip I took with my dad. But was there a lake? Well, time to find out.

The trip to the rim was about three miles long and one thousand feet up. The road meandered its way through Mountain Hemlock forests and rocky switchbacks. One switchback boasted an elegant gray rock building with a spring gurgling next to it. It looked like a historical land-mark, maybe a park service pump house from the turn of the century. It could have been carved out of the side of the mountain by a sculptor.

A sign at the end of the last straightaway pointed to Rim Village this way, Crater Lake Overlook that way. I veered left and out onto the Rim Drive, heading for the overlook. The park service snowplows had cut snow into fifteen-foot-high white walls on both sides of the road. Thick mist and melting snow wet the pavement. It looked as if the road had just been carved out of a massive block of snow. After about a mile, the road swung around a miniature white peak perched on the rim. I could see the scenic overlook up ahead. A long rock wall, about three feet high, separated the parking area from the great below. For now, this served as the end of the road and a turnaround for all those coming this way.

I drove my car cautiously through the slush and parked up against the stone wall. Over the side I could see patches of deep blue through swirling clouds. Above was socked in. I must be standing in the middle of a cloud.

I reached into the backseat for my parka because it felt like about forty degrees and the wind was blowing. The wind was eerie; no howling or whipping. Just the sound it makes when there is no other sound. Like it's breathing. A gust. Then nothing. A gust. Then still.

Turning to look in all directions, I could see only two man-made objects besides my beat-up Volkswagen. There was the rock wall that somebody had built years ago. And there was a sign that said, "road ends here." A tall, two-lane-wide block of ice stood guard behind the metal sign.

On either side of me, the land rose to rocky peaks, blocking my view of anything on the other side. In back of me, the land sloped down toward the mountain valleys many miles below. Every inch seemed to be covered by dense forests. A solitary mountain peak stood off in the distance. In front of me, I could see more of Crater Lake as the clouds cleared.

At about 5:30 the sun broke through and shot beams of light down onto the blue lake. Crater Lake is seriously blue. I sat on the rock wall, wondering if I'd ever seen such a rich blue in nature. Shasta Lake, across the border in California, had some blue, but mostly it had the emerald green tint that all mountain lakes seem to have. I thought snowmelt caused that color, but Crater Lake got at least some of its water from snowmelt. I could see green at the edges of an island close to the side of the lake where I sat. In the middle of the island was a volcanic cone. So the incredible blue must have to do with the extreme depth of the lake.

The enormity of the collapse that created this lake took my breath away. I knew that Crater Lake formed when Mount Mazama, a twelve thousand–foot volcano, collapsed in on itself after a violent eruption thousands of years ago. The lake water collected in the massive caldera, with jagged high and low points around the edge.

I was sitting on a rock wall at an altitude of about seventy-one hundred feet. The lake looked to be about five or six miles across. That means four thousand feet by five or six miles of rock came crashing down into the basin below. Rain and snow came pouring in to create one of the deepest lakes in the world. Nature was intimidating.

People have always accused me of being timid when it comes to climbing or jumping or swimming or skiing out in the wild and wooly world. Nature scares me. I love to watch the crashing ocean, but admiring nature doesn't mean I want to challenge it. It seems foolhardy to me to question nature's power and its oblivious attitude toward humans. Some people seem to think they can manage it. But if nature wants to pound you, no level of planning, physical skills, and worldly intelligence will save you. Russian roulette, if you ask me. It is only a matter of time. Nature doesn't care. It could be an avalanche, a shark, a tornado, a mountain caving in on itself.

From my rock wall, I couldn't see any access to the lake. I knew there was a boat landing somewhere, but I couldn't see it. I could only see two thousand feet or so straight down. In a couple places, rock and snow slides extended from the rim all the way down. In other places, the crater wall was solid rock with small trees clinging to the sides.

I got up from the rock wall and took a step closer to the edge. Looking down, my perception changed. You think you can throw a rock and hit the lake, but in reality, while the side of the rim is steep, at those dimensions the side juts out much farther than you can possibly throw a rock. And you can't see a small rock two thousand feet away, anyway. It doesn't look real way down there. You wonder what it would be like to jump. It's not real, nothing would happen. Right?

Chills from that thought and the dropping temperature startled me. So quiet. Just the wind breathing in and out.

Too bad my father had missed seeing all this. I wonder what he would think? I never noticed that he thought much about nature. But I didn't really know.

My dad was a lifer in the Air Force. Before he was stationed at Kingsley Field we had lived at Eielsen Air Force base in Fairbanks, Alaska. I hated everything about the military.

I always thought moving every two or three years to some place where I didn't know a soul caused me to be a social misfit. I can remember studying the map after my dad got his orders. Klamath Falls? What? My father had put in requests for air bases in California and Arizona, but he got Klamath Falls, a base that was practically closed. That meant someone above him was mad about something. Little did that person know he was not only screwing my dad, but also throwing me into a little farming community where everyone else had known each other all their lives. Not a great situation for a junior in high school with an inferiority complex already.

A rumbling in the distance became a green station wagon with cop lights on the top. I turned and watched the park ranger drive up. As he slowed down to park, I turned back to the lake. From miles away, the windblown waves look like wheat swaying on the plains. You can't see exactly what's going on, but there's a feeling of movement.

"Hey there, you don't want to get too close to the edge," said the ranger walking up to the rock wall. Tall and heavy-set, he wore a wide-brimmed brown smokey hat that seemed a little ornate for the task. "There's ice and underneath the rocks can be slippery."

"Okay, ranger. It looks like you could get people going over the side accidentally or not so accidentally. Does that happen?"

"Yeah, maybe one a year. It seems it's a different situation each year—a child slipping, a suicide. It's more dangerous than it looks. Why don't you come over to this side of the rock wall?" He kept his eye on me. "Are you working maintenance? I saw the helmet in your car."

"Yes, I am. First day today. Thought I'd come up to the lake. I'd never seen it before. It's unbelievable. It's so quiet. Sorry, my name is Sam Hunter." I stepped over the wall and shook his hand.

"I'm Ranger Bob Roberts. You watch how you drive; I don't want to give you a ticket. If you get two, you can't drive in the park, which could cause you to lose your job. And there won't be any excuses, I'll definitely give you a ticket. Okay?"

He looked out over the lake with an expression of respect. "It won't be quiet long. Mr. and Mrs. Winnebago will start arriving soon and then all hell breaks loose."

"No problem, ranger. I'll be careful."

He gave me a friendly look and headed back to his ranger-mobile. I admired him for how seriously he took his work. Anybody willing to call himself Ranger Bob Roberts and wear that hat was definitely into it.

I sat back down on the rock wall. I couldn't imagine this scene full of motor homes and screaming children. As the ranger's car got out of earshot, the stillness came back from wherever it had been hiding. I got an old towel from the trunk of my car. I laid it down on the other side of the wall and sat down with my back up against the cold rock.

I watched the water change to a darker, grayer blue as the sun slowly disappeared. The water fluttered in the wind. I noticed a small cabin-looking structure on top of a tall peak across the lake. A lonely post. I wouldn't want to be up there with the wind blowing. The view must be spectacular, though.

With twilight came a mean cold. I felt it knife through my parka. I wanted to stay, but Mother Nature insisted I go.

CHAPTER 4

TECHNICALLY,IWASN'TAPOLITICALAPPOINTEE.Butthatdidn't matter to the Crater Lake maintenance department lifers, the Vietnam army vets and Chiloquin tough guys slouching around the tables slurping bitter coffee. Chiloquin, a tiny town of several hundred, located about eighteen miles outside the east boundary of the park, had a reputation for street fighting and a pipeline to the seasonal maintenance jobs.

Political appointees got their federal jobs at a national park because their families were friendly with some politician. As far as I could tell, almost all the maintenance seasonals were political appointees of one sort or another—even the military veterans. I could make a case that everyone got their job because they knew somebody.

One of the regular seasonal veteran truck drivers had complained to me the day before about "those damn political appointees."

"That ain't no way to get a job when there's vets out there who should get all these jobs. You're one, aren't ya?"

"No, no, no, Billy, not me," I said. "My mother knows the office manager down in the Klamath Falls office. One of your brother vets dropped out at the last second and she called my mom to see what I was doing. That DOES NOT make me a political appointee. I'm just helping one of your guys out, right?"

Billy grunted grudgingly. "I guess so. But I hate those political appointees. That's not the right way to get a job. These jobs are for veterans." Billy didn't talk like an under-grad at UC-Santa Barbara, but the G.I. Bill did not discriminate. He drove trucks at Danang for a year. He even saw a couple mortars hit outside the fence while he was there. That was good enough for him to sit on his lofty perch.

Of course, my "technicality" argument didn't carry much weight when the jobs got divvied up for the summer. The maintenance department at Crater Lake National Park had a pecking order. A first-summer guy who wasn't a vet-eran or affiliated with one of the cliques had no chance of landing a decent position in the maintenance detail.

The handwriting on the wall spelled port-o-potty.

Down in maintenance, here's how it broke down. Frank Noble ran the "Roads and Trails" side of the house. Dan Jenkins oversaw "Buildings and Utilities." Both these guys worked full-time for the National Park Service as middle manage-ment, under the chief of maintenance. They lived at the park all year-round and they did pretty much as they wanted.

Frank was the bad boy of the year-rounders. He dated the park superintendent's daughter. Then, when that ended, he dated the park superintendent's other daughter. Dating may be the wrong word. Frank was tan and wore Jean-Claude Killy sunglasses. He drove his command green park service pickup like the Prince of Crater Lake. The rangers didn't mess with him. Dan never said anything when Frank ridiculed everything and everybody in Buildings and Utilities. Dan seemed aggressively uncaring about anything Frank said. That's just how it was and had been for a long time, apparently. Roads and Trails got all the he-men, macho veterans, and otherwise connected seasonals, while the dregs, political appointees, and females, well, they went to Buildings and Utilities..."where they belonged."

Dan Jenkins was ex-Air Force and still served in the reserves. Tall, but nonthreatening, Dan had a round face and was bald on top. His wife and two children lived with him in Steel Circle, across the main road from maintenance—where all the permanent park service people lived. And when it came to Frank's ranting, Dan seemed oblivious. Frank competed for the alpha male position all by himself.

An electrician and a carpenter worked for Dan. And, of course, in summer he got a load of seasonal flotsam like me. Frank had several truck drivers who primarily drove snowplows in the winter. The road to the rim had to be kept open all year and that took nonstop plowing much of the winter. There were also a couple mechanics to keep the snowplows and trucks running. These guys were all regular park service. Some lived off campus, but a few were housed across the road in Steel Circle.

Frank's favorite time was June, when his boys arrived. As their leader, he was going to grow these macho seasonals in his boyish image. He couldn't do much bossing in the winter because park service lifers only do what they themselves decide to do. Basically, "We'll all get along if you keep your 'alpha' to yourself, boss." Even Frank knew the maintenance manager's first rule: you only get to push around the seasonals.

So here we all were—stuffed into the maintenance office waiting for Frank to come in and let everybody know how it was going to be this summer. All the seasonals had arrived and the snow was melting fast. Back at the cabin, I could just see over the snow stacked against my window. Soon I might even be able to open a window to let out some of Sarge's pipe smoke.

Frank's speech was mostly a letdown. I guessed he saved the really good stuff for his crew. Basically, he said: drugs, you're fired; driving drunk, you're fired; weapons, you're fired; felonies, you're fired; insubordination, you're fired; crashing a government vehicle, you're fired; make sure you have some Pepto for the crud; lodge girls can't live in your cabin; softball season starts in a month; racquetball tourneys start immediately.

"Okay, boys and girls, let's have a great summer." Those were Frank's last words before we split up into the chosen ones—Frank's Roads and Trails group—and the dregs, Dan's Buildings and Utilities group.

The dregs went outside while the chosen ones stayed in the office. There was a lot more of them then us; that's what Frank wanted and Dan didn't care. So there we were. Out on the blacktop in front of the maintenance office.

Next to Dan, our mild-mannered leader, stood Andrew the permanent carpenter, dressed up in full park service regalia including the smallish park service cap. Two young girls who looked suspiciously like political appointees stood next to Andrew. The crew had been talking about the girls' arrival for days. For the first time, girls had been hired for the summer maintenance crew and the boys were anticipating opportunity.

Fair and blonde, Sally's cheeks were already pink from the sun. She had a pretty smile with deep dimples on both sides. Marcy had olive skin and brown hair. Sally wore her yellow hard hat and was clearly happy to have it on her head. Marcy held hers in her hand, probably looking for a way to lose it. Sally wore a short-sleeved sweatshirt, jeans and boots that looked new. Marcy had on a blue work shirt, a bandana around her neck and tennis shoes. She constantly ran her hand through her thick hair.

Sally looked around her—past the people—to the trees and snow. She was clearly taken by snow on the ground in June. This was probably as far away from home as she had ever been, and I was pretty sure she thought she had landed in heaven. Then her hard hat started distracting her. It didn't fit quite right, probably because it had only been on men-sized heads before. It kept sliding to one side. She kept trying to make it right, with no luck. She made me smile.

Marcy tucked her hat further under her arm, hoping no one would notice and make her wear it. She was deep into an animated discussion with Andrew.

Hazel looked like she was past retirement age. Her wiry gray hair was tied up in a tight bun. Her green Keds matched her park service uniform, and her eyes were a startling shade of blue. Her hands were the oldest things about her. They were worn and rough, but sported two big, almost gaudily set diamond rings. Hazel wasn't a seasonal. She worked all winter too, mainly taking care of the park headquarters building—cleaning the bathrooms, emptying trash, sweeping up. She had been off the day I had been enlisted to dump wastebaskets at headquarters.

There was an electrician on the crew, too, but he was on vacation. And, in a week or so a husband-wife cleanup crew and an assistant carpenter would join us for the summer. And Sarge.

I watched Dan carefully as he studied his troops. I give him credit for not laughing out loud, sighing in disgust, or throwing down his clipboard and just walking away. He probably deserved better. I saw a shadow of resignation show briefly on his face, quickly replaced by practiced indifference.

"Hazel, you and Sarge do the rounds on the rest stop at the park entrance, maintenance offices, and park headquarters. And, Hazel, don't forget to check in with Miss Clancy at headquarters and find out exactly what she wants done and when. I don't want to have to come up there and pull you out of the fire because you didn't talk with her first. Okay?"

"No problem, Dan," said Hazel.

"Heh-heh," said Sarge.

"Andrew, you take Sam, Sally, and Marcy down to Mazama Campground and open up the amphitheater."

Just as Dan completed his instructions, the maintenance office door swung open and out spilled the Roads and Trails crew in all its manly glory, young men bristling with swagger and little time to consider such things as maybe there was a meeting going on. They poured through us Buildings and Utilities folks with zero recognition that we were there, speaking in serious tones about softball teams and the new guy who got the honor of being on the trailbreaking crew.

But then they seemed to collectively notice something. Girls. There were two girls in the vicinity. The Buildings and Utilities girls. Right. Hold up men. What had been a torrent turned into a meandering, backwater of testosterone. Boys checking out the girls, pondering their chances, wondering what the line of succession would be in asking these girls out. The inevitable "How ya doin?" The girls smiling, happy to be noticed.

Marcy basked in the attention, obviously used to it. The herd of potential suitors was weighted to her side. She talked a lot—constantly pulling or brushing at her brown hair. The Roads and Trails stars talked with her, while the others stood a few feet away in little groups pretending to talk and glancing over every few minutes. Sally was on the edge of the group talking with a couple lesser lights. She seemed to work a little harder at playing her role—alternating earnest shakes of the head and little laughs.

I was embarrassed and depressed at the same time. Everything to do with girls embarrassed me. I liked to think it was just me being very sensitive and wanting to be very respectful of girls. But it had nothing to do with that. I was just plain scared to death. And I was depressed because, as I watched them, I knew I could never force myself to be a part of a group like that.

In high school I'd stand in the hall with a group of people, hoping to talk with one of the girls. And just when one of them was about to say something to me, a wave of jocks would roll in and the conversation would go a different way and, before long, I ended up walking in the opposite direction.

So I'm the guy with the lowest self-esteem in the world. So what?

Here's how bad it was. I can remember being a sophomore in high school and walking past the house of a girl that I had liked from a distance for three years or so. She knew I liked her because people had told her, but I could never talk to her about it. She was very pretty and a year younger than me, but definitely several steps above me in the social strata. She knew it and I knew it, but it didn't stop me from having a crush on her. Her name was Carol.

As I walked by I saw her sitting out on her porch. She called out to me, "Hey, Sam, come over and talk with me."

I blurted out, "Have you seen Gary Johnson, I'm looking for him, I need to talk with him."

Gary Johnson? I said to myself. Where did you get that from? What are you doing? She's inviting you over. You idiot. C'mon.

"No, I haven't seen Gary," she said. "Would you rather talk with him than me?"

Sam, she's even flirting with you. C'mon. If you can't talk to this girl you've wanted to talk to for years when she's asking you directly you might as well give it up. Shoot yourself or something. Idiot.

I lied. "I need to talk with him." And I walked away as fast as I could.

So as I watched the R & T boys chatting up Sally and Marcy I did what I always did—I walked away, pretending to look for Andrew's truck.

The Mazama Campground is quiet in June. It's the biggest campground at Crater Lake with about two hundred campsites. The fleets of Winnebagos wouldn't arrive for another few weeks, but it was going to take time to prepare the campground for the onslaught. The restrooms needed to be opened and cleaned. The wood shutters had to be taken off the amphitheater and ranger station. Debris that had accumulated during winter had to be cleared. Amphitheater benches needed repair. Because the campground was on the lower end of the park, the snow wasn't an issue anymore, except where the snowplows had piled it up next to the roads. During the summer, rangers used the amphitheater to give nature talks.

Andrew helped us take the shutters down and showed us what had to be cleaned. He went back to the carpenter shop to repair campground signs. Sally and Marcy started work on the ladies' restroom and I went to clean the men's, which I thought was funny. Like it made any difference. I quickly found out that I wasn't any good at mopping. There had to be a trick to it because I couldn't tell if the restroom floor's appearance had improved at all after twenty minutes of my mopping.

I was staring back and forth between the floor and the mop bucket when Sally and Marcy arrived on the scene.

"We're taking a break. Wanna join us?" asked Sally.

"Thanks, I need a break to rethink my mopping strategy," I said. "So far I'm not doing so good."

Looking around the floor, Sally suggested, "Maybe you're not cleaning your mop well enough. We'll brainstorm and see what we can come up with."

"You know, I think I'm going to take a walk around the campground to see what else is here," said Marcy, and she was out the door and down a path.

"Ouch. Was it something I said, Sally?"

"No, I just think she's coming to grips with the fact that she's going to be a janitor this summer," said Sally. "I think she probably believes this is a little below her station in life."

"Do you think someone told her she was going to be a ranger?" We both laughed at that.

On the way over to the amphitheater, Sally told me what she knew about Marcy. She was a sophomore at UCLA, pre-law, didn't admit to being a political appointee and was of Italian descent. Her mother gave lavish parties in Bel Air. Already was talking wistfully about the Southern California life. She dropped a few names Sally didn't know: Steve Garvey, Sam Yorty, Mark Harmon.

We sat down on the wooden benches at the amphitheater. I sat facing frontwards, looking toward the empty fire pit and stage area. Sally straddled the bench facing me. I could hear a car drive by on the way up to park headquarters or the rim. You couldn't miss it because there was no other sound but forest noises. I felt a little nervous sitting next to this girl I didn't know, all alone in Crater Lake National Park.

"So what about you, Samuel, how did you get here?" Samuel? Only my family called me Samuel. But a bigger problem loomed. The first thing I was going to say to this girl was "my mother got me the job." Damn. She must have seen me grimace.

"What?" she asked.

I was looking at a spot on the ground off to her left. "My mother knew somebody at the National Park office in Klamath Falls and they needed to hire another person at the last minute. And here I am."

"Well, that's not so bad. At least you're not a dreaded political appointee," she said. "And you better not tell anyone I told you that. My dad is a friend of a senator. That's the only way I could ever get a job like this. Pretty embarrassing. I don't care, though, this is such a great place it's worth it. I applied to parks all over, but I came here because it's the farthest from home—Pennsylvania."

"I don't think you have to worry about keeping it secret."

"Why?" she said, staring at me.

"I think everyone knows, Sally."

She let out a sigh. "Oh well. I guess I can stop lying to Andrew. He's asked me three times how I got my job. And I just keep saying I applied and got it. Pretty dumb, huh? Do you go to school?" she asked.

"Going to be a junior at the University of Oregon."

I could tell she was looking right at me. I would occasionally look at her when she asked a question, but then I would look away.

"What are you majoring in?"

"English."

"Samuel, are you going to talk to me or what?"

I looked back at her and she was smiling. She pushed me on the shoulder. I'm sure all the R & T romeos were thinking about Marcy—tanned, flirting eyes. Sally had something else. When she asked me questions it felt like she really wanted to know everything about me. That couldn't be true, but it sure felt that way.

Sally and Marcy lived in the old superintendent's house up the hill, back in the forest. The big stone house was where the superintendent used to live in the summers. In the mid-'60s it was decided that the superintendent should live in the park year-round, so a new modern house was built in Steel Circle.

Sally and Marcy had both arrived the Friday before and spent the weekend getting acclimated. Marcy had driven her own yellow sports car. Sally said she cracked up every night watching Marcy pull this special cover over the car to protect it. Sally's family drove her cross-country as part of a family vacation. Even her grandmother came along for the ride.

"It was so embarrassing when we drove into the park," Sally said. "We'd just driven three thousand miles singing *Annie's Song* along with John Denver on the radio. Seems like that was all that was playing the whole trip. And when we came to Annie Springs, the whole family started yelling. And my dad wouldn't keep going till I got out and let him take my picture next to the Annie Springs sign. There'll probably be a framed eight by ten hanging on the wall when I go home."

I don't think I could've shared a story like that, but it didn't seem to bother Sally. She just laughed thinking about it.

"How are you getting along with your roommates?" I asked.

Sally and Marcy shared the large Stone House with the seasonal female rangers and naturalists who were beginning to arrive at the Park. That hadn't been the plan. But park management had suddenly realized that it was probably a bad idea to house the two girls in the maintenance seasonal housing with all the men. There was clearly a class structure at the park and I suspect they were loathe to have the sanctity and purity of the rangers muddied by two maintenance girls. The alternative was just too scary because they were political appointees. Nothing better happen to them.

"The first day the ranger girls kind of ignored me," said Sally. "But then one of them—Amy, I think—picked up this writing pad I carry around with me. I had left it for a minute on the kitchen table. When I came back in the room, she asked me what it was. I told her everything is so beautiful here, I was trying to get it down on paper. Just a habit I got into from a short story writing class I had taken. Anyway, she seemed kind of surprised.

"Then she asked me where I went to school and what did I study. I told her I'm a Russian Studies major. I just finished my first year at Penn State. She said, 'Ohhhhhhhh.' I guess they don't expect us maintenance folks to be able to read and write."

I told her about my experience with Elizabeth Clancy at park headquarters on my first day of work and we laughed together.

"Why Russian Studies, Sally?"

For the first time since we sat down, Sally looked away from me. I think she actually blushed. "I don't know," she said softly. "Something about the passion, I think. The literature, the art, the history. I'd like to be that passionate."

"Maybe I could read your stories sometime," I said. *Oh no, Sam, where did that come from? You just met the girl. Don't scare her off.*

"I don't think I want any English major reading my stuff," she laughed. To my relief, she changed the subject.

"Samuel, did you know there's a party at our place Friday night? A get-to-know-you sort of thing. It was Frank Noble's idea. He stopped by over the weekend. He said the rock house was the best place for a party and that he'd bring the burgers and hotdogs. There's a big barbecue, so it should work out great."

Wow, I thought to myself. *That Frank Noble sure works fast.* Seemed pretty reckless to be fraternizing with young, female political appointees. I wasn't going to be on the invite list if it was a Frank Noble function. It's not the type of thing I would go to anyway. There would be too many people there who would look down on me because of where I worked. And, if you think about it, I was the only young guy who wasn't part of R & T—and I worked with a couple of girls. No, I don't think I'd be going.

"It's suppose to start around seven. You'll come, right?"

She looked right at me when she said it. For a second I thought she knew what I was thinking. *Don't get hysterical, Sam. Get it under control. You're just not used to talking to girls.*

She's a nice girl. Just because she smiles at you doesn't mean she's in love.

"Sure, maybe," I said.

"'Sure, maybe'? What in the heck does that mean— 'sure, maybe'?"

"It means I may have to practice mopping every night this week because I'm so bad at it. If I get the mop under control, maybe I'll think about it. Now let me get back to work."

She punched me in the shoulder again as she left.

I didn't see much of Sally or Marcy the rest of the week. They went on a different shift—starting earlier to clean various buildings. I was assigned to the carpenter. But I kept thinking about that smile.

After work on Friday, I took a shower, then lay on my bed wondering whether I should go to the party. I heard Sarge and Johnny talking about it. They were going, which meant it wasn't so exclusive an event that people would be turned away at the door. It certainly would make sense to go—meet people, get a free dinner.

That's a normal thing to do. It's the way of the world, Sam. I know. But here's what going to happen. I'm going to walk in and hope to find someone to latch onto so I'm not the weird guy everyone sees standing in the corner. When I don't find anyone, I'll go to the food table and take an hour or so looking and then choosing what I will eat. But then I will be the weird guy in the corner again. Hell, no.

At about 7:00, the door slammed behind Sarge and Johnny as they headed off to the party. Fine. I've got a stack of books to read. No problem.

At 7:15, I threw *Sometimes a Great Notion* against the wall and walked out to the stream that cut through the middle of the cabins. Rivers, creeks, and streams all soothed me. Some of it was the sound, but mostly it was watching the water. Twigs floating by. Eddies reaching out and capturing a leaf. Bugs swimming, making wakes behind them.

I got in my Volkswagen at 7:45 and drove across the maintenance yard, through the park headquarters parking lot and up the hill toward the Stone House back in the forest. Cars and trucks were parked everywhere. I had to turn around, go back down the hill and find a spot in the headquarters parking lot. The sun was almost down by the time I hiked back up to the mansion. I could hear party noise out back, but I still knocked on the front door. Nobody answered. The door was ajar, so I walked in. The punishing chords of "Smoke on the Water"—*Dun, Dun, Dun—Dun Dun Du-nah*—made the walls vibrate.

Crossing the dark, empty front room, I walked down a hall and stumbled into the kitchen. I could see a party going on through the windows. At the barbecue, one of the truck drivers was cooking what looked to be the last burgers and hot dogs. A patio table nearby held bowls of food, some buns and what looked like a battleground strewn with the onion and relish remains of what had been a condiment station. *Dun, Dun, Dun—Dun Dun Du-nah.*

Frank Noble held court on the back lawn. His entourage included about seven of his boys, Marcy, a ranger girl, and one of the young permanent truck drivers that worked for him. Oh my God, that wasn't a guitar leaning against his chair, was it? A couple picnic tables were full of seasonal rangers and another couple were full of park service management. I guess, for this one party each summer, all the different castes tolerated each other—but only from a distance.

Suddenly, Sally appeared right beside me. She poked me with an elbow. "Hey, could you open that door?" She was carrying a cake with chocolate frosting and a cherry pie and paper plates. "Glad you could make it," she whispered as she hurried by.

I saw Sarge and Johnny at the food table. I took a deep breath and headed into the traffic jam. It was easy in these circumstances to say excuse me and smile as you headed to some unknown destination. Didn't have to stop and talk because it looked like you were going somewhere. I said hi to Dan as I walked by. I nodded to Charlie the snowcat driver.

"Didn't think you were coming, Sam. Heh-heh," said Sarge.

"Can't pass up free food. Johnny can you grab me a bun there?"

"What did you say?"

"No problem, Johnny, I got it. Just needed a bun. I'm good now."

Okay. I had a paper plate, a hamburger. Now what? I looked around for Sally. I wanted her to ask me more questions. I don't know what about, really. Just talk. There she was, sitting next to an R & T guy, two spots down from Frank. She was part of the entourage. She was having a good time. Laughing. More at ease than that first day. The guy next to her seemed attentive. Maybe they were already a couple. That was fast.

I latched onto a group of maintenance people who were standing in a circle eating and talking. Sarge introduced me to the group. I nodded. The permanents acknowledged me and then resumed their tales of driving the big snow-plows during the wild and wooly winters at Crater Lake National Park.

I headed back to the food table, hoping that something edible remained. One disfigured hot dog. Hmmm. I didn't think the disfigurement was due to someone taking a bite. I weighed the risk versus reward. It could be a practical joke or it had been on the ground or whatever. How hungry was I?

I glanced over at Frank. He was giving a loud, animated rendition of some past adventure. The entourage—now about fifteen people—hung on every word. He had a beer in one hand, but set it down on the cooler next to him. He needed both hands to describe the next part of the story.

Sally slowly stood up. She stepped quietly toward a stream farther in back of the house. I could barely see her in the twilight, and the light from the party barely reached her. She stood there, looking at the water, arms crossed. For a second I wondered what would happen if I walked over. While I considered that unlikely event, I saw the R & T guy who had been sitting next to her walk up behind her and put a hand on her shoulder.

I'm so naïve sometimes I laugh at myself. I decided to pass on the hot dog and head for home.

"Well, Sarge, I've got my free food now, so I guess I can go. See you back at the cabin."

"See ya. Heh-heh."

I looked back at Sally and her friend. They were whispering and laughing quietly. Sally threw pebbles at the water. At one point, she leaned back against her new boyfriend. I shook my head and laughed at myself again.

I was surprised by the total blackout conditions when I stepped out of the front door. No stars. No moon. Pitch-black. Once I got away from the house lights, I had to stop for a moment because the depth of the darkness scared me. I waited to see if my eyes would adjust but, no, I still couldn't see a thing. How was I going to get down this hill? I couldn't go back to the party and ask for a ride. That would be humiliating.

I stood there alone for about twenty minutes trying to breathe in the dark. I heard insects, wind through the trees, water running, little animals in the bushes. I remembered the walk up and where the road twisted. I could feel the pavement. I knew where I was. Five minutes later, I had walked far enough to see the lights at park headquarters.

I expect I'll be walking in the dark around here a lot more now, I said to myself. A car coming from the party slowed down as it neared me. I waved it on. Walking in the pitch-black night felt good.

CHAPTER 5

THE CRATER LAKE CRUD roared down on the maintenance department like Mongol hordes. The Crud wielded invisible axes and swords that cut down R & T seasonals, as well as us lesser lights, in equal numbers. The once mighty maintenance crew quickly became just a rabble leaking bodily fluids from every conceivable orifice.

The sneak attack had been well executed. The Crud had shown up like it did every year. No one paid much attention. A few of the newly arrived seasonal workers got sick to their stomachs, stayed home a couple days, got better, and a couple others got sick. This would go on until about half the seasonals had been affected and then no more Crud.

Wrong. The Crud swept through Sleepy Hollow, crashing down cabin doors, holding the seasonal population tied up and gagging. No one was spared this time.

In an annoying aspect of the Crud attack, permanent park service workers weren't getting sick. They never got sick in all the years before and they weren't getting sick now. And that delighted them no end. It was just more material for their daily stand-up routines around the maintenance office coffee pot in the morning. The truck drivers would say something like there was no Crater Lake Crud at all. It was just the seasonals not being able to hold their liquor. Or they were sick of working. Or they took some bad pharmaceuticals.

I didn't say they were funny.

Even though the permanents weren't getting sick, some were willing to dish a little conspiracy talk. They mentioned some unnamed early-arriving seasonal ranger who took water samples and kept a record of the bacteria count each year. In June the bacteria levels always spiked, according to the story. The conspiracy part revolved around park service management people at Crater Lake who knew about it, but didn't want to tell their superiors for fear of attracting unwanted scrutiny.

The reasoning went: if permanents weren't getting sick and hardly anybody spent time in the park in June, why create a big commotion? Like all decent conspiracy theories, it was plausible because everyone knew that no one in government got anywhere by exposing big internal problems that weren't currently bothering anyone important.

Of course, if anyone had paid real attention to the carnage down in Sleepy Hollow, they might have figured out that in no way was any of this a normal occurrence. Vomiting and diarrhea were pretty much the only things going on down there. The boys referred to it as "coming out of both ends." Used in a sentence it was, "Yeah, poor Ole

Jack had it coming out of both ends." People were sitting on toilets, then leaning over and throwing up in bathtubs or shower stalls.

Most everyone had a theory about what was happening and it usually ended up back with the water. It seemed kind of elementary really. I had been assigned to Dave, the seasonal assistant carpenter, and we went over the evidence about once a day.

"Sam, you don't seem too bad off. You were one of the first ones to get here, right?"

"Yup. I've had some stomach issues, but you know I lead a pretty sheltered life. I don't eat up at the lodge, I eat out of cans. I go home to Klamath Falls on the weekends. I even boiled water the other night but I didn't drink it. I guess this is one of those times Pepsi is good for you."

Dave was a physics professor at Cal Tech in Southern California. He taught high-energy physics and did research for NASA. But during the summers he was a seasonal carpenter's assistant for the Park Service at Crater Lake. He brought his wife and teenage daughter with him in a trailer and they hooked up on the backside of the Sleepy Hollow loop. On the weekends they often took trips around the region.

Dave was probably in his early fifties, a slight, meek looking sort of man. But he always gave off a bit more authority when he talked shop with Andrew the carpenter. His voice would get lower and his words became precise and calculated. He'd look Andrew in the eye and hang on every word. Then he would turn toward me, so that Andrew couldn't see, and he'd make a goofy face.

It was funny to watch the permanent B & U guys around Dave. He was a university professor with a Ph.D in physics and worked with NASA, but the permanent guys wouldn't dream of giving him an inch. And anyone who made the mistake of actually calling Dave a carpenter would get back a very curt comment like, "Dave is not the carpenter. He's a seasonal assistant." Oops. OKaaaay.

Dave didn't care about any of that, which was unusual for a Ph.D. He left his ego in Southern California. But the trait of his I liked best was his kindness. He never once said out loud that I was the worst assistant's assistant on the North American continent.

About two weeks into the Crud attack, Dave and I were repairing a cabin wall. We got that sort of one-off carpentry job each day. I would have much more preferred to lug rocks or shovel dirt out on a trail somewhere. That was manual work. I could do that with confidence. This required knowledge of sawing and hammering, and not only that—you needed to do it right. I felt bad about it every day I was assigned to Dave. There weren't many seasonal bodies on the B & U side, so poor Dave was stuck with me. I tried to make it up to him by offering intelligent and witty discussion topics to help him pass the day.

"So, Dave, I'm not a biology major, but it's got to be the water, doesn't it?"

"You'd think so. You didn't see anyone already sick when they got here, did ya?" Dave kept trying to yank nails out of the damaged wood so he could put a new sheet of plywood up.

I stood by with the new nails. "No, I didn't. They keep saying it's just a bug in the water and it always goes away. It's just a little worse this year. Or the flu's been going around, or whatever. I'll bet they're up in the conference room at park headquarters right now, either trying to figure out what the hell it really is or working on how they're going to cover their asses."

Dave surveyed his work. "That's the government way, Sam. Deny, deny, deny. Until you absolutely have to let people know, then blame it on someone else. If I were a betting man, I'd bet big right now that whatever they come up with as the reason for this outbreak, it won't be the real reason."

Dave was as far away from being a gambler as anyone could be. He was a careful man. Later that day he decided to send his wife and daughter home. They could pick him up later in the summer. He twirled his bushy mustache when he told me the plan. "Maybe now I can go out dancing. Whatya think?"

As I handed him some nails, I said, "I don't think there are many people left that could go out dancing."

By June 23rd, forty percent of all park employees had reported firsthand experience with the Crud. To make matters worse, the couple hundred concessionaire employees were arriving and becoming sick within seventy-two hours. These unlucky college kids thought working at Crater Lake Lodge or the cafeteria or the gas station or the gift shop at a national park would be a great time. Getting that minimum wage with room and board taken out. Now these poor kids would get a bonus they hadn't figured on—The Crud.

The president of Crater Lake Lodge Company was an old man named George Haswell. From all accounts, he was an old-time, small-time robber baron. With his mane of white hair, he stormed through his little world, tormenting people as best he could. He especially liked dropping a dime on the park headquarters people. He would call the regional office complaining that the snow wasn't being plowed fast enough or signs needed to be painted or, most often, that park staff weren't listening to him and he was going to lose money. He liked to point out that the contract he signed said he got this and he got that and that the Park Service had to be responsive. And usually a congressman would be named or he'd let it slip that a friend in Washington would be visiting soon and he was going to tell them this and tell them that.

Mr. Haswell was a favorite topic among the seasonal maintenance workers. Almost as much as the college girls that worked for him up at Rim Village. With no TV and everybody sick, there wasn't much to do after work but talk.

In a normal year, softball was the activity of choice. The permanents had cleared a field out beyond Sleepy Hollow, in the middle of the pines, where no one could see it from any road. A lot of park service resources and land had gone into Frank Noble Stadium. The big game each year was between the under twenty-fives and over twenty-fives. That pitted mostly seasonals against permanents, though occasionally a longtime seasonal had to switch sides because of a birthday. Another big game was the maintenance department against Crater Lake Lodge. According to lore, no rangers had ever played in the games. Maybe it was out of protest. They didn't believe that even a single Hemlock should be sacrificed for a softball diamond. It was moot so far this year. There was a lot of running going on in Sleepy Hollow, but not around any bases.

After a tumultuous beginning, my cabin evolved into an oasis in the Crud storm. I had fought one major bout with diarrhea early on. Since then, it had been just a series of queasy stomachs with occasional throwing up. But the Crud ran both my roommates out of town.

Sarge was the first casualty. He wilted before our eyes. After a sleepless night spent in the bathroom, he packed his bag, crawled into his truck and "heh-heh'd" his way back to Medford. The last thing I heard him say was that the government was going to pay him anyway, he'd see to that.

A couple days later Johnny exploded—literally—in our tiny bathroom. A wave of Crud must have caught him by surprise after he ate dinner. Surveying the aftermath, it looked like he got caught in a moment of indecision. Toilet? Sink? Shower? Oh, fuck it. You can guess the rest. I banged on the door and asked if he needed help. I couldn't understand the response, so I opened the door just a little bit.

"GET OUT, GET OUT."

"Okay, man. Sorry."

To Johnny's credit, he made an effort to clean it up. He managed to get back upstairs to his room, grabbed his bags, struggled back down the stairs, opened the door, slammed it, started up his truck and I never saw Johnny again. The next day Dave helped me clean up the rest.

I was sorry Sarge and Johnny got so sick, but I can't say that I missed having roommates.

＊ ＊ ＊

A couple days after the Stone House barbecue, Chris James stopped by my cabin after work. He went to the University of Oregon, too. He said he recognized me because he had watched me play pool a few times at the Student Union—Erb Memorial Union, more commonly called the EMU. That wasn't hard to believe as I spent probably half my college life at the EMU—in the pool room playing for dollars, napping in the student lounge, eating at least one meal a day in the cafeteria, reading out on the lawn, and I even worked some in the bowling alley. Chris was a cook in the cafeteria upstairs and took his breaks down in the game area.

I liked Chris. The top R & T clique had chosen him for their trail team even though this was his first year. He was an army veteran with no apparent chip on his shoulder—probably because he had happily done his tour in Germany. He was older than most of the seasonals—twenty-five, I think, and there may have been something about his father being a big wig in the U.S. Forest Service. So maybe it was the bloodline, I dunno. But he didn't act like most of the R & T guys—at least around me—and that alone was enough for me to like him.

Chris starred in one of the most memorable non-Crud moments of the summer. After spending a cushy school year in Eugene, his first workday at the park was at seven thousand feet, chain sawing, and then carrying, huge blocks of ice off a tourist trail at the rim. His new trail buddies never told him to pace himself, or reminded him of the altitude, or told him he was likely to get sick if he didn't take it slow and steady. Sort of an initiation prank—Roads and Trails–style.

At the end of that day, Chris unloaded himself from the truck in the maintenance yard and just stood there for a moment, looking ahead with one of those thousand-yard stares. His body started to lean forward and it looked as if the momentum of that weight shift caused him to take a step forward. And then he rocked back, then forward and another step. People yelled out to him and there were shouts of encouragement, but he just kept moving forward, one step at a time. You really couldn't call it walking. Drape some bandages over him and he WAS the Mummy.

Chris dropped by the cabin every few days, so we could spend time talking about the University of Oregon Fighting Ducks and how crappy the football team was going to be next year. The Ducks were a big deal for him and there weren't any other U of O folks around, so I guess it was me or nobody. Plus, he and Sally had become an official couple and I'm sure she encouraged him to visit, especially after my roommates departed. Occasionally they arrived at my door together and invited me to do things with them, like go to dinner at Fort Klamath or drive to the Lava Beds National Monument for a weekend hike. It was part of Sally's crusade to get me a life.

When I said I couldn't go, Chris didn't seem that unhappy. But it always annoyed Sally. There'd be an awkward moment or two and a silent test of wills. I'd have to refuse two or three times before she'd let it drop. She didn't approve of my solitary life, and she would give me a look to make sure I understood that. I thought it was pretty obvious that I didn't go because I didn't want some mercy invitation.

The ironic thing about a person like me is I wanted to be asked to go somewhere. And I really wanted to go. I just couldn't.

Despite Sally's claims that I never went anywhere, I did go with them every now and then. One night we all went to Beckie's out on Highway 62 on the Medford side of the park. This coffee shop–looking place was located at Union Creek next to one of the bigger campgrounds along the Rogue River.

Once we settled into our booth, Sally looked quite satisfied. "Now, Samuel," she said, "aren't you glad you came this time?"

"Have you ever thought, Sally, that I don't accept most of your invitations because I don't want to intrude?" I said. "I'm trying to be respectful of your private time."

She looked straight at me, an exasperated look on her face. "We ask you because we want you to come. Don't you get that?"

"Chris, could you speak to her about the facts of life— you know, boys and girls and third wheels?"

Chris just smiled. He didn't want to get involved. If I were him, I would be thinking, "Yes, Sam I would rather be out with Sally ALONE." Poor Chris.

That night I ordered something I'd never eaten before—a chicken-fried steak. Both Sally and Chris highly recommended it, so I figured what the heck. Steak encased in a deep-fried crust, topped with gravy. Why hadn't anyone told me about this before? I felt like swooning after the first bite.

Chris and Sally laughed at me.

"See, Samuel, you need to get out more," Sally said.

I barely heard her. My eyes were closed as a bite of chicken-fried steak settled in the back of my mouth. "Don't start with me right now, I'm really happy."

"Better than Beanie Weenies, huh?" she teased.

"Chris, would you get your woman off me?"

Sally glared.

Chris laughed and threw up his hands. "Sorry, you are officially on your own, pal."

Sally continued to give me the death-ray stare. If she had been standing up, her hands would have been on her hips, elbows out. But I don't think she was really, really mad. I tried, but I just couldn't imagine her really, really mad. That was part of what made Sally and Chris seem the perfect match. They both were just so darned nice. And the funny thing was, they both kinda looked alike, too. Both had blonde hair, blue eyes and really big, easy smiles. They belonged together.

The first time he dropped in on me, Chris talked about Sally. He didn't know I had seen them together by the stream at the barbecue. He asked me whether I knew which of the two girls he liked. Obviously I knew, but I shook my head no.

"Most of the guys are all worked up about Marcy— and I guess she is the prettiest one. But I think Sally's the special one."

Chris wasn't giddy, but he seemed content. I don't know any other way to describe it. Maybe it was like eating chicken-fried steak for the first time. I was heartbroken when I put the last forkful in my mouth.

"Don't be sad, Samuel," said Sally. "You've probably never had fresh Marionberry pie, either."

It wasn't just fresh Marionberry pie. It was warm, fresh Marionberry pie with a huge scoop of vanilla ice cream melting on top. I was stuffed from dinner, but my stomach accepted my apology and in it went, bite by bite. How was I going to live without this?

✳ ✳ ✳

Sally and I saw each other about three times a week somewhere on the job. She worked an early shift, so our lunch and break times might intersect and we'd have a chance to talk. Sometimes I might see her walking around after she got off work and I'd take a few minutes to see what she was up to.

I definitely liked Sally. There had been that moment of instant attraction when I first saw her fiddling with her hard hat outside the maintenance office. I saw that smile, and it was a done deal. I could pretend all I wanted to, but the truth was, I liked her. I'd really enjoyed our first chat on the amphitheater benches. She was funny and smart.

The unnerving part of it all was that she seemed to like me, too. Not romantically, of course. I wasn't that dumb. For some reason, she seemed to want to know things about me. She was often shy about herself, but always full of questions about me. We'd run into each other somewhere, say hello, and then she'd just start in. Where else had I lived? What was my family like? Had I been to other parks? What did I like about them? What was I reading? Once, she actually asked me what I wanted to be when I grew up.

She always listened to my answers. It was like she was entirely focused on me. She never really pushed, except maybe in a teasing kind of a way, but she'd watch me as I talked, nod or smile, and just listen. And sometimes she'd bump into me when we were walking along. On purpose. It didn't feel like she was flirting, just making contact. But I never got used to it. Every time she touched me, it shocked me. I didn't know how to deal with a human being like that. Especially a female human being.

I wanted the attention, but, truthfully, it intruded on my comfort zone. I'd never had a girlfriend. There had been a couple of times when I thought a girl might like me. Once, when I was a freshman at U of O, this girl in my contemporary fiction class starting timing it so she'd be walking out the door with me at the end of class. She'd talk to me—ask how I liked the book we were reading, or make a joke about something the teacher had said in class. But she never gave me any concrete evidence that she liked me—like a marriage proposal or something—so I never got around to asking her out. After a while, she started timing it so she didn't walk out with me.

None of my guy friends seemed interested in much more than shooting hoops and drinking beer. So how was I to know what all this "sharing" with Sally was supposed to mean? I didn't want to make a fool of myself.

One morning Sally and I found ourselves in the Mazama campground at the same time. I was down there with Dave, putting in new redwood signs. She was helping clean the restrooms. It was Sally's lunchtime, so we walked over to Annie Creek for a break. That was one of the best things about this park. You could turn a corner and feel like you were in the middle of nowhere—a very beautiful nowhere.

As we approached the creek, Sally grabbed my arm and whispered, "Oh look, Samuel."

Just ahead of us stood a doe. I expected her to bolt. But she didn't. She just stood there watching us while we watched her. Neither Sally nor I moved.

I turned my head to Sally, but she held her fingers up to her lips. And then the doe turned and melted into the shadows of the pine trees that lined the banks of the creek.

Sally pulled a red apple out of her lunch bag and laid it on the ground near where the doe had stood. "She might come back," Sally said.

We sat with our backs up against a large tree trunk. I tossed a stone into the creek. She looked into her lunch bag again, but grimaced and quickly crumpled it closed. There was a soft breeze. We relaxed, listening to the gurgling of the creek.

Out of the blue she asked, "Do you like working here, Samuel?"

"Yeah. I do. But you can't tell anyone. It'd ruin my reputation. What about you?"

"I love working here. I think this is about the most beautiful place on earth. Every morning I wake up and I can't believe I'm here. I don't care that I spend most of my time cleaning toilets. I'd do just about anything to be here." She turned to look at me. "But you know, it's tough being a girl in this park."

"What do you mean?"

She laughed. "Oh, nothing. What a dumb thing to say." Then she changed the subject. "You know, I'm having second thoughts about my Russian Studies major. It's gonna mean an awful lot of time cooped up in the library. I can't seem to remember why I wanted to do that."

"Is this all of a sudden, Sally?"

"Not really. Maybe." She paused and I threw another pebble into the creek. "I'm not seeing things very clearly right now."

"What things?"

"Oh, my life. I seem to be having an identity crisis. Everything used to seem so simple. I thought I knew what I wanted. I could look ten years down the road and see it happening. But now I'm just not so sure. I seem to keep making mistakes. Maybe my major is just another one."

"What does Chris say about it?"

She looked over at me. "He says to do what will make me happy. I just don't know what that is anymore." She pulled up her knees and leaned forward. She rested her chin on the back of her hands. The yellow helmet sat in the dirt next to her. "What do you think, Samuel?"

I threw a bigger rock down stream. *Kerplunk.*

"First of all, changing majors isn't a big deal. Who doesn't change their major at least once? I started as a journalism major. That was stupid. But I think it happens to everybody, so don't let it bother you if you decide to change. And second of all, I'd like to see you change your major. I've never understood the Russian Studies thing. I don't think it's really you."

"So, Mr. Hunter, who is the real me?"

"I don't know exactly. Somebody who helps other people somehow."

"It's that simple?"

"Yup. From where I'm sitting anyway."

We both leaned back against the tree trunk, listening to the creek, thinking about the other. At least I did.

* * *

"You won't believe what I saw today," Chris said, closing my cabin door behind him.

"What now?" I asked. I was laying on the couch reading *Jaws*. With no more snow or ice covering the cabin windows, I could actually read by natural light.

"The crew stopped in at the store at Rim Village during a break. Wanted to get some canned stuff, some Cokes, some beer."

"How can you drink beer with all this crap going around? Wait a minute. You had beer in a government vehicle?"

"Uh, no."

"Right. Okay, what happened?"

"We walked out through the cafeteria. Looking around, you know. I swear at least three of the girls at the buffet line looked sick as dogs. They were serving the tourists. They obviously had the Crud. Isn't there a law or something against that? I almost gagged thinking about it. Man, there's going to be a trail of sick people all up and down this state."

"From what I've heard, Mr. Haswell will let them vomit in the food before he'll let someone off work."

"SAM! OH, don't even say that. I'm going to puke right here."

"Chris, this could be anything. We're so isolated. We don't have the slightest idea what's going on. Do you have any confidence that the park bosses have a clue at all about this? I'm thinking someone might have to die before anything's done. Okay, maybe not die, but MAYBE—"

"Well, if you saw those girls on the buffet line today, George Haswell certainly thinks that." Chris took a seat in the plastic covered chair next to the furnace.

"Chris, have you heard any management people say that the water was a possibility at all? Because I haven't. They don't even entertain that idea. It's the flu. It's the flu. We called the doctors in Klamath Falls. It's the flu, okay?"

"Why did I bring this up with you? How stupid can I be? Not even you can believe the Park Service would knowingly put us at risk. You don't, do you, Sam? I mean, c'mon."

"Well, let's review the possibilities. One, it's the flu. Two hundred people get the most virulent strain of flu seen on the West Coast in fifty years. And, oh, by the way, no other community in the country has seen anything like the high percentage of sick people that we have. But we all eventually get better. Two, it's the flu and some of us die. Three, it's something in the water and the Park Service doesn't know it. Some of us die. Four, it's something in the water and the Park Service does know it. Eventually they fix it and maybe some of us don't die. Five, it's a bubonic plague thing nobody knows about until some of us die. Six, an alien race has dropped a biological bomb in some sort of reverse *War of the Worlds* thing and most of us die."

Chris got up from the chair and looked out the window. I continued.

"See what I mean? So out of the six things that might be happening only one scenario has nobody dying for sure. I don't know about you, but I think someone needs to be working a little harder on this problem."

Chris turned around and looked at me. "So, Sam, who do you think shot Kennedy?"

"Don't go there, Christopher. You have that look of a Republican to me. Don't make me bring up the big W. You did watch your boy Nixon give it up last summer, right? Watergate. Big-time conspiracy. You remember that, right?"

"I'm outta here. No wonder you don't go out much."

"Say hi to Sally for me. Go Ducks."

As he headed out the door, Chris said he hadn't seen Sally today because she was sick. Apparently she had the Crud bad and wasn't receiving visitors. I was sorry to hear about Sally. I hoped the Crud didn't do too much damage to her happy disposition. Maybe I'd try to visit. It might shock the Crud right out of her if I showed up.

Things could be better, but as long as I didn't die, life in Sleepy Hollow wasn't so bad. Just the occasional stomachache. A cabin to myself. Dave for a boss. Sally. The Park Service was still paying me despite my total ineptitude. I had had sort of a rough start, but despite the Crud outbreak I had gotten into a comfortable groove at beautiful Crater Lake National Park.

The next morning was bright, crisp and quiet. No fog pouring over the cliffs. A beautiful day had arrived.

When I got to the maintenance office, I saw a piece of paper taped to the door. It looked Park Service official. It had these words hand written on it: "Sick employees are instructed to use Kaopectate for their flu."

CHAPTER 6

I STRADDLED THE PEAK of the cabin roof, scooting on my butt to where Dave perched, tapping in shingles. If I slipped, gravity would take over and there would be a collision with the ground. This cabin wasn't tall, but I knew I could reasonably expect a broken bone if that happened.

This stone cabin was one of several situated on the high ground behind park headquarters. Seasonal rangers lived here. While digging it out, a snowcat had put a dramatic gouge in the roof.

I don't like heights, which was embarrassingly obvious to anyone watching. Dave had sprinted up the ladder and quickly walked across the rooftop. Me? I scooted along on my butt. Dave didn't stare or laugh. He just kept positioning, then nailing, the shingles. I could have stayed on the ground. Dave wouldn't have cared. But I felt I should at least make an effort.

Actually, it wasn't so bad once I got there. I looked around, momentarily relieved.

"Hey, Sam. I didn't see you there. How ya doing?"

"Just came up to offer some tips. Your shingle work looks a little rusty."

"Great. I need all the help I can get. I don't get much shingle practice back at Cal Tech."

For some reason I could handle exposing my frailties in front of Dave, though I was loathe to in front of any other person on Earth. I suppose I had no choice. I had nowhere to hide out on a job. I often imagined him going home after work and stomping around his trailer complaining to his wife about that dumb-ass assistant he had to put up with. Nah. I'm sure there were chuckles, but no unkind ranting. At least I hoped not.

"Dave, I've been wondering what you think of your students' liberal political views. You get a fair amount of demonstrations down your way."

He laughed as he pounded a wooden shingle into place. He reached for another one. He split it to fit the next space.

"I try to be very nice to them," he said. He looked up from his work for a second. "It's so sad when they find out what the world is really like. I feel bad for them."

"What does that mean?" I asked. I wasn't actually helping Dave. But I was working hard at not falling off the roof.

"Well, take the 72 election. The students were talking big about McGovern this and McGovern that. The eighteen-year-olds were getting to vote for the first time. The Vietnam War. It was a done deal, McGovern was going to win. Poor guys, it was a real blow. They think the whole world is like the five people they know. And you know what, Sam? The voting results for the major universities in California showed Nixon won in a landslide there, just like everywhere else."

"I voted for McGovern, Dave."

"Sorry, Sam. I guess you didn't buy that stuff about the silent majority, either."

"Nope. Still don't."

"What's it going to take? McGovern got about a hundred votes, didn't he? You've got to remember that there are a fair number of liberals on the coasts, but everyone in between IS conservative. Never underestimate how conservative this country is. When I see the student activists around campus I sometimes think about some officer leading troops into battle. He jumps out of the trench and runs at the enemy yelling, 'C'mon boys.' He's charging forward, then looks behind him and he's all by himself with the enemy's guns in his face."

"So you're against liberals. I didn't think you would be."

"I'm not against liberals, I'm against being an idiot."

"THOSE DAMN STUPID COLLEGE KIDS," I yelled. Dave laughed. He was back to fitting shingles.

"Hey, Sam, look who's coming down the road. Isn't that Sally?"

It sure was. She was walking slowly down the road that led to the Stone House.

"You better go down and see how she's doing." Great. Of course, I wanted to go check on Sally. But the thought of maneuvering across the roof again so soon didn't thrill me.

"Are you trying to get rid of me, Dave?"

"As a matter of fact…"

"Fine, I'm outta here."

Luckily, Sally was still too far away to see me shakily duck-walk across the roof and very deliberately climb down the ladder. Once I was firmly on the ground, I stood next to the truck and waited for her.

She didn't look so hot. The closer she got, the paler she looked. She had on her standard Building and Utilities crew garb—tennis shoes, jeans, and a Penn State t-shirt. But she was trudging more than walking. She looked wobbly.

"Hey, Sally. What were you doing at the house? Skipping work today?"

She grabbed the tailgate to stop her downhill momentum. Without saying a word, she turned her body so she could rest more comfortably against the truck.

I knew enough not to say something like, "You look terrible" or "What happened to you?" or "My God, Sally, what's wrong with you?" or even something as neutral as "Are you okay?" but I didn't know what to do.

Sally looked at me. Tears rolled down her cheeks. Her whole body shook and slowly she slid down the side of the truck till she was sitting on the ground.

I quickly knelt down, putting my hand on her shoulder. "Sally?"

"I wish I'd never come to this damn place," Sally said in between sobs. "I wish I'd never come."

I could hear the ladder rattle as Dave climbed down off the roof. Sally heard it too and quickly stood up. She wiped her face with her shirt and took a couple of big breaths.

"Hey, Sally, what's going on?" Dave called as he walked over.

She turned to me. "Don't say anything. I'm fine, just a little sick."

"What's the matter?" I whispered.

"Shhh. Not now, Samuel. Please."

Dave came walking around the corner, a hammer in one hand and a can of nails in the other. "Hey Sally, you look terrible."

I tried to save Dave from the mistake he was making. "She's all right, Dave—" but Sally cut me off.

"Oh thanks, Dave. Just what a girl wants to hear. Samuel, can you teach your partner some manners?" Her smile wavered, then took, and—just like that—everything seemed back to normal.

When it came to understanding people, I was always a little behind. What just happened with Sally? And how in the hell did Dave get away with saying that? I would have been skewered.

"Had the Crud bad, huh, Sally?" asked Dave.

"Yeah, this whole week. I have two new friends: Mr. Toilet and Mr. Garbage Can. I've become especially close with Mr. Garbage Can. I dunno… Maybe it's something to do with all those toilets I love to clean. My firsthand observations indicate there are a lot of sick people in this park. I'll spare you the details. I've only drunk water that's been boiled, so I don't know what it is."

While we were talking, Ranger Bob pulled up in his park service green station wagon. He had turned out to be a good guy. He always waved when he drove by. And despite that dire warning he gave me the day we met, I know for a fact that he let a couple maintenance folks off when he could have easily given them a ticket. He was my only access to the mysterious world of the park rangers.

"Hey, Bob, got any news on the killer Crud?"

"Well, I got a few little news items, if you don't quote me on them."

Dave and I moved closer to his car. Sally stayed where she was, keeping one arm on the truck. Ranger Bob leaned out his window, looked around and started in on his report.

"Some of the permanent park service guys have gone to the superintendent and asked him about the water quality. They also asked if they could take some water samples down to the Klamath County Health Department. I guess the superintendent told them that the water is tested frequently. Although, between you and me, I don't know who is doing the testing. I've worked here for six summers and I haven't heard of anybody who had the job of testing the water."

Ranger Bob was clearly enjoying his role as Deep Throat. He looked around again before going on.

"The superintendent said that Klamath County had no jurisdiction in a national park. And he told them that nobody was taking any water samples anywhere. He said it would be a waste of time.

"And one other thing. We're starting to hear reports of tourists getting sick after they leave the park. Gas station people are complaining of soiled restrooms all the way to the California line."

"So, Bob, what do you think it is?" I asked.

"That's way above my pay grade, Sam. I just report the news, I don't make it."

"I think you should start an underground newspaper."

Ranger Bob made the motion of zipping his lips and with a little salute, slowly drove down toward park head-quarters, around the parking lot, and out onto the main highway, headed toward the rim.

"We're dead men," I said.

"And women," Sally called from over by the truck.

Dave grinned at Sally. "Well, I don't want anybody dying before I have to make a honey run," he said. "I've been informed that we three will be honored with that task this year."

The dreaded honey run. About a third of the way around the rim was a steep trail down to Cleetwood Cove where tourists could get a boat ride to Wizard Island and then around the Lake. It was the only access to the Lake. I hadn't been there yet, but from what I'd been told there were two port-a-potties at the bottom and another on Wizard Island that periodically needed to be emptied—by hand.

It wasn't unexpected news. I had predicted I would be getting that kind of duty, being a newbie. Sally fit that cat-egory, too. But poor Dave.

When Dave had said "honey run," he just started laugh-ing. Actually, anyone who said it laughed. For Dave, I think it was a defense mechanism. He got the job every year. It must be the maintenance managers' joke. Honey runs didn't fit the job description of assistant carpenter, but he was a Ph.D. so they probably saw it as a fun way to make sure he remembered his place. Every day, from that point on, Dave would find a way to get honey run into the conversation. Then he would laugh.

"So, Sally, you want a ride back to your house?" I asked.

"No, I don't want to go back there. I've been cooped up long enough."

"Well, I'm not trying to say anything negative but, you know, you looked kind of wobbly walking down here," I said.

Dave ended the discussion neatly. "It's a long walk up to your house, Sally, let Sam drive you. Lie out in the sun and rest up. You don't want to see Mr. Garbage Can later tonight, do ya? Sam, go ahead, drive her."

Dave opened the passenger door of the truck and gently pushed her toward the seat. "C'mon, let's go. Go on, now."

"All right. Damn." She smiled at Dave before she slid in.

Thank God for Dave. I don't think I could have talked her into going home. Dave really could switch on that air of authority when he wanted. Later he'd brush it off, saying something goofy like, "Yup, I got a way with the ladies."

Sally and I were quiet as the truck wound its way up the hill toward the Stone House. Sally leaned back against the seat and closed her eyes. She looked sad again. That's what kept eating at me. She didn't just look sick. Her spirit was missing.

"I could bring you up some dinner later, Sally."

"Thanks, Samuel, but a can of Beanie Weenies is not what this stomach needs. I plan on skipping dinner tonight. Go to bed early."

Then she turned to me. "Samuel?"

"Yes."

"Don't say anything. Okay?"

"About what?"

"You know what. It's nothing."

"It wasn't nothing."

"Don't say anything to Chris, okay? I know you're thinking about telling him, but don't. I'm serious. It's nothing."

I drove into the Stone House driveway. Sally got out and slowly walked around to my side of the truck.

"I know you won't say anything. I'll tell you someday, honest."

She turned toward the house. I hadn't said anything. I didn't know what to say. I had patted her on the arm. How did she know I wouldn't say anything?

The next day Frank Noble called an all-hands-on-deck meeting for 11:00 a.m. at the maintenance office. Someone had decided it was time to give the folks at the bottom of the information totem pole a carefully crafted message from park headquarters. From the carpenter's shop I could see trucks starting to pull up with the crews about five minutes before. Dave was in the back of the shop gouging out a sign from a block of redwood.

My job was to watch for the perfect time to head out to the meeting. We didn't want to be early because the office was small and the smoke was thick. Some of the permanent truck drivers liked pipes and almost all of them smoked something. Plus, if you got in there too early you got squeezed from people pushing to be near Frank and thus bask in his majesty's glow and good will.

Dave and I wanted to avoid all that by positioning ourselves in the hall, just close enough to yell, "Yo" if Frank barked out, "Are Dave and Hunter here?"

I saw Hazel and Sally. No Marcy. Sally looked like a different person today. She was striding, not trudging, and talking animatedly with Hazel as they walked to the maintenance office.

I counted the folks arriving for the meeting. I'd say we were down almost half of the thirty seasonals who had started work this summer. The permanents were still going strong, even those that lived on campus. Rumor reported a sick child or two across the street at Steel Circle, but I hadn't heard that firsthand. It fed perfectly into the conspiracy theories. "They're just not telling us. They don't want us to know."

"Hey, Dave, it's time. Let's go, man."

As I opened the maintenance office door I heard Frank yell out, "Okay, listen up. Is everyone here?" Dave flashed me a thumbs up. We couldn't see Frank. He was down the hall and around the corner, but only twenty feet away from where we were leaning against the wall, so we could hear everything just fine.

Down the hall I could see people squished in around a table and along the wall in back of the table. Hazel and Sally were pushed in against Chris and his trail crew brothers.

"Headquarters wants me to get you people up to date on what we know about the flu problem we're having. It's not a whole lot, but here it is. The water is being tested and no one has found anything wrong with the water. Period. Nothing. So we need to stop spreading rumors. It just makes matters worse. We don't want to be whining like little girls about this.

"The people who are supposed to know say IT IS THE FLU. That should be good enough for us.

"Starting tomorrow we're going to have visitors in the park, looking for whatever is causing this. There will be State Health people, as well as Federal Public Health people. And, just in case, they will be looking hard at the water supply. So I don't want to hear from anybody that we're not doing anything to find out what the problem is.

"We're sending out B & U people with these health folks to do whatever they need.

"I've heard that a few less people are getting sick, so maybe it's almost over. I don't know. The thing I do know is it's holding up softball season and I can't wait to kick some seasonal butt.

"Any questions? Or maybe I should say, any questions I can answer?"

A trail guy raised his hand. "I heard the superintendent had refused to send samples out to be tested."

"That's crap!" Frank smiled, realizing he had made an unintentional pun. There were a few uncertain chuckles. "I was at headquarters today and was told by the boss himself that everything that could be done was being done. He said it was just one of those things and we were going to have to fight through it."

"Anything else?

Pause.

"All right then, let's take an early lunch and then get back to work."

Dave and I rushed out the door. We stopped at the carpentry shop so Dave could put his tools away before we headed down to Sleepy Hollow for lunch. While I waited for Dave, I saw Hazel and Sally come out of the maintenance office and walk toward their truck. They worked an earlier schedule, so they had already eaten and needed to get back to their cleaning rounds.

Everyone else was still in the maintenance office eating lunch or deciding where to go eat lunch. Sally walked about halfway to the truck, then stopped. She turned around like someone had called her. She looked back toward Hazel and gave her an I'll-be-right-there-so-go-ahead wave. She took a couple steps back toward the office and stopped. She was waiting for someone.

Out of the corner of my eye, I saw Frank jogging toward her. That was odd. Frank wasn't her boss. What could he possible want with Sally? He reached her, stuffed his hands in his front pockets and bent down slightly. It looked as if he was talking directly to her ear. Sally listened, but stared off at about a ninety-degree angle. Her body was tense, her face blank.

Abruptly she walked off at a brisk pace. Frank watched her for a second, then marched back toward the maintenance office.

Dave bumped into me. "Hey, ready to go, bub?"

"Dave, have you noticed that a lot of weird things are going on around here?"

"Well, Sam, I'm sure that some day you're going to be a genuine college graduate. How do I know that? Because you are such a fast learner."

I opened the door. "Dave, was that a shot?"

He pushed me out the door. "C'mon, lunchtime."

* * *

I got in the habit of taking a nap after work. It was dead time. I had nothing to do, and it was depressing thinking that I had nothing to do, so sleeping worked just fine. I usually woke up right as the sun started to go down. Just in time to eat a quick dinner and head out for a walk in the twilight.

My dinner consisted of Beanie Weenies most nights. I bought the little cans by the case. It was inconvenient that they only came in tiny cans. I could get big cans of pork and beans, but I liked the Beanie Weenies. Something about those little hot dogs. But because they came in the small size, I had to eat at least three cans to make a meal. I'd open the can by yanking off the pull top and set the can in a pan on the stove. The Beanie Weenies got warm in the can and voila.

At school I might pour the Beanie Weenies into a pot and warm them up, but at Crater Lake I wasn't washing any pans in that questionable water, no matter what the superintendent said. I didn't drink the water; I wasn't too sick. End of story.

I'd grab a Dr. Pepper and I was out the door.

There's nothing like the cool summertime evening air in the mountains. Not really cold or even chilling, unless you got out in the wind somewhere on the rim. Cleansing. Refreshing. Out with the bad air, in with the new. The aches disappeared and the swelling went down.

The landmarks around me were familiar by now, some even good friends. The cliff above the maintenance yard was Castle Crest Ridge. The valley where we worked and lived was Munson Valley and the little stream in back of the maintenance building was Munson Creek.

On the park headquarters side of the maintenance yard there was a two-story wooden shed behind a more modern storage building. We stacked the snow poles in the old shed. Out behind the wooden shed was the only man-made treasure at Crater Lake Park—*The Lady of the Woods*. *The Lady* is a partially finished nude, sculpted out of the top of a six-foot-tall chunk of volcanic rock. *The Lady* is small—maybe thirty-six inches tall. She sits on a rock chair, leaning forward against the rock with her head buried in her arms. She made me sad every time I saw her. Park literature says she's a "sleeping beauty." I don't think so. I visited her quite often. I wished she were sleeping, but to me it looked more like she was crying.

The sculptor, Dr. Earl Russell Bush, was a surgeon for the U.S. Engineers stationed in Crater Lake National Park. He began chipping away stone on October 4, 1917. When his tour of duty ended fifteen days later, he left *The Lady of the Woods* unfinished.

Park literature speculates that *The Lady* sleeps, waiting for the sculptor to come back and finish his work. Dr. Bush did visit her once—thirty-seven years later. He offered no explanation.

For the record, this is his only official comment on his work: "This statue represents my offering to the forest, my interpretation of its awful stillness and repose, its beauty, fascination, and unseen life. A deep love of this virgin wilderness has fastened itself upon me and remains today. It seemed that I must leave something behind…if it arouses thought in those who see it, I shall be amply repaid. I shall be satisfied to leave my feeble attempt at sculptural expression alone and unmarked, for those who may happen to see it and who may find food for thought along the lines it arouses in them individually. It would be sacrilege to assign a title and decorate it with a brass plate."

The Lady was Dr. Bush's first sculpture. He went on to take sculpting classes with esteemed artists, but never again created anything that had such an impact on so many people.

I give Crater Lake credit for that. The power of this place could make the man. If only Crater Lake could straighten up the bureaucrats running the park. Actually, I'd settle for them just not killing me with bad water or furnaces.

And now there was this new problem with Sally. I didn't want her to become another *Lady of the Woods*. Should I ask her about Frank? Should I talk to Chris? Should I demand she tell me everything? Could I do anything?

The Lady of the Woods lives back in the Hemlock forest, and night had snuck up on me. I could handle pitch-black if I was out on the pavement, but I hadn't learned to go cross-county quite yet. I laid my hand on her head. "See you later, *Lady of the Woods*. If there's anything I can do, let me know. Please."

CHAPTER 7

THE NEXT MORNING DAN JENKINS led a Building and Utilities convoy up the road to the Munson Springs pump house. Dan, Andrew, and I were in the command truck. Don the electrician took two new guys in the second truck. Behind them came two orange crew cab trucks stuffed with eager high school kids and counselors. Every one in this parade wore a bright yellow plastic hard hat.

The high school kids represented a new federal program called the Youth Conservation Corps. The idea was to get teenagers out into the national parks to work on conservation projects. In this, the first year of the program, Crater Lake National Park got its share of YCCers. Twenty-five or so lived in the old Ranger Dorm next to park headquarters, about half a mile from Sleepy Hollow.

The YCC hadn't been in the park long, but they had one thing in common with the rest of us—many had been sick as dogs. The different factions—maintenance workers, rangers, lodge kids, YCCers—worked in different worlds across this huge park, but when it came to the Crud, word got around fast.

The Munson Springs pump house sat at the top of Munson Valley. It was the elegant, square, one-story, rock structure I noticed on my first drive up to the lake. Park headquarters was about a mile back down the road, less as the crow flies. The road to the rim did a switchback around the pump house and Munson Springs, then continued up and back around the next hill. Because the pump house was the only man-made structure around, it stood out. But the old rock walls also helped it blend in. I'd never seen anyone there before, but I had a feeling its solitary days were over.

Dan parked the truck on the side of the road across from the pump house. One of the YCC trucks pulled in behind us. Don and the other YCC truck went by and up the hill toward Rim Village. I had no idea where they were going, but the precision of our B & U unit was impressive.

Dan had kept the mission plan to himself. Normally easy-going, today his face was tight and a bit red. He looked like someone who had just been reamed by his boss, or maybe it was just a sunburn. We had waited in the maintenance office for about an hour, wondering when he would show up. All I had been told was "wait in the office, Hunter, you won't be going with Dave today." Dan eventually showed up with the YCC in tow. He was clearly unhappy. Frank sat at his desk and chuckled just loud enough for everyone to hear.

"Let's go," Dan yelled. No one chose to ask him where we were going.

The maintenance office wait had given me time to talk to my new roommates. Tom and Paul arrived at the park that morning, just in time for work. For bookkeeping purposes, they replaced Sarge and Johnny, but they were hired for a specific B & U task—painting. They were told to bunk in my cabin. Tom was rough looking, with a five o'clock shadow and clumps of brown hair sticking out in all directions from under his helmet. Paul was about six-foot-five, looked fifteen, and wore a bright orange Oregon State sweatshirt spattered with different colors of paint.

We sat at the table waiting for orders, Tom and Tall Paul drinking coffee. "So, did they tell you guys about the Crud down at the regional office?" I asked.

"The WHAT?" Tom blurted out.

"They didn't say anything to you about a problem we were having up here?" I threw in a look of disbelief.

"Nope."

"What about the flu? Did they say anything about that?" Now I shook my head for full effect.

Tall Paul answered. "Yeah, they did say the stomach flu was going around, so bring some Kaopectate just in case."

I started laughing. "I swear, some day someone's going to write a book about the summer of 75 at Crater Lake National Park. Boys, you've walked into the middle of an epidemic of biblical proportions. There are more than one hundred people sick as dogs in this park. And I'm not talking oh-I-have-a-headache sick. I'm talking your-mother-better-come-for-you-if-she-ever-wants-to-see-you-again sick."

I had their full attention now. From the corner of my eye, I saw Don the electrician hurrying down the hall with a scowl on his face.

"Remember these words: don't drink the water," I whispered. "In no way let that water into your body or you're going to be puking up stuff you ate in high school."

"No one has proved that there's anything wrong with the water, Sam," said Don, with an exasperated look on his face. "Don't listen to him, you two. There's a lot of talk going around, but it's some kind of bad flu and it will be gone soon. Happens every June to the seasonals. Just not normally this bad. Did you get some Kaopectate?"

They both nodded. They were both now giving their coffee cups a funny look.

Don gave the thumbs up sign. When the electrician walked away Tom and Paul gave me inquiring looks. I pulled an imaginary zipper across my lips, stood up and walked down the hall.

When we arrived at Munson Springs, Dan got out of the truck and huddled with Andrew and the thirty-something leader of the YCC gaggle. Dan delivered his orders, crossed the road and walked down the path to the pump house. The YCC leader met with his troops. Andrew came over to brief me at the back of the truck where I was standing.

"Sam, what we're going to do is look around the watershed and see if we can find anything out of the ordinary. Look through those trees in back of you. See that clearing in about seventy-five yards? That clearing is a little valley that goes all the way up to Crater Lake Lodge. The Lodge is not that far up there. Because the road winds around, you think it's a long way up, but it really isn't. Anyway, that valley and its surroundings is the watershed for the springs. If there is anything contaminating the spring, it could come from there."

"What am I looking for?" I asked.

"I really can't tell you. I guess it would be anything that could contaminate the water supply. But I don't know what that would be. Maybe the Russians are flying over dropping chemicals bombs and it's seeping into the spring."

Andrew was perplexed. He stared through the Hemlocks, then turned and looked over at Munson Springs.

"You know, what about the Viet Cong?" I said. "The Japanese floated those balloon bombs over during WW II. Maybe the Viet Cong did it before the end of the war and they're just getting here now. What do you think?"

Andrew ignored me. "I doubt there's any chance we'll be able to see anything because, once you get past the trees, the snow's probably at least six feet deep. That valley is protected from the sun by all the trees. The YCC's got some antique snowshoes, but I don't know if that's going to help them get in there and see what's up. Don the electrician and his group went up to the Lodge to look down into the valley and, if possible, walk down into the watershed to look around."

I really, really wanted to say something smart like, "Gee, Andrew, you mean it might not be the flu?" But even I knew that would be unwise. Actually, I had to admit they had a sound strategy. Even if you didn't believe it was the water, you'd better make darn sure because you don't want anybody coming in from outside and showing you up. That definitely would be a career-ender. And the pressure was on—I'd heard that, for the first time, a state health official was in the park looking around.

As I watched the enthusiastic YCC kids scramble up the snow-packed hill, I wondered just how much the regional headquarters in Klamath Falls really knew about the situation up here. I couldn't believe they would knowingly send two new recruits up if they thought there was something out of the ordinary going on.

Andrew and I went to work searching the ground closest to the road. We let the YCC kids go up and play in the deep snow. We scraped at the frozen ground with shovels. If we were going to see anything, it likely would show up as some discoloration in the snow.

After awhile Dan popped out of the pump house. He stared hard at the creek coming from the spring. Andrew left to join him. Together they hiked down the hill, studying Munson Creek as they walked.

Just about then, the YCC leader appeared out of the forest. He jumped down to the road from a rock outcropping. He looked friendly enough for park service personnel. He didn't wear a uniform and had un-park service-like long blond hair. Maybe I could get some firsthand information from him. He brushed snow off his pants.

"Hi. I'm Sam Hunter. See anything up there?"

"Mark Johnson. Not really." He stopped brushing snow to shake hands. "I don't think we would see anything if it were there because the snow is so deep. The kids up there are mostly just flopping around. There's really nothing they can do. I think it's worth looking because this situation is so bad, but…"

"Wow, you're the first park service person I've heard admit that this is a bad situation."

He laughed.

"Well, YCC isn't park service. We're a federal program, but paid for by another agency. We're just visitors that the park service puts up with because they have to. This IS a bad situation. I'm responsible for these teenagers. It's my job to worry. You know, I've been in to see the superintendent more than once about this, but he just blows me off. I told him I'd like to take water and stool samples down to the Klamath County health people, but he told me, rather emphatically, that I shouldn't waste my time. I left him with the impression that I was going to let it drop. But you know what?

I shook my head no. "What?"

"Keep this under your hat, but I took some samples down to Klamath Falls yesterday after work. We should hear back soon."

"Oh my God, you ARE the man, Mark."

He looked around to see if anyone could hear him.

"Well, I'm not absolutely sure, but technically the superintendent can't fire me because I don't work for the Park Service. I'm a political appointee. And if push came to shove I think I could make the case that, in a situation like this, especially with kids involved, it's better to be safe than sorry. You know what I mean? Seems like a good defense."

"Mark, you are my hero. I've got to write this time down. 10:45 a.m., Wednesday, July 2nd, 1975. The first time I heard a lick of sense at Crater Lake National Park. I'm glad I was here to share this moment with you."

I shook his hand again. He laughed and walked a few feet down the road to where he could watch his teenagers.

The tourist traffic had picked up as we talked. By this time of day, almost eleven, the campers and Winnebagos were winding their way up the hill to the rim. I wanted to run out in the middle of the road and flag each one down and warn them about the water. "Don't drink it, please." But if I did that the park rangers would wrestle me to the ground then escort me off the premises. I felt bad. Some of these tourists were going to get sick.

But how about this new player, Mark? Obviously he wasn't a government management type, talking like that to a stranger. Only a political appointee would so brazenly ignore the chain of command.

I could see Dan and Andrew walking back up the hill toward us. Mark took that as a cue to go round up his boys and girls. Dan didn't look any happier after his little hike.

Fifteen minutes later we drove past the Rim Village Store on our way to the Lodge parking lot to join the other half of our B & U battalion.

Then I heard, "Oh Shit" and the truck accelerated. I could see two people arguing up ahead. "Andrew, when we get there, tell Mark to get his YCC kids back down the hill; we won't need his group the rest of the day. Tell him to move it." Dan got on the radio and called headquarters. His message was, "Get somebody with authority up here, right now. Haswell and the state health guy are screaming at each other out in front of the Lodge."

Yup. George Haswell was putting on a show. His hands flailed over his head. He danced back and forth in front of this poor state guy. Haswell was old, but he still looked intimidating. And he was tall—about five inches taller than the state guy. The state guy wasn't saying anything. His jaw was pushed out and he was staring hard at the crazy guy jumping around in front of him.

The confrontation must have just started. They hadn't attracted any civilians yet, even though they were in voice range of the Lodge entrance. Don, the two new guys and the other YCC group watched the hoopla from about fifty yards down the short road that goes to the lodge employee dormitory.

Dan screeched to a stop about ten yards behind Haswell. That slowed the concessionaire down. He looked around, saw it was Dan and turned to make his case. Dan barely got out of the truck before Haswell was on him.

The old guy wore a white dress shirt, open at the collar, and a light blue, unzipped windbreaker. I figured he got to act like he did because, in this land of odd behavior, he was king. No natural predators. He was bulletproof. In the real world, he'd be dumped by the roadside because no one was going to take that kind of crap. But here he could blow up on anyone until the inevitable day of reckoning.

"Dan. What is this asshole from the state doing in a National Park? He has absolutely no jurisdiction here. It's illegal for him to be sniffing around."

"Mr. Haswell, you need to calm down. Someone from headquarters is coming up to talk with you about it. They will be here in a just a minute. But I'm sure they're not going to talk with you unless you calm down."

"Calm down? This state guy just said there are a lot of sick people in Crater Lake National Park and someone has to get to the bottom of it. Where did he get that? There are NOT a lot of sick people here. We have about ten sick people and they're not that sick. We give 'em a little Bubble Up and they're fine. What's he talking about? He can't say stuff like that. It's going to get out and people are going to stop coming to the park. It would be a disaster."

This was getting good. Andrew had ordered the YCC to retreat and was now walking down to find out what Don and the new guys knew about what was going on. I got out of the truck and nonchalantly stood behind the cab, in hopes I'd go undetected and get to hear all the juicy details.

"Mr. Haswell, you were informed that a state official would be in the park today."

"Someone said something about it, but I didn't expect to find one nosing around my property unescorted, Dan."

The state guy didn't like that. "I wasn't nosing around," he barked. "I was just trying to get the lay of the land. Trying to see if there was anything that could be contributing to possible contamination. That's my job." His jaw was still stuck out.

"It's not your job on federal property," yelled Haswell. "I can't believe this. I'm going to call regional headquarters."

"Mr. Haswell, we've gotten reports that many more than ten people are sick. Maybe I could go over to your dorm and interview your employees."

Haswell jumped around again, arms flailing. "HELL, NO. I won't let you or anyone else interfere with the privacy of my employees. Get the hell out of here!"

George got red in the face. He yelled. I got the impression this was his act, rather than a spontaneous burst of anger. He didn't miss a beat. He didn't mess up any words. He didn't sputter. He didn't get into anybody's personal space. It seemed well rehearsed.

The superintendent's car pulled up, carrying the superintendent and the chief ranger. In back of them was a green station wagon driven by another ranger. With that development, all conversation ceased. Everyone turned toward the cars and waited for what might happen next.

The superintendent got out of the passenger side and motioned to Haswell. "George, could you come over for a second?" The old guy pouted, then grudgingly made his way over to the superintendent.

This was only the second time I had seen the superintendent. He wore glasses. His face was non-committal. The uniform and hat mostly covered him up, so not much personality seeped out.

"Jim, the state has no...."

"George, we're not going to discuss it here. C'mon, get in. Let's go have a cup of coffee."

Haswell got in the backseat of the car. He pretended not to realize that this was the logical next act in the show he was starring in. The wheels turned in his head. He would fight all the way, you could just see it. He didn't know how not to fight. The ranger cars drove off.

The state guy stared at the cars as they drove off. Then he turned to Dan. He shook his head, then took a deep breath. "Those maps you gave me really didn't help me much, Dan. They're a little sketchy. I couldn't find many landmarks around Rim Village.

"Yeah, I know. It's all we have. The people who drew those maps when construction was going on are long gone and the regional office doesn't have anything."

"I did find one thing, Dan. It looks to me like the parking lots in the Rim Village drain into the Munson Springs watershed. Now, the good news is that I didn't see any contamination around that would be going into the watershed through those drains, but you guys have to fix that right now. If the chlorine system is working right, that will take care of anything from a parking lot, but there could be a chemical spill or something."

Then he pointed out to the snow covered meadow in back of the Lodge, at the top of the Munson Springs watershed.

"I couldn't see any problems out there, Dan. I tried to hike out there some, but the snow was pretty deep. I scanned the area with binoculars, but saw no signs of contamination. So at least that's good. Can I look at your water testing records after lunch?"

"Sure. Such as they are. But right now I want you to show me the parking lot drainage. Let me get Andrew and we'll all look at it together. Hunter, go tell Andrew to get over here and tell Don to take you back to the office."

"Okay, Dan."

Damn it. I was getting used to hearing the news first-hand. It saved a lot of time developing my conspiracy theories. It also shed some light on the characters in this drama. George Haswell was definitely as advertised. Dan had some skills. More than I'd given him credit for. He had done excellent damage control on what could have been an international incident. And Mark Johnson, the YCC leader—finally, a hero.

* * *

After work I jogged to catch up with Dave. He had a head start toward Sleepy Hollow and I wanted to tell him all the firsthand news I had collected at the rim earlier in the day.

"Hey, man, wait up, I've got the scoop," I said.

"Can't stop, Sam. I got to get to the trailer before there's an accident."

Dave focused on taking one quick step after another. His head tilted slightly, face down. He was struggling. I knew the signs. The Crud had got him and he needed to get to the privacy of his trailer's bathroom. My report would have to wait.

"Dave, can I get you anything? I was going down to Fort Klamath anyway to get some untainted supplies. What do you need? I could get you some canned stuff, fruit, juice?"

We got to my cabin and he kept walking. I'm sure he thought talking would take away from his focus and risk an accident right there in the road. "Yeah, bring me some canned stuff," he said without slowing down. Then I heard a muffled, "And don't forget the Kaopectate." I couldn't tell if he was joking or not.

"HEY, SAM." I turned around. Chris motioned me to wait a minute. I leaned against my Volkswagen and waited for him to arrive.

"We need a fourth for tennis, Sam. We're going to those courts by Agency Lake—on the other side of Fort Klamath. It's Sally, Andrew and me. Are you in?"

"Andrew the carpenter?" I asked.

"Yup."

"I'm in if you can dig up an extra tennis racket."

"I can."

"Okay, then. I have to stop at the store in Fort Klamath for some supplies, so I'll meet you guys down there. You need any tennis balls? I think they have some at that store."

"Yeah, pick up a can or two. We'll be heading down there as soon as everyone gets changed."

✳   ✳   ✳

About an hour later we all converged on the two sad looking tennis courts at the neglected county park. The nets sagged. Leaves and branches covered the court. The surface had cracks. Andrew, Sally and Chris had all crammed into Chris's Honda and I was waiting for them when they drove up. Right away, Andrew and Chris went to work tightening the nets. I swept the court with a broom I found leaning against the fence. It was amazing how often my B & U experience came in handy.

The only annoying thing about this outing was I wouldn't be able to talk about all the new information I'd gathered that day. With Andrew—a park service regular—around, that might be a problem. I wasn't going to trust anyone with the water sample news.

For the record, Sally, Chris and I had each played recreational tennis at college. Each of us had even taken the one credit tennis class all schools offer. But none of that mattered with Andrew playing. He was a freak. He was about thirty-four or thirty-five, six feet tall and extremely fit. The carpenter got to every ball, no matter where it was hit. That was especially galling because he held the tennis racket like a ping-pong paddle and still beat us. He also wore his stupid park service cap while he played. He had no serve. He ping-ponged it over. Didn't matter. Chris and I tried to load up on that serve, but we'd smack it past the baseline almost every time.

At four thousand feet above sea level, you had to hit the tennis ball with a little more skill to keep it in play—the thinner air let the ball fly out of control. That didn't stop Chris and me from trying to blow winners by Andrew. Wrong. Out. Out. Out. Out. Out. When we just tried to keep it in the court, he outlasted us by playing like a backstop. We switched teams a couple times, but mostly it was Andrew and Sally against me and Chris. If you were on Andrew's team, all you had to do was cover about five feet of court and let him run around like a mad man. Sally seemed happy to let him do just that. Her last bout of Crud seemed to have sapped her energy. Andrew delighted in making us college boys look stupid.

Sally laughed at our frustration. I admit the macho thing got to us. We got beat silly by a guy who held his racket like a ping-pong paddle. The final humiliation came when Sally made a big show of holding her racket like a ping-pong paddle, too. She and Andrew beat us, 6-1.

"That's it. I'm going home," I announced. Andrew laughed and held his arms straight up in the air in celebration. There was talk of lessons and rematches and then

Andrew struck a pose showing off his ping-pong grip. Okay, I had to admit that was funny.

Sally shook Andrew's hand and said, "Thank you, partner." He bowed.

"I hope the Crud gets the both of you."

"Don't be a bad loser, Samuel," said Sally.

"That ballerina game isn't going to work for you next time, Andrew," Chris said in a bitter tone.

"Well, if you ever win a set, I'll start to worry."

What's a little more humiliation when you work B & U at Crater Lake National Park? I was still glad Chris had asked me to play. I would have liked to talk with Sally, but there really wasn't much chance. I still didn't know what was going on with her. It worried me. She caught me watching her a couple times. She just smiled.

Night was nearly here and, with the massacre over, it was time to get back to the park. Andrew rode with me. We took off while Chris and Sally were still packing up their gear. I disliked driving through the lower end of the park at night because of the deer. Cars routinely ploughed into the poor animals. At least the deer gave you some warning. When a car was coming toward them, they always looked up and you could see their bright red eyes in the headlights. Still, they were unpredictable. You had to keep your eye on them until you passed because, at the last minute, they might leap right out in front of you, thinking they were being chased. I dreaded the thought of killing one of those beautiful animals.

Andrew was more cavalier about the deer danger. He viewed accidentally running into a deer as an opportunity.

"If you know how to field dress one of those guys, well, you got yourself a load of good venison. You know how much that's worth? And the best thing is I might be the best cook there is when it comes to venison. Yeah, run over a deer and we got a party."

"You're going to hell, Andrew."

"Oh, you're not one of those bleeding hearts, are you? I know you ain't no vegetarian."

Yes. That was a problem. I hated seeing animals hurt or killed, but I liked my steaks medium rare. I might as well just shut up about that kind of stuff in this crowd. At least the animals could take some solace in the fact that people didn't treat people any better than they did animals. Except for the eating part.

"Andrew, what's it like up here in the winter? There's only about ten or twelve park service families at Steel Circle, right? And you only get two TV channels? Seems like that could be bleak."

"I will have to admit, it's different. It can get a little crazy when you get snowed in day after day. And you only see the same few people month after month. We all get good reception on the two channels. For the most part, we get along. We have a racquetball court and the activity center where we can have potlucks, etc. And there are a few snow-mobiles we have access to. It's not too bad. But there can be some peculiar things that go on. And it's funny, people know about stuff but never talk about it."

"Peculiar things? Like what? You guys wife swapping up here or something?"

"Lucky guess, Sam. But maybe not like you were thinking. Two winters ago, a maintenance family was living next door to the garage manager. The garage manager lived alone. You know the houses we live in are duplexes? So it was RIGHT next door. Anyway, one day the wife of the maintenance guy packed up her two kids and walked out the front door of her house and up the stairs into the garage manager's house. She's still living there. Everyone knew about it—including many of the seasonals—but officially it never happened. The maintenance guy transferred out and we heard he committed suicide."

"Christ, Andrew, that's not just a little peculiar."

"Oh, I dunno. When you have people living together out in the middle of nowhere—and cut off from the rest of the world for nine months at a time—peculiar things are going to happen."

"What other weird things go on? And what about Frank and the superintendent's daughters? That's odd, too. Doesn't anyone else think that's odd?"

Andrew laughed. "Now that you mention it, I guess it is a little odd." Andrew laughed out loud again.

"So what's the deal?"

"Well, last spring when the supe's oldest daughter came home from college, she moved in with Frank for awhile. Everyone thought an atomic bomb would go off. That was even nervy for Frank. But nothing happened. Nothing. Then the supe's other daughter graduated from high school and there were some people saying that she wanted to live at Frank's and has been auditioning for that role."

Now it was my turn to laugh out loud. "Are you kidding me? How can he get away with that?"

"I think the maintenance boss is afraid of him because he's 'dating' the supe's daughters. And the supe's afraid of him because he knows he's got some wild girls and, if it all hit the fan, this might be his last superintendent's job. He's probably just trying to weather the storm.

"We all have to keep an eye out for Frank, especially in the winter. Who knows what else he's doing? He's drunk a lot and he's a mean drunk. He crosses the line sometimes. While he probably thinks he intimidates people because he's a tough guy, it's really about working for the government. Do you want to take him on and create some blowup that hurts your career over some ego issue? He apparently doesn't care, but everyone else does. So far no one's thought it worth taking him on. And eventually in these jobs, people move to another park."

"Now there's a formula for success, Andrew. Maybe he should write a book."

"It's worked for him so far. Sam, watch out for the deer on the right. I see at least four."

"I see them. Maybe I should aim for 'em, Andrew. You know we could have a party. What if I try to hit one for dinner? Will you stay quiet about the tennis match?"

Andrew laughed. "Sorry, Charley. There's not enough venison on the hoof in this park for that to happen. College-boy tennis pros suffer humiliating loss to old carpenter who never plays. The crowd goes wild. Ahhhhhh."

CHAPTER 8

IT WASN'T A NEWS FLASH WHEN Dave didn't show up for work the next morning. When I had dropped his supplies off the night before, I could see he was in bad shape. He lay spread-eagled on the bed, no shirt. He still had his work pants and boots on. His hair was heavy with sweat.

"Dave, man, you've looked better." He raised his head an inch, gave me the thumbs up sign. That was all the energy he could muster. His eyes closed.

I got his cooler and filled it with ice from the refrigerator. Then I stuffed in as many bottles and cans of juice and sodas and water as would fit. I lugged it over to his bed. I'd bought a box of soda crackers and a bag of sugar cookies, which I put on the nightstand.

Dave's trailer was a good size, but even a good sized trailer is small. The tight bathroom took some thoughtful maneuvering. With that in mind, I pulled a trash can out from under the kitchen sink and found another one in a bedroom. I lined them with plastic bags and set them next to the bed. I spread a towel out along the edge of the bed. All Dave had to do was lean over, if it came to that.

Last, I made sure there was a clear path to the bathroom—and that the door stood wide open.

"Can you think of anything else, Dave?" I had asked.

Lying on his back, eyes closed, he said, "How about a giant glass of cold Crater Lake Park water? We could toast."

"Sure, Dave. Coming right up. Now, here are the rules. You can't fight the Crud. Just lie back and let it pound on you until it's had enough. Drink as much liquid as you can. Then drink some more. If you feel like you can eat something, there are crackers over there. I have left you two garbage cans for your vomiting convenience. I'll be back tomorrow morning to check on you. Okay?"

Dave gave a feeble salute, then groaned a goodnight.

Andrew let me check on him a couple times during the day. Dave's biggest problem was a phone call he was supposed to make to his wife that night. She didn't know he was sick and he didn't want her to worry if she didn't get the expected call. After a couple of animated discussions, I finally talked him into letting me make the call after work just to let her know what was going on. He needed to stay in bed. I wrote down the number on a scrap of paper and began my hike to the closest phone available—the pay phone outside the front door of park headquarters.

I walked because I was mad and needed to cool off. How could so few people screw up a 249-square-mile national park? Maybe it was me. Maybe someone was upset that I got lucky and got a plum job in a national park. To get back at me, they dropped a pint-size plague on everybody.

Or maybe I had actually died in a fiery wreck on the drive up in that snow storm and this was hell. You know, thinking you were in paradise except everything keeps going wrong forever. Okay, that was a reach. But JESUS, C'MON. Hundreds of people can't get sick and no one do anything about it. This isn't a third world country. This is the United States of America.

I stopped. I needed to get a grip before I made that phone call. I had reached the maintenance yard, and I turned and looked back down at Sleepy Hollow. The cabins looked quiet and peaceful, despite the carnage going on inside the wooden walls. All around were miles and miles of dark green forest. The cooling air was sharp and fresh. A couple of deep breaths. Okay, let's go.

There were only a few cars in the park headquarters parking lot when I got there. This time of day, campers sat around their campfires eating dinner, and probably talking over tomorrow's Fourth of July plans. The Lodge guests sat on the veranda drinking hot chocolate or gin and tonics. The day tourists were driving to Klamath Falls, Medford, and Eugene to check into motels.

But something did catch my interest. I saw some ugly, brown, government cars parked close to the headquarters building. State of Oregon cars. All the lights were on inside the building. Three men were having a serious discussion on the steps out front. To the left of headquarters was the YCC dorm. My new favorite government employee—Mark Johnson—huddled in the doorway with his counselors.

Something was happening. I walked up the headquarters steps slowly, my ears cocked toward the talking men. Damn it. Nothing meaningful. Somebody was arriving tomorrow. Some reference to testing equipment. That's it. Oh well, maybe I could get something on the way back. I had to make this phone call.

Betty answered right away.

"Hello, this is Sam Hunter. I'm not sure you know me, but I work with Dave at the park."

"Hello, Sam. I know who you are. Dave talks about you all the time." Betty paused as it occurred to her to worry. "Sam, is Dave all right? He was supposed to call me tonight."

I told her about his Crud attack. I didn't want to alarm her, so I said that he was in pretty good spirits, all things considered, but I had talked him into resting and he had fallen asleep.

"I didn't want to wake him. So I decided to call you myself. Dave gave me the number in case something happened," I said.

She paused again, thinking over what I'd said. "Sam, I'm thinking I need to come back to the park. What do you think?"

"I think that would be a great idea."

Betty thanked me for calling. And for taking care of Dave. She was in Southern California and would start out first thing in the morning with her daughter. Depending on how the drive went with all the holiday traffic, she would arrive late tomorrow night or early the next day. She would call this number at six tomorrow evening to deliver an update and find out how Dave was doing. Great. Mission accomplished. Except I knew Dave was going to be pissed because he wanted his wife to stay safely away. Hmm. I had never seen Dave pissed. Well, we'd see what that was like.

With the phone call done, I went back to my investigative work with the three official-looking men on the steps. They were catching their breaths or doing a group think or something, because no one said anything as I passed by. I looked at them directly enough that one of them noticed and half-looked at me. *Whoops. Sorry, don't get up, I'm just passing through.*

Dead end there, but I bet my new friend Mark Johnson had news. He seemed like someone who just couldn't help himself. He was a burned-out teacher's worst nightmare. He just couldn't let anything go. He was going to correct or challenge every mistake or oversight. I wondered if it came from having lived in a rich family or something like that, where you weren't used to anybody telling you no. In that environment, you grew up with no fear of the common folk and certainly not of anyone wearing a uniform.

Who knew? I just wanted to get the scoop, so I walked across the parking lot toward the Ranger Dorm. As Mark noticed me, I saw Sally walking down the road from the Stone House. She was still four or five minutes away, but I waved and pointed to where I was headed. Mark came off the porch and met me halfway.

He walked toward me like a man with a mission. Full strides. A serious expression.

"Hey, Sam, remember that test I told you about," he said in a low voice, with one eye on the headquarters building.

"Of course I remember. I can't wait to hear what comes back."

"Well, I've got it."

"What! What does it say Mark?"

"Shhhh. Don't tell anyone. I haven't been able to talk with the people that did the testing yet. I just got some brief written results. It said the water wasn't up to purity standards for drinking. There were no pathogens, but, get this—there's fecal coliform present in some of the samples."

"Oh, don't tell me that's…."

"I don't know what it is exactly. That's why I have to talk to the people in Klamath Falls."

"Well, I bet those people know," I said, nodding toward the men on the headquarters steps.

"Yeah, I'm waiting for them to leave so I can make some phone calls. I may just have to drive down to K-Falls tonight and knock on some doors."

"Need some help?"

"What do you know about the permanents in maintenance? Are there any I could talk to?"

"I don't think so. At least not until you get the final word on these tests. I don't think you want to say anything to anybody until then. I'm sure your kids aren't drinking the water, right?" I looked through the windows of the noisy dorm. There was a ping-pong tournament going on inside.

"We've had some sick kids, but we haven't been drinking the water for a couple weeks."

"That's good. What are you going to do next?"

"Wait for the word on this test, I guess. I have to get it tonight or first thing in the morning, because we're taking the group camping outside the park for the holiday weekend."

"Well, if you need me to help with something, come down to Sleepy Hollow and get me. I'm working tomorrow, but then I'll be gone Saturday and Sunday. I'll be at my parents' house in Klamath Falls."

Just then Sally arrived. "Hey!" Mark and I stopped talking abruptly.

"Oh great, you were talking about me," she said.

I laughed. "Yeah, it's all about you."

"Mark, this is Sally. She's a member of our B & U misfits."

"Hi, Sally."

"He's the YCC boss, but, more importantly, he recently became my hero."

"Your hero?"

"Sam, I've got to go. Remember—don't say anything. Nice meeting you, Sally."

"Bye. Nice meeting you, too." Mark hurried back inside the dorm. "Don't say anything about what?"

"We all get to have our own secrets."

"I hate you. And to think I was walking all the way to Sleepy Hollow just to visit you."

"Lucky you ran into me, then, because I'm not there. Where's my Duck brother Chris, anyway?"

"He's off with the boys to Chiloquin to play some softball against the locals. I was invited, but I'm not really the cheerleader type. I guess it's up to you to entertain me. So what are we doing?"

"I don't do much entertaining, Sally. Let's see. I guess we could go over and visit *The Lady of the Woods*. But then I have to go down and check on Dave."

"Okay. I'll take that. Let's go."

Because of the tourist interest in *The Lady of the Woods*, years ago a trail had been carved out so a visitor could walk from park headquarters across the parking lot, past the backside of the Ranger Dorm, and over Munson Creek to the quiet spot behind the wooden storage building. As we walked over the little bridge I couldn't help looking at the water in a totally different way. I thought I might see things I didn't want to see floating down the stream. Every twig or bit of leaf had now become suspect.

I was glad when Sally diverted me from my morbid inspection of the water. "Tomorrow, Chris and I are driving to the coast for the weekend. We're meeting up with some friends of his and we're going to camp at Crescent City. I'm really looking forward to it. There has been so much going on around here, it will be nice just being some place different. I love the ocean. Chris says the water will be cold."

"Yeah, bone-chilling, Sally. But I think you'll like it."

"Why do you think that?"

"Because you like everything." Which made her punch me on the shoulder.

"Hey, listen," she said, "I've about finished all the books I brought with me. Do you have something I could borrow?"

"Yeah, I've got a few I think you'd like. You can take a look at what I've got when you get back."

"Thanks. Are you going anywhere for the weekend, Samuel?"

"Actually, I'm working tomorrow. I guess all the permanent B & U guys are working, so I'll be the designated gopher for them. Which is fine with me. Love that holiday pay. Then I'll go home Saturday."

"Why are the permanents working?"

"They're worried about the water, I think. There are a bunch of state folks here and they're going to be looking around. Park management doesn't want to get surprised, so we'll probably be tailing the state folks all day, making sure they don't find something the park guys don't know about. That's what I was talking to Mark about. We worked together the other day, looking for anything that could be wrong in the Munson Springs watershed above the pump house. We're developing some excellent conspiracy theories."

"So I've heard. Chris thinks you're a nut. Tell me your best conspiracy theory."

"Can't. I'm sworn to secrecy. Although it's not a big secret that I think the Crater Lake Crud comes from the water. The question is why no one in authority can figure it out or even admit it. See, nothing very exciting."

Sally stopped walking and turned to me. "I bet I know something you don't know about the water."

"Tell me."

"I don't think so. You're not telling me any of your secrets." Sally continued down the path.

"You can't do this to me, Sally. I'm the senior water conspiracy guy in the park. I need to know anything you know about the water."

"Okay. Technically, I guess it's not really a secret anyway because I overheard it from the rangerettes up at the Stone

House. I heard them talking about how peculiar it was that the rangers down at Annie Springs haven't been sick."

I stopped and stared at Sally. That revelation fit nicely into the case for the Crud being in the water. The Annie Springs Ranger Station was home to two rangers who manned the park entrance where tourists paid their two dollars per car to get into the park. Mazama Campground was across the street. Both places got their water from Annie Springs, not Munson Springs. If nobody down there was sick that put the Crud in Munson Springs.

"That's award-winning information, Sally. Keep eavesdropping on those rangerettes for me, will ya?"

Sally wasn't listening. She was running her hand slowly over the head and back of *The Lady of the Woods*. She followed *The Lady*'s outline down to her legs and back up to her arms. She stroked the hair chiseled out of volcanic rock. Then she put her hand softly on the front of *The Lady*'s head like she was checking a child for a fever.

Sally looked up at me. "She's so sad."

"Yes, she is," I said.

"I like this place. It's so peaceful and seems so far away from everything else."

"Sally, are you going to tell me what's wrong?"

She stood up slowly. "No, I don't think I can."

"I might be able to help."

"Samuel, no one can help. I've got to figure out what to do myself. I've made a really big mistake. I have a little time. Then maybe I can tell you." She reached over and tugged on the sleeve of my jacket. Please don't say anything to Chris. I know you're worried. But I need you to wait. Okay?"

I wanted to ask her about Frank and their brief encounter in the parking lot a few days ago, but I couldn't gather the courage. I told myself it probably had been nothing. Except I knew it wasn't. The look on her face that day had made that clear. I just hoped there wasn't any connection between her problem with Frank and whatever was making her sad now.

"It's getting dark, Sally. I need to get you back to the Stone House so you can do more eavesdropping on those rangerettes."

"I want to go see Dave."

"That's a nice thought, Sally, but I can guarantee you Dave is in no shape to be taking visitors. He'd hit me with a sledgehammer if I brought someone into his Crud-riddled trailer."

"Well, I don't need anyone to take me home, so just go take care of Dave, then."

"You're such a pain. I've walked that road to your house at night and you need to take my word for it—I should go with you. Besides, I'm going with you no matter what, so just get used to the idea."

Sally let out a big sigh. Then she turned back to *The Lady*, barely visible in the fading light, and bent down to kiss her on the forehead. I was glad when she took my arm as we headed off in the dark.

"I hate you," she said.

"I know. Me too."

* * *

That Fourth of July was not a holiday if you were an administrator for the Crater Lake Park Service. The headquarters building swarmed with state health and medical people. They had brought a truck full of testing equipment. I helped them carry the equipment into a room in park headquarters where it looked like they were setting up for the long haul.

People were tightlipped. I was the last person they would ever talk to, but it was obvious they were here to test the water.

I had hoped to see Mark Johnson jumping up and down in front of park headquarters, waving a damning water test in the air, but he was gone on his YCC camping trip.

You could say I spent the morning on call. I'd wait in the truck for Dan until the state people bumped me from the truck so Dan could ferry them to some undisclosed location to get water samples. Then they'd come back and go inside park headquarters, and I'd get back in the truck to wait some more. Until I got bumped again. By eleven, tourists filled the parking lot, so I figured I'd be on call someplace else after lunch. And that's what happened.

I was needed to dig a trench in back of Rim Village. Dan wasn't expecting the Panama Canal on the Fourth of July, but I would have to earn my holiday pay with some digging. I was told my trench would be the new drainage for the rim parking lot. I paced myself and thought about Sally at the ocean.

I'd have liked to be at the ocean. The southern Oregon and northern California coasts are something to behold. To the south you have the thousand-year-old redwood giants living in the dense clouds. The beaches north of the ancient forests—for a hundred miles—are loaded with warehouse-sized boulders rising out of the waves. I liked sleeping on the beach with the fog.

Snap out of it, Sam. You have the Panama Canal to dig.

Dan picked me up about 3:30. We had a heart-to-heart talk about the water problem on the way down the hill.

"What are all the state people doing here, Dan?"

"Doing tests."

"On the water?"

"Some."

"Have they found anything yet?"

"No."

"What do you think is causing it, Dan?"

Pause.

"Today I heard the superintendent say it was the flu. I heard George Haswell say it was the flu. I heard a state person say it was probably the flu. So, until further notice, it's the flu. Okay, Sam?"

He looked over at me waiting for an answer. I nodded. Yes, it must be the flu.

CHAPTER 9

THE GOOD NEWS WAS THAT, when I drove up to the ranger station entrance at Annie Springs late Sunday night, the park was still open for business instead of boarded up with a huge red skull and crossbones spray painted across it.

The ranger on duty waved me through.

I guess the bad news was that the park was open for business instead of boarded up with a huge red skull and crossbones spray painted on it.

Before I drove to my cabin, I had rounds to make. I wanted to stop by the Ranger Dorm to see if Mark Johnson had more news on his water tests. And I needed to drive by Dave's trailer to make sure everything was in order there. I had talked with Dave's wife Friday night and she told me she would arrive no later than noon Saturday to take over the nursing duties.

As I pulled into the park headquarters parking lot, I was disappointed to see the Ranger Dorm dark except for one hallway light. The YCC campers must be coming back tomorrow. Next-door, the park headquarters building was anything but quiet. Government sedans and park trucks were scattered across the parking lot. Lights blazed inside. A couple of older guys were taking a smoke break out on the front steps.

Damn. Events were obviously unfolding fast and I was at least two days behind the news cycle with no hope of catching up until later Monday. The maintenance office wouldn't be any help tomorrow morning. That's the last place I could get any real news. The only person there who had any idea what was going on was Dan and I had already heard what he had to say.

Maybe I would run into Mark or Ranger Bob during the day.

As I drove through the dark maintenance yard on the way to Sleepy Hollow, I couldn't help thinking that whatever was going to happen would happen this week. This epidemic could not be just the flu and, as more and more outsiders got involved, something had to break.

I drove around the Sleepy Hollow loop to Dave's trailer. I didn't know why I was so worked up. I had no vested interest in the situation. Whatever happened wouldn't affect me any more than the next guy. I couldn't do anything about it anyway. I needed to calm down and just go with the flow. I was here to make college tuition, not join any unruly rabble calling for the king's head.

Oh good. The family station wagon was parked next to Dave's trailer, and lights were on inside. The reunited family guaranteed Dave would get better care than I could give. With my rounds completed, I headed for my cabin and a little rest before the storm I knew would come.

Unfortunately, rest wouldn't be on the agenda because I faced two sick roommates as I walked in the door. Paul lay stretched out on the couch, his long legs dangling over one side. His face was chalky and he was moaning. Tom was in the bathroom throwing up.

It would have been wrong of me to shout out, "I told you NOT TO DRINK THE WATER." But I did think it.

Paul moaned a little louder. He knew what I was thinking. "We didn't drink any of the water, Sam. Not one drop."

Tom stuck his head out the bathroom door. He was wild-eyed. "We need to go see the doctor or nurse or whatever there is up here. Where do we go?"

"Sorry, guys. You'd think there'd be some medical person for 120 or so national park employees and another few hundred Lodge employees. But there's nothing here and nothing close by, either. There's Medford and Klamath Falls, but they're an hour away. I guess we're supposed to ride it out because we're he-men. And as you know, the Park Service believes Kaopectate is the solution."

"Well, screw the Park Service," yelled Tom, unwisely using up the last bit of his energy before the next wave of Crud yanked him back to the toilet bowl.

"I can drive you two down to the Klamath Falls emergency room tonight or after work tomorrow. That's the best I can do, I think. Otherwise you just have to drink a lot of bottled fluid and give in to it."

That news didn't make either of them happy. They got even with me by moaning and retching all night. Nobody was happy.

* * *

Management floated a rumor that the Crud was subsiding. Monday morning in the maintenance office shot that full of holes. Dave was still out, my roommates were no shows, and a couple of R & T seasonals, who had already been sick, were out again. In a real scary development, Stan, the garage manager, and one of the truck drivers were out sick. They were park service permanents. They weren't supposed to get the Crud.

Nobody talked about it while we waited around for our day's assignments. Frank was on the prowl. He looked around the office, daring someone to start complaining. He had made it clear that he didn't want any babies on his crew. Suck it up, damn it. No whining.

Chris came up to me while we were waiting and I asked how the trip to the coast had gone.

"Oh, it was really nice. Except Sally seemed pretty sick a lot of the time. But you should have seen her. It was her first look at the Pacific. She just stood there in the wind with the biggest smile on her face."

Andrew drove me up to the Panama Canal construction site in back of Rim Village. He left me with only these instructions, "Keep digging. I'll come get you this afternoon." I tried, but my old tennis buddy wouldn't spill any beans. He said he really didn't know anything except that the CDC was here.

"What's the CDC?" I asked?

"The Centers for Disease Control. They're federal. They'll decide what's what, once and for all."

I guess I felt better knowing that. But that was all the news I got for the rest of the workday. I worked in isolation, trench digging. I did get a brief visit from Dan and five official looking folks in the early afternoon. Fortunately, I was actually digging at the time. They stopped about thirty yards away from my excavation and pointed in different directions for a couple minutes, then they were gone.

It was a full news blackout. On top of that, Andrew forgot me. At about 4:00 I made the command decision to call a halt to the digging and start formulating a plan to get back down the hill to the maintenance yard. I figured if I stood next to the road out at the end of the parking lot, a ranger or a maintenance crew would drive by and give me a ride.

The problem with this plan was that there were tourists around and I might have to talk to one. The parking lot was half filled—pretty typical for a late Monday afternoon. With clear weather and a soft breeze, it was a good day to see Crater Lake. But the tourists always wanted to know stuff, and my yellow hard hat made me look official. Maintenance workers were not park naturalists and I would hate to disappoint some little girl when she asked what kind of squirrel that was or what mountain peak she could barely see a hundred miles away over there.

I did have answers for the two most commonly asked questions: Why is the Crater Lake water so blue? The extreme depth, coupled with how the light is refracted, and, Where are the toilets? Over there.

A few tourists came dangerously close while I waited, but then I saw a ranger car coming from the direction of the lodge. Bingo! It was Ranger Bob. Flagging him down wasn't hard since he was trolling at about ten miles an hour.

His passenger seat window was open.

"Hey, Ranger Bob, can I get a ride? I've been left stranded in all the excitement."

"No problem, Sam, get in."

"Thanks, man."

"It's okay, but you can't ask me any Crud questions."

"Oh no, you're Deep Throat. You're my main source of inside information."

"Well, the truth of the matter is, I don't think anybody knows anything more than they did last week. There is one thing, but...."

"Oh c'mon."

"I think we'll be putting up a flyer that tells visitors that there have been reports of sickness in the park, but the water continues to be tested and is fine."

Ranger Bob made a left-hand turn and we were headed down the hill toward park headquarters. I wanted to laugh at this newest park service idea.

"Uh, Bob?"

"Yes."

"Was that your idea?"

"No."

"Okay. Could you then explain the reasoning behind that to me?"

"You must be confusing me with someone who makes decisions around here. I'm just a soldier doing my duty.

Maybe I shouldn't be telling you these things. And don't tell anyone, because it may never happen. Hard to know anything for sure just yet."

"You're right, sorry. Didn't mean to make you mad. It's just a little unsettling, you know? We peons are doing a lot of asking, but no real answers are coming back. And people seem to be getting sick all over again. It's really hard not to think there's something in the water."

"You haven't been talking to Mark Johnson, have you?"

"Why do you ask?"

"Bad idea, Sam. Bad idea. He's been at headquarters all afternoon meeting with the head guys. They even had a couple people come up from Regional in Klamath Falls to point out to him that he really isn't a water testing specialist and that if he's spreading bad information then that's irresponsible."

"Ranger Bob, you were holding out on me."

"Just remember, Mark isn't a favorite of the National Park Service right now. He's liable to be a little hot, so maybe you should stand clear until the situation is resolved. I'm not telling you what to do, I'm just trying to help you out."

"Thanks."

"Where do you want to be dropped off?"

"The maintenance office. Just in case somebody missed me."

"No problem."

I got out of the green station wagon and thanked Ranger Bob for his help and advice. I looked through the glass into the office and saw nobody. I walked home demoralized. My roommates were nowhere to be found when I got back to the cabin. I went right to bed. Maybe life would look a little better after a nap and a couple cans of Beanie Weenies.

Neither helped at all.

Not even the cool mountain air could make me feel better as I started my twilight walk out of Sleepy Hollow and across the maintenance yard. I felt a little sick to my stomach, but I hoped that had more to do with being wound too tight than the Crud. The Mark Johnson situation bothered me. He was like a one-man band against the Park Service's stupid response to the Crud epidemic. I talked a lot about it, but Mark actually did something. Nobody was helping him—including me—as the Park Service started to circle him like wolves.

Despite my big talk and self-professed knowledge of what was making everyone sick, I couldn't stop Dave from getting sick. I couldn't keep my new roommates from getting sick. All I could do was talk. If you penciled it out, I really didn't know a thing and hadn't been any good to anybody.

I rounded the storage shed and came face-to-face with someone else I'd failed—Sally. She and *The Lady of the Woods* were leaning against the same rock. Sally's face looked puffy and I knew she'd been crying. I kicked some branches on the ground as I walked up so she'd know I was coming.

"Well, you're not exactly Daniel Boone, are you?" she teased as I got closer. "I could hear the brush crackling a mile away."

"Nice to see you, too. And what are doing at my secret spot, anyway?"

"Some secret spot. There are signs and a well-maintained trail right to it."

"I hate you."

"Me too," she said softly. She wiped her eyes with the sleeve of her gray sweatshirt. I didn't know what to say. I sat down on a rock a few feet away and decided to keep quiet. Maybe she would tell me what was wrong.

There was a very long silence, maybe five or six minutes. I really didn't mind just sitting there, looking at Sally, but her sad face broke my heart. I didn't understand why she wouldn't let me help her.

Finally, she sighed and said, "I've been feeling really lousy. It pretty much ruined my trip to the coast. I'm not sure Chris is still speaking to me. After work today, I tried to sleep, but I needed some air and ended up here with *The Lady*.

"The Crud is hitting a lot of people for the second time, Sally. You'll be past it soon."

"I'm sure you're right. You must think all I do is cry." She smiled. "How's Dave doing?"

I gave her the full update on how his wife was here and taking care of him now. I told her he might be back at work Friday.

"You know," she said, "there's a lot of buzz from the rangerettes about the Crud crisis. I don't really think they know anything, though. They seem to be mostly talking about which government folks have arrived. And they were talking about some controversy at the YCC camp. I didn't get much."

"The YCC controversy is all about my hero, Mark Johnson. You met him the other day."

I told her my brief history with Mark and what he was into. I replayed my conversation with Ranger Bob and told

her how sick I felt about the whole Mark thing and how useless I felt and how almost nothing seemed to be going right
this summer. It was a real whine fest. But it felt good to let it
out. I think Sally was taken aback a little because I hadn't let
loose like that with her before.

We were quiet for another good long time.

"You know," she said quietly, "None of it's your fault
and you're not in a position to do anything about it, even if
you could. We're just innocent bystanders."

✳ ✳ ✳

Tuesday was not much different than Monday except
that I had help on the trench. My roommates were back,
which surprised me. They had gone down to the emergency
room at Klamath Falls yesterday and felt like they were
ready to work again.

The two of them lasted about forty-five minutes. I went
into the rim store and called down to headquarters to get
someone from maintenance to give them a ride back to the
cabin.

There was some good news. Andrew remembered to
pick me up at the end of the day. He had apologized for
yesterday's mishap. In fact, he had remembered me at about
6:00 yesterday and driven to my cabin. When he didn't find
me there, he drove up to the rim, thinking I was still there.
Served him right, but I thanked him for the thoughtfulness
anyway.

As we made the right-hand turn into the park headquarters parking lot, I saw Mark Johnson and some of his
crew packing equipment out in front of the Ranger Dorm.

"Hey, Andrew, can you stop and let me out here? I want to see what's going on with Mark."

"They're packing up and moving out of the park."

"Oh. Okay, let me out so I can say goodbye then. It's quitting time. I'll walk back."

Andrew stopped the truck and I jumped out and headed over to the Ranger Dorm.

Mark saw me and said something to the people he was supervising. Then he walked toward me. "Hey, Sam, come to see us off?"

"Yeah, I guess. What the heck is going on? I heard a rumor that you were taking on management again. Is that right?"

Mark laughed. "I guess you could call it that."

"So I take it you showed them the test results."

"Oh, yes. I sure did."

"Well, what did they say?"

Mark looked around. I looked around. Mark motioned to the dorm and we both walked over to the front door and went inside. Most of the kids were busy talking and packing up their things. A few were setting the long table where they ate their meals. It smelled liked spaghetti was on the menu tonight.

"Well?" I asked again.

"I guess you could say they went a little crazy. I felt like I was in a hatchet fight without a hatchet. First, the superintendent read me the riot act. Then the chief ranger read me the riot act. They had a couple state people come in and basically call me an imbecile for thinking I could take accurate water samples. And, if you can believe it, they called in a contingent all the way from Regional in Klamath Falls just to tell me I was an idiot. But the coup de grace was a ranger coming over this morning to wake me up because I had a phone call. It was the head of the YCC program in D.C. He wanted to know what the hell I was doing."

"Jeesus. What did you say?"

"Nothing. I just answered yes or no and said once or twice that I thought it was the right thing to do. It wasn't intended to be an exchange of ideas, so I just let them pound on me."

"So I take it their goal was to put the fear of God into you?"

"Listen, Sam. I'm thirty-five. I've been in the Army—Vietnam. I teach school in downtown Los Angeles. It was all I could do to not laugh in their faces.

"So your boss ordered you out?"

"Not really. We came to a mutual decision. I'm afraid for my kids, basically. We really shouldn't have stayed this long. If I had known how dumb these people are—that they're willing to put people at risk—we would have left three weeks ago."

"It's too bad—for all our sakes—that you couldn't win the day, Mark. I want you to know I have a lot of respect for what you did, even if it failed."

"Thanks, but I don't look at it that way. I don't think I failed. Listen, Sam, a lot of people over the course of your life are going to try to tell you that you failed at something. You didn't win the game, so you failed. Your department didn't reach its goal, so you failed.

"If you live up to what you say you're going to do, or what you should do, then in my book you've succeeded. When the going gets tough, not very many people will do the right thing. Self-preservation and other priorities get in the way and maybe sometimes you have to accept things the way they are. But you never fail when you stand up and do the right thing."

Mark flushed a little and shook his head. "Sorry, got a little carried away."

"I'm sorry, Mark. I didn't mean to say I thought you'd failed."

"I know. There's just a lot of REAL failing going on around this park right now and I wanted to make sure you understood the distinction."

"So when are you guys heading out?"

"Dawn, tomorrow. The kids are excited. We're going to try to camp at as many parks as we can on our way back to Southern California. You know, I haven't told you the best thing yet."

"Oh yeah?"

"I talked to a CDC doctor about an hour ago. I showed him the water report. You know what he said?" Mark paused and looked me in the eye. "He said, 'It looks like you've been drinking human waste.'"

* * *

On Wednesday the following flyer was given to all visitors coming into the park and posted at all park facilities and campgrounds, as well as at the Lodge.

To all visitors:

Over the past several weeks there has been an outbreak of gastroenteritis in Crater Lake National Park. The illness is characterized by diarrhea, abdominal

cramps, nausea, vomiting, and chills. It can last anywhere from a few hours to several days. It is unclear
how this illness is contracted or how it is spread. We
have professional U.S. public health personnel actively
working on this problem now.

While using the park facilities, we recommend
using no water that hasn't been pre-boiled, or treated
with iodine or chlorine tablets, for drinking, for food
preparation, or for brushing teeth. Water may not be
a factor in contracting the illness, but we feel this
precaution is important.

We hope to correct this situation as quickly has
possible.

Thank you,
Superintendent
Crater Lake National Park

Dave came back to work Wednesday. He was down a
few pounds and moving a little slow but seemed in good
spirits. Andrew gave him a new task—to build a shed near
the trench I had been digging up at Rim Village. We didn't
know quite what it would be for, but Andrew said Dan
wanted it and he wanted it sturdy.

Dave's reaction surprised me. He had that Ph.D in physics and was very handy with a hammer, but I got the feeling that maybe he hadn't actually built any kind of wooden
structure from scratch before.

"I guess I shouldn't have mentioned all those LA sky-
scrapers I built on my resume," he chuckled nervously as we
drove up to the rim.

"Dave, why didn't you just tell them you hadn't built anything like that before?"

"Now why in the world would I tell 'em something like that? They want me to build them a shed, I'm going to build them a shed. It might fall over on top of the first person who opens the door. But they're going to get a pretty little shed. With big red polka dots."

We both laughed at that.

When we got to the site, we performed quite a song and dance, checking out the ditch and deciding on the best place to build what we were now calling our "Fort." Dave did some thinking out loud.

"Maybe eight foot tall and a little bit bigger than a regular-sized bathroom. What do you think, Sam?"

"Dave, why are you asking me? I do think you should put in a cement floor."

"Cement! I was thinking expensive Italian tile. Maybe a nice earthy terra cotta. It's gonna be a pretty one."

Now came the hard part—actually starting the project. Dave had brought a pad of paper, a measuring tape, and drawing tools. Apparently, he planned to increase his comfort level by drawing the heck out the project before building anything. Andrew had said the shed was supposed to be out of sight, but near where the ditch was going in. Eventually some sort of pipe would go in the ditch and it would be covered up, but for now instructions were "near the ditch."

When I was no longer needed for taking measurements, I took a seat on the edge of the parking lot. Dave was going to be a while—drawing, erasing, pacing, remeasuring.

An explosion coming from the rim parking lot shattered our tranquil work environment about fifteen minutes later. It was either Mount Mazama exploding again or George Haswell screaming at someone from the Park Service.

I got up and jogged toward the front of the Rim Village Store. When I got there, I found Haswell nose-to-nose with one of the seasonal park rangers I didn't know.

Every time I saw Haswell he was in the middle of a screaming fit. It was a miracle he had gotten to be this old without having a stroke.

"I'm going to have you fired," yelled Haswell. He waved the park service flyer at the poor ranger. Apparently he had found it tacked to the front of the rim store and he didn't like it one bit. "Then I'm going to rip every one of these sons of bitches down."

"I wouldn't do that, sir," said the ranger through gritted teeth. "This is an official park service memorandum. You'd be subject to arrest."

"Yeah, you're going to arrest me. Right!" Then Haswell stepped back and tore the memo up into tiny pieces and threw it down on the ground in front of the ranger. "So arrest me, Mr. Park Ranger. I'm going to do the same thing to every one of these flyers I find. Well? Arrest me!"

The ranger had no choice but to retreat, which was smart as this was definitely a no-win situation for him. He went around to the driver side of his car, reached in and pulled out the hand-mike for his ranger radio.

This action didn't slow George down.

"I tell the Park Service what's what in this park, not the other way around. If there are any flyers to be put up on my buildings, I'll put them up. If you put up more, I'm going to tear the mothers right down again. Tell that to whoever you're talking to. You got me, Mr. Park Ranger?"

The park ranger looked right at Haswell as he talked on the radio.

"I can't believe you park service people are trying to ruin my business with this crap."

The park ranger leaned in and put the hand-mike back into its place in the car. He straightened up, stared at Haswell and said, "Mr. Haswell, the superintendent would like to talk with you at your earliest convenience."

"Fine. But I'm going to be talking to my friends in Washington first. You people. I don't know what you're so worked up about. Nobody's died yet. Christ!"

With that, the ranger got in the car and drove off. By this time Dave was standing next to me. We watched as the seven or eight tourists that had gathered walked off with quizzical looks on their faces. I turned to Dave and said, "You know, I'm beginning to think old George is running the show in this park."

"Maybe I should have asked him how big to build the shed."

It was good to see Dave feeling better. He had recovered quicker than I thought he would. I imagined having his family around had something to do with that.

After the George Haswell show ended, we headed back to the carpentry shop so Dave could do some really fancy drawing on the Fort project. I swept the floor. I found sweeping strangely similar to mopping in that I wasn't very good at it. How could you not be good at sweeping? Yet when

I looked back at my work I could see I was clearly bad at it—dirt and dust were everywhere. A mystery I hoped to solve one day.

As I pondered my lack of sweeping skills, Dave announced that he was ready to get back to the rim to stake out the Fort's new home. They'd already given us the sad news that neither cement nor Italian tile were options. We would have to do our best without them. Still, Dave was determined to create a masterpiece.

On our way to the site I asked Dave to stop by the water fountain near the front of the rim store. I wanted to see who was winning the water memo war.

The memo taped to the fountain said: "This water has been adequately chlorinated and is tested daily by the U.S. Public Health Service."

The winner and still champion, George Haswell.

CHAPTER **10**

THE PARK SERVICE DIKE HOLDING BACK the Crater Lake Crud mystery sprang new leaks every day. Park management had stood firm as the water kept rising. But when the dike finally gave way, it took little more than twelve hours for history to be made. Crater Lake became the first national park in the country to close in peak season, shutting out thousands of tourists.

All the action took place in the Munson Springs watershed, at the Munson Springs pump house, and the offices of park headquarters. I never knew exactly what happened until the end of the summer, when Ranger Bob showed me an unofficial log he kept of the events.

Thursday, July 10th, 1975
- A state test reveals that four out of ten water samples show evidence of sewage contamination. The state testing

people feel the results are sufficient, in their opinion, to close Crater Lake National Park.

- The Lodge food service manager, following a food service inspection by CDC and state doctors, decides to close the Lodge dining room to consolidate employees who are still well enough to work in the Cafeteria.

- The ranking CDC doctor on site is still concerned that the transmission method is unknown, but feels there is "insufficient evidence" to close the park. A state doctor, disturbed about the indecision, calls CDC headquarters in Atlanta for a ruling. CDC headquarters believes there is insufficient evidence to support closure of the park. Several more calls by the state doctors finally reach the director of the CDC in Atlanta. The local doctors are told, "Let's consider this overnight and we'll give you a call tomorrow." Several of the doctors now feel the method of illness transmission is "person-to-person" contact.

- One of the doctors digs through the snow pack to find the chlorine line at Munson Springs and finds that the chlorinator's position and lack of mixing allows the water in the headquarters line to bypass the chlorinator completely. Another chlorinator is installed on the headquarters line. The doctor then digs through the snow to take samples from the headquarters reservoir.

- At 7:30 p.m., the maintenance chief discovers an area directly below the Lodge (in the Munson Springs watershed) where the snow has fallen in. An overflowing manhole on the sewer line leading directly from the Lodge has covered the exposed ground with sewage, solid waste, and toilet paper.

- At 8:10 p.m., fluorescein dye placed in a manhole above the Munson Springs overflow appears at the plugged manhole a few minutes later. Forty minutes later, the dye appears in Munson Springs. The doctor crawled onto the collection caisson at the springs and finds evidence of dye coming in from the collection pipes. A medical team pries the cover off the collection caisson and discovers solid sewer waste floating in the cement box.
- The medical team walks the watershed between Munson Springs and the Lodge checking all holes in the snow. Solid human waste and paper are visible. The odor of human waste is very evident.
- At 10:00 p.m., a flat six-inch rock is removed from the sewer line. The superintendent is notified and park rangers start a massive house-to-house operation to warn residents to stop using the water immediately. When dispatcher Ranger Larry Smith asked a CDC doctor why the residents couldn't just continue to boil the water, the doctor answered rather agitatedly, "You can't boil out human feces." Memos follow. All park residents are notified by midnight. Since the seasonals did not have telephones, patrol rangers had to knock on doors.
- Gamma globulin shots are recommended to all who visited Crater Lake National Park, as precautions against hepatitis. The doctors recommend closing the park.

Friday, July 11th, 1975

- The superintendent contacts the General Superintendent of the Park Service shortly after midnight. After talking with the Lodge concessionaire and more health specialists, they decide to close the park. More dye placed in the sewer lines soon appears in Munson Valley sewer lagoon. Lime and chlorine are spread on the raw sewage around the overflowing manhole.

• At 8:15 a.m., Crater Lake National Park is closed to the public with all entrances manned twenty-four hours a day. This becomes the first closure of a national park in the history of the National Park Service.

CHAPTER **11**

FRIDAY MORNING WAS OVERCAST AND COLD on the rim at Crater Lake National Park. As I looked down Munson Valley from the Lodge parking lot, the scene looked much like it always had. Mostly it was a snowfield. But now there were unorganized footpaths in the snow and a couple of ugly looking brown spots, the biggest starting about thirty yards from where I stood.

The park had been closed because of those brown spots.

Next to me was a stack of sacks filled with lime. Along with Billy and Craig from R & T, my job this morning was to shovel lime wherever we saw brown. I had been told to wear boots I never intended to wear again. We would be reimbursed for the boots. Somebody had started the task, but now it was our turn.

The Park Service had developed a story. They didn't know why the Lodge's sewer lines were built directly above the park's water supply, but it was definitely unlucky that a six-inch rock had found its way into the line and caused a backup and overflow of sewage that traveled undetected under the snow right into Munson Springs.

We carried lime across the snow, broke through the heavy sacks and threw shovelfuls of the white powder onto the offending areas. The lime was supposed to soak up the brown stuff. Even though it was cold for July, the snow kept melting and the brown areas kept getting bigger.

"Billy, we're going to need a lot more lime. I hope they're ordering it up by the truckload."

"Don't talk to me about it, I'm not planning to be here much longer," he said, disgusted. "I drive trucks and fix roads. This is nasty B & U work. I expect Frank to drive down here any minute and get me back on the road. He said he was sorry but it was an emergency and that he would relieve me as soon as he could."

"Hey, one for all and all for one, right?"

"NO, this is a Buildings and Utilities deal. I'm Roads. See the difference? If B & U had taken care of the water the right way, we wouldn't have had to close the damn park down. You should have to clean up your own mess."

That caught me by surprise. Actually, it made some sense and I'm sure Frank was telling everyone just that.

As I walked back to the parking lot to get another couple sacks of lime, I saw three cars—packed up to the windows with boxes and suitcases—driving out of the lodge employee parking lot. With no tourists there wasn't much need for concession employees. First they get the Crud and then they're out of a job. Talk about a bad summer. And all of the non-law enforcement seasonal rangers had been temporarily furloughed until the water issue was resolved. All the still-walking maintenance folks stayed to do what we do.

I was studying the sacks of lime when Frank drove up. I always noticed his truck. It was just a little better than all the rest. A sharper green color. The tires looked bigger. And the size of the front end gave the impression it had a bigger engine. A huge radio antenna sat on top of the cab. Sort of a park service version of a mean green machine. And driving it was a cool guy with black sunglasses.

"Hunter! Come here."

I walked the twenty yards over to his truck, slow and deliberate. He sat back in the seat with his elbow hanging out the window. He never wore a park service hat like most of the other permanents did. His black hair curled over his ears, very un-park service-like. He was looking straight ahead.

Before I even got there he said, "Hunter, tell Billy that he and Craig can get back to the road work." He was still looking ahead. "The two B & U painters will be up in thirty minutes or so. They worked late last night."

"Okay, Frank." And I turned back toward the lime sacks.

"And hurry it up, Hunter. We need to get lime spread on that shit as soon as possible."

I didn't say anything. With Frank, it had been hate at first sight. Some people you could just look at and know they were trouble.

I hoisted a sack of lime on my shoulder and started my walk back. Frank drove off. The R & T boys had figured they were relieved and had put down their shovels and started taking off their gloves. I threw the sack on the ground and started back for another.

"Hey, did Frank say we can go?" asked Billy.

"Yup, you are free to go. I hope you'll think kindly of me when you're filling those potholes."

"Yeah, we'll think kindly of you all right. We'll think how it's better you than us knee-deep in this shit. See you later, sucker."

They double-timed it back to the truck and were out of there in a hurry, just in case someone changed their mind. And, yet again, I was alone with a shovel and without a truck. I wondered how long before my roommates showed up. There really wasn't any rush. The damage had been done. The sewer lines were shut off. The pump house was closed down. We were officially closing the barn doors after the horses had galloped off.

Actually, my roommates—Paul and Tom—had been right in the middle of the action last night. They had been commandeered by the head of maintenance to work late and help the army of state, federal, and park service folks track down the source of the Crater Lake Crud. They were the only B & U seasonals who could be found quickly.

Someone had decided to give the watershed below the lodge another look. Bingo. Tom and Paul came busting into the cabin about 10:30 that night with big news and stinking boots. They blurted out the headlines and Tom talked crazy about a six-inch rock and said that he had found it. But all I could think was, *Wow, such an easy answer to such a big problem.*

Shortly after that storm blew in, rangers knocked at the door with the official news: Don't Drink The Water. Don't Use the Water For Anything!

With the official news, came the answer to a mystery that had been a thorn in the side of my best conspiracy theories. "How come people who didn't drink the water still got sick?" Stupid me. If you washed dishes, washed clothes or took a shower using the water, you were contaminated. And, of course, the biggest joke was boiling it didn't do a thing. You can't boil out human waste.

Actually, I was hoping the roommates would show up so I could get the unofficial story of what happened. Last night they just gave me the headlines. There was too much hoopla for anything else. And I'm sure the official version we heard this morning at the maintenance office lacked some juicy details.

This poor park. I hoped the lime would help.

About an hour later Tall Paul and Tom arrived. They got out and leaned against the truck surveying the scene. Maybe they had noticed I was down to the last five bags of lime and were hoping that the longer they waited the less they would have to shovel.

I decided not to let them wait me out and headed over to talk.

As I walked up, Tom said, "Don't let us stop you, you're doing great."

"Thanks for the encouragement. You guys are heroes now, so you don't have to do any shoveling, right? You were part of the great expeditionary force that found "The Rock.""

"Yes, I'm proud to say that we were part of the great sewer line hunt," said Tom. "But not only did I help find the rock, I was the one who actually identified it as the culprit rock."

Paul looked at his partner. "I don't think you should be talking about that, Tom."

But Tom was basking in the limelight. "Yes, I AM a rock star. When the bosses were standing there staring at the sewer line saying, 'woe is me,' I was there for them. I said, 'Fellas, I think I've found the problem.' And that's when I walked a few steps and picked up a suspicious looking six-inch rock and told them it looked like this came out of the sewer. And, you know, it really could have. 'It's probably been blocking that line for years,' I said. Their sad little faces lit up like neon lights. And that, my friend, is how I became a rock star."

I was, at least for a moment, without words. But at least I now understood what part the rock actually played in this melodrama.

"Now, roomie, if you repeat that little story I'm going to deny it until the bitter end. I'm a made man now, the Park Service is my friend. You're a known conspiracy kook so no one's going to believe you. Ah yes, it's good to be me." He waved to the nonexistent crowd and acknowledged their cheers. Tall Paul and I had to laugh. Tom made an unlikely park superstar with his four-day growth, ripped jeans and ratty hair almost down to his shoulders.

A fleet of vehicles arrived, ending Tom's rock briefing. There was a ranger car, another government car and a flat-bed with two pallets of lime. We had no forklift, so we'd have to unload the lime by hand.

Charlie was driving the truck. He said, "Have at it, boys," meaning he'd be waiting in the cab for us to finish, so hurry it up. I climbed onto the truck and began ripping the plastic wrap away. I grabbed dusty sack after dusty sack and laid them on the edge of the truck so my partners could pull them off and stack them at the very edge of the road. I straightened up for a second to give my back some relief, just as a roar came out of the forest below. Up popped a helicopter. It followed a line right up the watershed toward the Lodge parking lot. It was small—maybe a four or five-seater—but it made the noise of something ten times bigger. It passed in front of us and swung around toward the Lodge parking lot where it hovered.

I saw Ranger Bob standing in the road south of the Lodge to block any traffic and another park service person—who I think was the chief ranger—acting as landing guide for the helicopter. He had a radio and waved the helicopter to the spot he wanted it to land.

I assumed the helicopter carried some sort of big time politico or governmental management type who needed to see whatever it was firsthand before he or she deemed it an official debacle and could pronounce it as such to the media and their colleagues. But if that were the case, wouldn't there have been a mandatory welcoming party made up of the park's leading citizens?

Well, we'd find out in a minute. The rotor blades were slowing down and somebody would eventually get out.

"C'mon, Hunter, let's get these pallets unloaded," barked Charlie. "I've got to get down to the Community Center to get my gamma globulin shot."

"What about us?"

"A few must be sacrificed for the many. Now get that lime off the truck."

I wondered if Charlie would forgo his shot if I stuffed a hunk of lime down his damn throat. I lifted another bag to the edge of the truck. One pallet down, one to go. I looked back over to the helicopter. Three people had gotten out. One talked to the chief ranger and the other two appeared to be unloading equipment.

The visitor talking to the chief ranger pulled out a notebook and started writing.

Mystery solved: The Media had arrived on scene.

I could hear Charlie grumbling and my housemates were waiting, so I had to pick up the pace. Once I got all the sacks off the truck, everyone could calm down and go about their business and I could concentrate on this new turn of events. I wondered who it was. I had to think the equipment was a television camera. Newspaper reporters didn't need gear. I guessed it could have been supplies not related to the person talking to the ranger.

This is where the rubber met the road. How believable would the Park Story be to civilians? Surely the six-inch rock theory was going to sound thin.

With helicopters flying in and park rangers milling around, our little trio of B & U workers turned into a crack lime-spreading crew and performed with military precision. Bust open a bag, spill some lime, carry the bag across the brown spots, leaving a trail of white as you went. Then go back and push the lime around with shovels to make sure all areas were covered sufficiently. Then back to the road for more sacks of lime.

As I worked, I could see that the equipment coming out of the helicopter definitely included a television camera. We were about seventy-five yards away. And then one of the men put the camera on his shoulder, just like you see on TV. Then he put it back down. The first visitor finished his talk with the chief ranger. Ranger Bob got introduced. Maybe he was going to be the media guide.

The two other men carried their equipment over to Ranger Bob's patrol car. The reporter walked slowly out of the parking lot onto the road where we had our lime stacked. Ranger Bob walked about ten yards behind him.

Yes, it was time for more lime. I figured I could time it just right if I went and got a sack, brought it back and then went to pick up another. Given the speed the reporter was currently walking, I should get there the second time just as he arrived at the spot. It reminded me of an S.A.T. question: If train A left Klamath Falls at 11 a.m. and Sam left the sewer spill at 11:30, what time would the reporter ask Sam about the Crud at the stack of lime sacks?

I was off by one trip to the lime sacks. The reporter stopped before he got to where he was supposed to go. But when I arrived for the second time I got a good look at him from only about fifteen yards away. It was John Iwasaki. JOHN IWASAKI.

John Iwasaki was ABC's high profile overseas correspondent. When I saw him on TV he usually had one hand holding a microphone and the other holding his helmet on with the sounds of gunfire all around him. He was a big time war correspondent and spent years in Vietnam. What a comedown. But with the Vietnam War mercifully over, what's a combat correspondent to do?

I was star struck and almost fell into the snow when I tripped over the curb. I held it together and packed another sack of lime to my team. They didn't know that we were in the presence of a TV celebrity. They only knew that people were watching, so they better be working. I had a more sophisticated view of life and headed back for another sack of lime.

When I was about ten feet from the stack, my eyes met Iwasaki's.

He walked over to the lime stack. He wore a tan trench coat with the collar up and his hands jammed in his pockets. This was okay weather for Crater Lake in July, but I imagine it would signal a coming ice age if it hit Southeast Asia. He looked just like he did on TV, but maybe a little older—late thirties, early forties.

By the look on his face, I think we were both wondering what the hell he was doing here covering a sewer leak.

"This is it, huh?" he asked.

I could see Ranger Bob lurking behind him looking uneasy. I wasn't going to start anything. Ranger Bob had been good to me, so no way was I going to make him look bad. Anyway, John Friggin Iwasaki would see right through this charade. He didn't need me.

"Yes," I said.

"Lime, huh?" he asked.

"Yup," I said.

"Tough job," he said.

"Yeah, but I don't mind if it helps clear this mess up so the park can get back to normal," I said.

With that we both gazed out on the Munson Springs watershed and my hardworking roommates spreading lime. We must have stared out there for hours, two kindred souls searching for the truth.

Probably it was more like sixty seconds before I blurted out, "Mr. Iwasaki, shouldn't you be out covering some war or something?" I saw Ranger Bob turn his head to stare at me.

It was too late; I couldn't take it back. He said nothing for about a minute. While I waited to see if he would say anything, atomic bombs exploded in my brain. What an idiot.

"I was flying back from Thailand and my boss told me to stop here and see what was going on. So here I am."

I thought hard about whether I should say anything else. I was sure Ranger Bob preferred I didn't. And before I could gauge Iwasaki's state of mind, he turned and walked away. No farewell, no whispered questions about what the real story was or plans for a clandestine meeting later where I could tell him to follow the money. I was deflated.

As he walked toward the Lodge, Ranger Bob asked him if he wanted to go down to headquarters now. John Iwasaki nodded yes, and that was the last I saw of the famous war correspondent.

He didn't care. No one was going to care. Hundreds of government workers and innocent park visitors suffered a serious illness due to government bungling. But the real crime was park service management refusing to help the sick workers until it was proven beyond a shadow of a doubt that it was their fault. Now they were going to try and convince people it was an act of God and everything was fine.

I was pretty sure that was going to work.

Of course, people would be fired, careers lost, and lawsuits filed. But by the time those things happened, Crater Lake would be out of the news, no one would know about it, the problem would be officially compartmentalized, and the Park Service would move forward without even the smallest blemish on its record.

At lunchtime my roomies and I were picked up and driven down to the Community Center in Steel Circle to get our gamma globulin shot to protect us from hepatitis. We also got to listen to a lot of information being dispensed about what our world would be like for at least the next few weeks.

Fort Lewis in Washington State would send down a water purification unit and soldiers to run it. All the Munson Creek water would be thoroughly cleaned before we drank it. All the water lines would be blasted with chlorine before that. Until the purification unit was up and running, a big milk truck would bring as much water as we needed from Annie Springs. No showers, no washing machines, etc., until the Fort Lewis equipment was up and running. That could be two weeks. The Park Service hired a water treatment plant expert. There were medical people available to treat anybody who was sick. The tone was "ain't it great, we're as good as new."

The Park Service had turned the page at the worker level. It was all about the adventure now. How you survived by straining the big pieces out with your teeth. Sponge baths.

And how you had a whole national park to yourself in the middle of summer.

After lunch, an R & T crew went up to spread lime for a while. They went because Frank had heard that the continually arriving news crews were going to be shooting film sometime during the afternoon. If anybody was going to be on TV, it was going to be his boys.

Fine with me. The only downside for me would be seeing Walter Cronkite on the news saying, "According to Frank Noble, the sewer spill was all the fault of Building and Utilities. He says it's a crying shame his boys have to clean up their mess. And that's the way it is, July 11, 1975."

I saw Andrew and went over to ask him what I should do next.

"R & T has commandeered the lime fields, so I guess you lucked out there. Maybe you should just take a ride around the rim." He gave me a you-know-what-I'm-talking-about look. "Start a check on the wooden outhouses in the rim picnic areas. See if there are repairs needed. Get a truck back at the maintenance office. That will keep you busy the rest of the day, right?"

"YES, SIR," I said. I almost ran out the door.

This was not an uncommon practice for maintenance employees. When there was nothing to do, or your supervisor got tired of working, you could drive somewhere and then drive back or, in this case, around the rim. The good news: the drive was pleasant. The bad news: the drive around the rim didn't take nearly long enough.

I always enjoyed the moment that I turned left rather than right when I got to the rim road. Right went to the tacky

Rim Village. Left went to one of the great nature drives of all time. The first thing I checked for was the color of the lake. It could be anywhere from a muddy gray to brilliant blue, like a giant sapphire. Then I looked for waves. I couldn't actually see individual waves from the rim road because I was so far from the surface of the lake, but I could see patterns. Moving patterns. There could be a huge patch of lake that was blowing one way and the rest could seem flat. Or there could be a large rectangular motion pattern on one side of the lake, then clear, than a large patch blowing a different direction.

When I looked across the lake, it seemed like a trip around the rim should take at least a day. But it was only a thirty-three-mile journey and it took less than an hour to make the circuit. If you didn't stop.

Rim Drive was really a series of switchbacks around high points—the bits and pieces that remained of Mount Mazama before it fell in on itself. One of those high points was Hillman Peak. I liked getting there because I could get a good look at the Pumice Desert off to the northwest.

The Pumice Desert is a several-square-mile patch of bleakness—a town-sized piece of the moon, right in the middle of a pine forest. Except, instead of moon rocks, there are crunchy little pieces of pumice. Pumice rocks are reddish, light, and pockmarked. They look like tiny petrified sponges. Only a couple of midget pines grow in that desert. Nothing else. It's reddish pumice, flat and that's it.

Before Mount Mazama imploded, it spent a few thousand years sending avalanches of pumice and other volcanic rock down its sides. For some reason, volcanic rock collected in this spot more than one hundred feet deep. The volcanic rock has no nutrients. There's plenty of water, but nothing grows. It's been more than seven thousand years since the Mount Mazama event and still nothing grows in the Pumice Desert.

I didn't know what kind of Eden might have flourished there before all the volcanic activity, but that lifeless desert seemed like some primeval, biblical form of revenge to me. Mother Nature wields a heavy hammer and she must not have been pleased. Total devastation. But that was the thing about Mother Nature—even her devastation was beautiful.

I checked out a couple of picnic sites then headed for my favorite spot on the rim road—Kerr Valley.

It was a miniature mountain valley just east of the tallest point in the park, Mount Scott. I liked looking at Crater Lake, but for some reason this pristine little high plain got to me. It wasn't a significant enough landmark to be mentioned on anything but geological-type maps of the park. But there was a spring and hidden creek down in a line of trees. You could hear the creek murmuring if there was no other noise.

In my short time at the park, I'd driven by maybe nine or ten times and, each time, I had seen a herd of twenty or thirty elk about a half mile out in the distance. I asked a few of the maintenance permanents about the herd, but no one remembered ever seeing elk in the valley. They said the elk herds usually stayed in the southeast part of the park, at lower elevations.

As I pulled to the side of the road I could see the elk out in the distance. Tourists didn't stop at Kerr Valley since it had no parking and no maintained trails. I could only stop here now because the park was closed—obviously no tourists would slam into my park service truck. I assumed the patrol ranger had plenty of other stuff going on just now, so hopefully I wouldn't get a ticket. I pulled over onto the shoulder.

I opened and closed the door very gently because I didn't want the elk to hear me and run off. I had no prior experience with elk. When I was a kid in Alaska I would walk up on the occasional moose, accidentally. In that situation, it was always clear to me that I was the one who needed to go.

Elk are beautiful animals, more majestic than deer and much more handsome than moose. I wondered how far I could walk out into the valley before the elk would bolt. I just wanted a closer look. The terrain seemed easy enough, so I stepped down off the side of the road onto the grass. Okay, so far, so good. I took another step. The next step, I tripped and fell.

The elk herd stampeded, shaking the earth and kicking up a huge cloud of dirt and pumice as they went. It sounded like the start of the Indy 500 or what buffalo must have sounded like on the Great Plains. In less than thirty seconds, they were out of sight. I could still hear the rumble, but they were gone.

I tripped because the ground felt spongier than it looked. It was sort of a mix between a bog and tundra and it felt like walking in mud. If you didn't pick up your feet, you were going down. I hadn't expected that. So I hit the dirt and caused the earthquake. Or maybe the valley was just reacting angrily to what I was tracking in on my boots.

I still wanted to explore, but the elk were gone and I didn't have the proper footgear for this muck. I decided I could at least make it to the invisible spring and creek hidden in the trees about fifty yards away. I slowly made my way over and was happy to see proof that the herd wasn't a mirage. Elk droppings were everywhere.

I pulled back a tree branch and there it was—a little bubbler of a spring. A trickle of water that became a tiny creek about thirty yards further down. Water sounds are peaceful. I sat and rested against a tree and just listened. I wondered if this water eventually ended up in Klamath Lake.

With a start I sat up and looked at my watch. It was almost 4:00. I had been dozing for almost an hour. I stretched my arms and neck. I rolled over onto my knees and peeked through some branches out into the valley. About two hundred yards away was a bull elk and several cows, a few with calves.

I shivered. It was getting cold in the shade. I needed to leave if I didn't want to be late getting back to the maintenance office.

The reddish-brown bull was easily seven hundred pounds. A six-point rack crowned the stately king of Kerr Valley. Against the backdrop of the slopes of Mount Scott, the herd could have been posing for an oil painting. At the edge of the tree line, I lay on my stomach and watched as more elk appeared. I was going to be late.

CHAPTER 12

My family lived in Pine Grove, east of Klamath Falls. It wasn't a town, it was an undeveloped area out in ranch country on the way to Lakeview. My father had bought the house on an acre of land shortly after I graduated from high school. Before that we lived in Falcon Heights, base housing for Air Force families stationed at Kingsley Field.

I liked coming home to Pine Grove during school breaks or for long weekends. I liked walking down the dirt road to the main highway to get the mail. Across the road, the high plain stretched down into the Klamath Basin. Hogback Mountain rose off to the left and everything else seemed to be rectangles of brown and green. Some horse ranches, but mostly lots and lots of hayfields. Sometimes you could watch the shadow of a cloud walk across the fields.

When I got home Friday night after the park shut down, I grabbed the plate of steak and steamed carrots my mother had saved for me and went out to the porch picnic table to watch Dad and Ginger. My father loved his horse. When I was home I often sat on the back porch and watched him brush her. She was a smallish horse, tan, a little on the chubby side. Dad bought her from a local rancher for my sister to ride, shortly after the family moved here.

As usual, Yapper, our collie, was in the corral, too, sniffing and milling around Dad and Ginger. But she was easily distracted. If a rabbit happened by, Yapper took off after it, running fast and barking as loud as she could. The rabbit, not looking too worried, would let the barking dog get tantalizingly close and then bounce ninety degrees to the right, leaving Yapper chasing air. It took about thirty yards for her to realize she was running after nothing. Then she'd trot back, head held high, happy as a dog could be.

Puzzled, I watched my father brush the horse. There had been the '58 Chevy he waxed every weekend years ago, but that horse was the only living thing I had ever seen him show any physical affection. He knew the words a father or husband should say. And sometimes he actually said them. But he was never playful with my sister or me. And he never touched my mom with any affection while I was around. Maybe it was the former military police sergeant in him. He was a tough guy. He wasn't supposed to show emotion.

But with Ginger it leaked out. I don't think Dad even realized it. Gentle strokes. Making sure to get every spot more than once. His lips moved, but I never heard his sweet-talk. He might pat Ginger a few times and then pull some treat out of his pocket for her to eat. My sister had lost interest in riding, but my dad kept Ginger anyway. She was his horse.

I watched and ate as twilight ended the ritual. My father patted Ginger goodnight and walked toward the back porch.

"Hey, there, what's the latest Crater Lake news?" he asked as he sank into a wicker chair next to me. "You made the national news tonight. Congratulations."

"Yeah, sometimes you have to eat a little crap to get on the news, but it was well worth it."

I told him what I knew about the closing of the park. From Mark the YCC leader to the six-inch rock. Just talking about it made me mad and I gave my unfinished plate of food a shove across the table.

"Dad, I don't understand people in charge. They get opportunity after opportunity to do the right thing. But they just don't. They ignore what's right in front of their faces."

My dad sat back and thought for a few seconds. He was wearing old baggy pants and a green sweatshirt with the arms cut off. The screen door opened and Mom came out with a ginger ale and ice. She took my plate off the table and took it back to the kitchen. My dad took a long drink.

"Samuel, the world you think is out there doesn't exist. You have all these quick answers and you think you know what's right or wrong because it's so obvious to you. Well, welcome to the real world. If you pay attention, in another twenty or thirty years or so, you might start to understand.

"You don't believe me now. And you don't think I know anything, but you're going to see eventually."

That shut me up for a minute. I had no idea what he was talking about.

"Are you saying what the Park Service did was right?"

"See, that's your problem. You're going to find that the world doesn't run on right or wrong, or fair or unfair. Of course I don't think the Park Service actions turned out to be RIGHT. But I understand how it could happen and why it happened.

"Right and wrong are obvious in moral dilemmas. And maybe with families and friendships. But in the big, bad world things happen because of money, people protecting what they have, everyone trying to get ahead and keep ahead, stuff like that.

"Let me give you an example. My supervisor has pretty much complete control over my career. He writes my evaluation. If my evaluation isn't excellent, I'm not getting a promotion. So I aim to please. And if something goes a little wrong in his group, he knows I'm going to do everything I can to fix it. You don't go outside the chain of command in the military, even if it's over something big. Because the moment you do, your career is over. No one will trust you to work for them. Someone willing to jeopardize what they have—and what everybody else has—is a big risk.

"You read the Serpico book. Serpico was attacked by his fellow officers because, when he didn't take the money, he jeopardized what they had going. They couldn't trust him if he didn't take the money. So, eventually he got shot in the face with a shotgun. He survived and testified and a couple people went to jail. But now he lives in Europe because he's afraid. And I bet the corruption is just as bad as it ever was.

"Do you see what I'm saying? People are going to protect what they have. I'm not going outside the chain of command because there are things I want. I like living out in the country and having money to help put you through college. I'm not going to jeopardize that for anything."

We both stared out at Ginger. The hawks flew overhead in their long, lonely circles. Yapper sniffed through the brush searching for rabbits.

"It sure sounds like you're telling me that I should ignore injustice in the world. Or something like that."

He took a sip of ginger ale. His lower lip jutted out, like it always did when he was mad. He shook his head,

"That's what I'm talking about, Samuel. The world is not that black-and-white. People in this country want to work thirty or forty years, get the benefits, get the pension and retire. Nobody wants to get tossed out in the cold, cold world and start all over at, say, forty. You're risking everything you've made and everything you'll ever make. When you have something and people depend on you, you'll understand.

"It's just not as simple as you think it is, Samuel."

He got up, picked up his glass and walked in the house.

❊ ❊ ❊

Saturday was a big day. It was the first time I got to READ about the Crater Lake Crud. The Oregonian was a morning paper published in Portland, so it didn't get to Klamath Falls until midday. My dad drove into town to pick up the paper on weekends.

When he got back, there it was—on the bottom of the front page. "Contaminated water supply closes Crater Lake—Sewage leak found." In black-and-white, the superintendent confirmed that raw sewage had contaminated the park's main water supply. But no other quotes, that was interesting. I was glad to see it said "250 to 275 of the area's 300 summer residents and employees have been sick." That was the truth, not a watered-down number. It also mentioned that five hundred to one thousand tourists were affected. Get that lawsuit money ready, boys.

Sunday's story got a lot more interesting. I didn't know that Oregon Senator Mark Hatfield served on the Senate Appropriations subcommittee responsible for the National Park Service. That was just awful luck for the Park Service. The story quoted Hatfield as saying he'd already called the Secretary of the Interior and that everything possible was being done.

With this new piece of information, I had to admit there would be more pain for the Park Service than I had predicted. They were too close to the fire not to get singed now.

Sitting at dinner Sunday, my father asked me if anything he'd told me the other day had sunk in.

I knew I should be careful. So I took a few bites before saying anything.

"I dunno. It just seems like such a negative outlook on life."

My dad picked at his baked potato. My mother sat quietly. There wasn't anyone else at the table because my sister was over at a friend's house.

"It's because you're putting inexperienced values on things," he said. "Right, wrong, fair, unfair, negative. It's nothing to do with that. You should know the rules most of us have to play by before you start charging off assigning guilt."

I finished dinner, thanked my mom for feeding me, picked up my clean clothes and the front pages of the Oregonian. I wanted to get back to the lake early. I didn't want to have to run a gauntlet of deer in the dark.

"Thanks. See you guys next Friday," I said as I closed the front door. "Everything should have calmed down by then."

I don't know why I said that. Every minute that the park stayed closed would be tense for management and those in charge of picking up the pieces of the water system. That unhappiness would trickle down to us on the lower rungs.

I kept thinking about my dad's lecture on the "rules" of life during the drive back. My liberal proclamations rarely got a rise from him. He might laugh, or sneer, or shake his head, but never did I get anything more than some quip attacking my naiveté. I didn't know what was different this time.

I pulled up to the cabin just as twilight faded into night. I opened my car door to the pounding, incoherent musical stylings of Uriah Heep. Or was it Humble Pie? My room-mates had it bad for these two bands and I didn't know why. I expect the bands were not really incoherent, but even Frank Sinatra would have been unintelligible at this decibel level. Personally, I felt if you were going loud, choose Led Zepplin, there was no substitute.

Tom and Tall Paul had joined the seasonal maintenance party circuit as soon as they got past their first bout of the Crud. They were gone almost every night drinking beer somewhere. But tonight it sounded like the party was at our house.

I opened the door to yells of "Sam Hunter!" I saluted the crowd packed into the tiny living room of our cabin. Tom,

Paul, Marcy, her current R & T boyfriend, another Roads and Trails guy with his girlfriend and Craig from my recent lime spreading crew. "Hey, give Hunter a beer, would you, Paul?" Tom blasted. I took the beer that was handed me, toasted the room, took a sip and then dragged my duffel bag full of clean clothes into my room and shut the door.

The Sleepy Hollow community was pretty good about not bringing marijuana into the park, because that was a federal offense, but I'm sure someone was smoking somewhere. That was a very common aroma back at college and hard to miss.

I stepped out of my bedroom into party central. Paul came over and said that if I needed water, the milk truck was full and open for business. He said they also had a few portable showers set up—cold water only.

"Good idea, Paul. Thanks. My cooler's still in my car, so I guess I'll go over there now."

I did have a cooler in my car, already filled with cold Klamath Basin water. But it was a good excuse to get out of the house and see what had gone on while I was away. It was 9:00 p.m. now, so maybe by the time I got back order would be restored and I could go to bed.

I would have preferred to walk, but I wanted to keep up the illusion, so I cranked up the Volkswagen and drove to Steel Circle. To get there you drove out of Sleepy Hollow, turned right to the main road, stopped, looked both ways, drove across the main road and you were there. The Community Center sat in the middle of the permanents' residential area. And now, parked next to the community center, was a big tanker filled with Annie Springs water. There were also three port-o-showers on the other side of the truck.

I didn't need any water and I didn't need a shower, so I walked over to the picnic tables just off the road. I took a seat on the top of one, lay back and looked up. The night sky at Crater Lake had its extremes. Some nights you couldn't see anything, sky or a hand in front of your face.

Then there were nights like tonight. You could see four or five times more stars than in a Eugene night sky, or even Klamath Falls. The sky was more than a one-dimensional ceiling. The depth let you see the Milky Way for what it was—a galaxy.

I wondered again why my father had reacted so strongly to my unkind attack against all things Park Service this weekend. He'd heard plenty of my moronic self-righteous outrages over the last few years. And I had heard "you think you're smarter than me" many times before. Maybe he'd just had it with me thinking I was smarter than I was.

According to stories, Dad barely got through high school. Everyone always said he was a rough-and-ready kind of guy, who didn't take to school at all. He enlisted in the Air Force after trying a couple menial jobs. He'd been in the military ever since.

He was a conservative man. Slow to act when it came to making a big decision, like buying a car or anything else that cost more than fifty dollars. He never took any chances that I knew of. He was quite proud of himself when he made an investment in a certificate of deposit that had a good interest rate. That was as risky as he got.

But he had a house, a car and a truck, a nice family, and a horse. Scuffling around back in his hometown, he probably never saw himself doing this well. Maybe he thought the only reason he got here was because he followed the rules very closely. And that was a lot tougher than his big-talking kid could ever know.

The stars blazed down at me. I thought about taking my shirt off and getting a star tan.

* * *

The next morning Dave and I were a team once more. Dan told us to hurry up to Munson Springs where Andrew was waiting for us.

"This could be an interesting day, Sam," said Dave as we drove up the road to the pump house. "These park service guys are really nervous. They're not used to being in the middle of the bull's-eye with all the important people looking hard at every little thing they do. You're liable to see some things you've never seen before."

"You mean things worse than what has already happened?"

"Way worse. You might see people just lie their asses off to any of these people who come from the state or the Feds. And the people right next to them will lie their asses off, too, because they know their best chance is to stick together—at least until the dam breaks and it's every man for himself."

"Somebody up the chain will want to get to the bottom of it, won't they?"

"Not likely. It's the same way with any big organization. Deny, deny, deny. Then hunker down and it will eventually go away, because it's in no insider's best interest to make everyone look bad. In fact you're liable to get promoted if you lie well enough."

"Man, Dave, you're sounding like my dad. And I was so looking forward to the peace and quiet of a shut down national park."

Dave gave me a look. "I'm serious, Sam. If a park service regular hears you say some of the things that you say to me about the water and management, you're liable to get tossed out of here. They'll find some excuse, trust me. Their careers are on the line and, in comparison, you don't matter to them at all."

The Munson Springs pump house was a happening place this sunny Monday morning. We pulled up behind a long line of parked green trucks and cars.

The Army had rolled into town. They'd brought a couple of big, camouflaged water treatment trucks and trailers full of machinery, and parked them on the side of the road next to the pump house. I didn't see a single military uniform anywhere, but most likely they were sleeping off the long drive from Washington State. It was unlikely the Park Service was ready for them anyway.

It wasn't for lack of trying. The pump house swarmed with people in park service uniforms, people with CDC hats, guys with short-sleeved white shirts unbuttoned at the neck and a few folks in tan work clothes. A State of Oregon car sat on the road that rose above and behind the pump house. Standing next to it were three people wearing ties.

Dave said he'd go find Andrew; I should stay put and he'd be back in a minute. I didn't want to get caught hiding in the truck, so I got out and stood next to the driver side door. I was careful not to lean against the truck in case someone thought I might be slacking in this time of crisis. I stood strong, leaning forward, one fist clenched, obviously someone willing to come home on his shield if the Park Service just said the word.

I started daydreaming about galaxies, and how the stars I looked at last night were probably long gone because of how long it takes light to travel. Then I heard, "Hey you, you with the yellow hat, why is Crater Lake so blue?"

"Hi, Sally."

Marcy and Sally pulled their truck up alongside me. "Guess what? We're going to spread lime. How about that? Finally something important." Ever since the beginning of the summer, Sally had been mildly annoyed by the jobs given the female seasonals—her and Marcy. After their first few days, it was just expected that they'd take over the cleaning of the outhouses along Rim Drive.

"Well, I guess you two are moving up in the world." I leaned against the truck window. "Hi, Marcy, how are you?"

"A little hungover from the party at your house last night."

Sally looked surprised. "What party?"

"Oh, did I forget to invite you? I'm so sorry."

Marcy rolled her eyes. "He's kidding you, Sally, he wasn't even there."

"Was too."

"For about five minutes. Where did you go anyway? You were still gone when we left."

"I was there, you were just too drunk to see me. Who was smoking the weed anyway?"

"Shhhhhhhhh. There wasn't any weed," Marcy whispered.

"Well," Sally said, pretending to be mad, "no one told me about any party."

"No one told me, either," I said.

"Can we all just stop yelling?" begged Marcy.

"You know, Marcy, I hear lime is great for a hangover."

"Bye, Sam."

Sally just waved and smiled as they drove off.

* * *

A few minutes later Dave headed back, purpose evident in every step.

In a serious tone he said, "We've been asked to take on a very important mission. One from which we may not return."

"Not the honey run?"

That broke Dave up. "This damn park closure. It's really cut into my honey run time."

"Okay, what's really going on now?"

"We've been asked by the park service higher ups to build them a house. See that huge army water treatment unit over there? It needs to feel like it's at home, so we're building a house right over the top of it. They knew who to come to for a quality job. They must have seen the work we did on that shed up at Rim Village."

"You mean the shed we haven't built yet?"

"Yes, that's the one. They must have seen the plans and gone, damn, those two sure know how to build a rock-solid structure."

"Dave, you haven't built anything else in the last couple days while I was on other jobs, have you?

"Nope, you know I can't do the big stuff without you."

"So that means you've STILL never actually built a wood structure of any kind before, right?"

"You sure are a negative Nellie."

* * *

Back at the wood shop, Dave was about an hour into his drawing of the planned water filtration house when Andrew burst through the door. I had been examining my broom work, trying to decide whether I was actually getting better at it or not, when he stormed in. He was out of breath.

"Dave, it's been more than hour, what in the hell are you doing? We're not building the Great Damn Pyramid here. We just need to do some framework, so we can get a roof over the damn filtration unit. Are you ready?"

"Yes, sir."

Dave said 'sir' in such a normal way that Andrew didn't seem to notice and headed back out the door.

I noticed. I stared straight at Dave.

He stared back. He turned his body a little to the right so I could see his hands in back of him. He had his fingers crossed.

It took Andrew, Dave and a couple of Army guys all day to get a rickety roof up. It was held up by four corner posts braced by two by fours. As this was an important task and people were watching, I didn't try to hammer a single nail or climb up on any ladders. But I tried to be as good a gofer as I could, and I did it all day long. I drove back to the shop four times. I helped carry lumber. I ran Army guys back and forth to their new camp at Mazama Campground. I even did some clean up inside the pump house.

When it got close to quitting time, I started carrying our equipment to the truck. With all the people we didn't know working here, Dave wanted to take all the carpentry tools back to the shop. It took me about thirty minutes to get everything packed into the back of the truck.

Dave came walking up and whispered, "Let's get out of here before the Great Pyramid blows down."

After we put all the carpentry tools back into the shop, Dave and I walked home to Sleepy Hollow. It was after quitting time and I needed a nap.

"Sam, why don't you come down for dinner? We're firing up the barbeque and we have plenty of chicken. I told Betty you probably wouldn't come because you favor those Beanie Weenies, but whatya say, just this once?"

"I don't really have anything to bring."

"We got plenty of everything. The daughter's off with Dan's daughter and wife doing something in Klamath Falls. They won't be back until dark."

"I know, I can bring the Oregonian for your reading pleasure. You can see what they're saying out in the real world."

"All right, then. Why don't you come over around 5:47. Okay?"

"Got it. See you then. Thanks."

When I got to Dave's trailer later that evening the lawn chairs were out and the little Weber was fired up. Betty was putting on the chicken and Dave was sipping a beer. He wore a Dodger baseball cap and a long-sleeved shirt. Glen Campbell's "Wichita Lineman" was playing on the cassette deck.

"Hey, Betty. Hey, Dave."

"Hey, it's Sam. I haven't seen you in a while. I hope you don't mind our old fogies music, but the daughter's away, so it's our only chance."

Betty smiled, then told Dave to stop loafing and get out the folding table for dinner. She had to go shuck the corn.

I put the newspapers I had brought down on the table. "I think you'll enjoy these, Dave, though there's not much there we don't know. It should start getting a little more interesting once people start blaming each other."

"Thanks. You need 'em back?"

"Nope. I'll wait for the good stuff to start my scrapbook."

Betty grilled the corn out of the husks. I'd never had it that way before. It was great. So was the chicken. She served a lettuce and tomato salad with oil and vinegar dressing and, after all that, came homemade cherry pie. I was thinking, *Oh, no, back to Beanie Weenies tomorrow.*

Betty's hair was all gray, cut short and feathery. She wore gold wire-rimmed glasses and had the Northwest look down pat—jeans with a red and green plaid shirt. She was wiry just like Dave.

"How do you guys stay so thin eating like this?" I asked.

"She doesn't let me eat except when there's company."

"Poor, poor Dave," I said.

Betty asked me about my family and my parent's house in Klamath Falls. I told her about Yapper and Ginger and my sister and what my dad did for a living.

"Your father must be very proud of you, working your way through college," Betty said.

"Well, I'm not sure he really believes I'm going to get through college, not to mention pay my own way. We don't exactly see eye-to-eye on things. I guess that's probably par for the course."

Betty and Dave both got quiet.

"Dave, I wanted to ask you something. My dad and I were discussing this Crater Lake fiasco and I complained about the behavior of the park management team. You know I get a little excited about that. Anyway, he got a little worked up himself and said I was making a judgment about things I didn't know anything about. That the situation here, no matter how I saw it, was not as simple or obvious as I was making it and I should recognize that nothing is black-and-white."

Dave took a sip of beer. "I know what he's talking about, Sam."

"Now wait a minute, Dave. You've been blasting the Park Service almost as much as me."

"I'm a college professor. I've been a college professor since...well, a long time. I'm around college kids every single day for nine months at a time. And, while I like a lot of them, they all suffer from the same thing—they don't know what they don't know. That's your problem. YOU don't know what you don't know. How could you? You're only twenty years old. I've found that the older I get, the less I know. I think the difference between your dad and me is that I've just gotten used to the frailties of youth.

"Look at what your dad's accomplished. With a high school education, he has a nice house with a little land out in the country. He has a horse, for God's sake. Sam, do you really know how bad the military pays?"

"I guess I don't know what he makes. Actually, I have NO idea."

"People make this a dangerous world to live in, Sam. You get more than two people together and things get political. I lived in terror for my family until I got tenure. You wouldn't think that working at a major institution of learning would create so much fear. You can bank on nothing ever being what it seems like on the surface. I'm sure your father has had to deal with a big dose of that over the years.

"I'll give you an example. When the Nixon thing blew up, all my college kids were telling me what a hero that Deep Throat was. Someone stood up to the evil administration. What a guy. That's crap, Sam. Deep Throat was someone defending his turf. He was in some agency in Washington, losing a battle with the Executive Office, and the only way he could fight back was getting the newspapers to do his dirty work for him.

"You don't know what you don't know. And let me tell you something else. If I drove down to Klamath Falls and visited your dad, I guarantee you he would spend an hour yakking my ear off, telling me what a great son he has."

Dave was pissed. He'd never got in my face about anything before. I didn't know what to do or say. I looked deep into the forest on the other side of the dirt road.

Dave suddenly stood up and walked over to a stack of coolers by the trailer. "Betty, we're going to need some more water to clean up. I'll go fill these up."

"I can do that, Dave, I want to."

"No, Sam, that's all right. You're the guest. You can help Betty put things away if you want. I'll be right back."

Dave gathered up his various water containers, put them in the back of his truck and drove away. I watched as he drove to the fork in the road where he veered right to the maintenance yard.

I felt a hand on my shoulder.

"I'm sorry, Betty. I didn't mean to upset Dave."

"Sam, don't worry about Dave. He'll be fine." Betty pulled me around so she could look at me. "We lost a son a few years ago in a car wreck. Bobby. He and Dave had a very hard time. They didn't even speak the last year before the crash. Dave has trouble with that. It might take him a few extra minutes over at the milk truck, but he'll be fine when he gets back. It would be nice if you were still here waiting."

CHAPTER 13

P EOPLE LIKE TO SAY THAT every dark cloud has its silver lining. I didn't believe in that proverb. I'm more in tune with the church of It Can Always Get Worse. But in this one case, the saying was true. A window of opportunity opened and it suddenly got good to be a seasonal worker in Building and Utilities. All because of the Crater Lake Crud.

I read in the newspaper that the park would be switching over to Annie Springs water and closing shop at Munson Springs. That was baloney. There wasn't any pipe to connect Annie Springs and the park's water system. Even if the Park Service brought in every Army plumber on the West Coast, that couldn't happen in less than a couple months and they wanted the park open NOW.

The Army guys spent a week blasting the entire existing water system with a strong chlorine solution to sterilize every pipe that carried water. Park service folks and outside contractors got down on their hands and knees to clean out all the pump house equipment, as well as the spring and the ground around it.

The Munson Springs water was pumped through the Army purification units, sent into the pump house where a god-awful amount of chlorine was added and, voila, the park had water again. Here came the silver lining. The powers that be wanted the chlorine levels watched. They wanted a lot of chlorine in the water, but not too much. A large gauge in the pump house monitored the percentage of chlorine in the water going out. A black line marked the highest it could go before the chlorine needed to be turned off, so it would drop to the proper level.

The chlorine almost never hit that black line, but the Park Service wanted to be careful. Better late than never, right? So someone had to watch the gauge twenty-four hours a day, every day. That's where the B & U seasonals came in. Dan asked for volunteers. We'll pay overtime, he said. The shifts were six hours, six to midnight and midnight to six.

My arm shot up. That's what I was there for—the money. Sally, my two roommates, and the custodian couple from Mazama Campground also signed up.

The next day Chris caught up with me as I walked home at the end of the day.

"Hey, Sam. Wanted to talk to you for a minute."

"Yeah, man, what's up?"

"Well, you know tomorrow's Sally's first shift at the pump house. She's got six to midnight. I don't think she really wants to do it. She just doesn't want to look like a wuss."

"Dan's not making people do it. Marcy didn't sign up."

"I know. I told her unless she really needed the money, it was no big deal. Anyway, I didn't win the argument."

"Dave and I could try."

"Are you kidding? The more people make an issue of it, the more stubborn she'll get. And she'll be mad at me for saying anything. I'm just worried about those army knuckleheads. I've been in the Army. I don't know those guys, but I know those guys. They're going to be hanging around all the time taking care of the equipment—or at least pretending to."

"That reminds me, Chris. What were you doing in the Army?"

"Long story. So listen, I'm going to be visiting a lot during her shifts and I was wondering if you could help me out with that?"

Chris didn't have to tell me about Army knuckleheads. As a criminal investigator in the Air Force, my dad dealt with the worst the military had to offer. According to him, the services were full of drug dealers and users, thieves, and gangs. That didn't mean the park's recently acquired knuckleheads were any of those things, of course. But it was enough that they were guys. I wasn't thrilled with Sally being alone with them at the pump house late at night, either.

"Sure, Chris. What shift do you want me to take?"

"I don't care. If you take two hours I'll do the rest."

"Okay. I'll do ten to midnight. You need your beauty sleep."

"When's your first shift?"

"Tonight—midnight to six. Graveyard, baby! I'm ready to go."

"Geez. You sure you want to do the thing with Sally tomorrow?"

"I'm on it. I'm going to eat some Beanie Weenies and then I'm going to bed. I'll be fine. See ya."

"Thanks. I owe you one."

"I'm writing that down," I said, as I hopped up on the porch.

*   *   *

Thump, thump, thump filled the air when I got out of my car at the pump house. The Army generator didn't sound so loud in the middle of the day, but in the midnight mountain air it reminded me of a jackhammer with a silencer on it. *Thump, thump, thump.* But slower.

Things were a lot better inside the rock walls. When I closed the door, the generator noise disappeared. As an added bonus, I got to kick Paul awake. When Dan explained the job to us volunteers, the only thing he got worked up about was staying awake. "DON'T FALL ASLEEP or I'll have your hide."

Paul was sitting on the floor with his back up against some boxes. I looked over at the gauge to make sure we weren't poisoning everybody. Then I kicked Paul in the butt.

"DON'T FALL ASLEEP OR I'LL HAVE YOUR HIDE."

Still mostly asleep, Paul scrambled to his feet. He got his bearings, looked around and saw me.

"Asshole."

"Is that how you greet the person relieving you of duty so that you can go home and get into your warm bed?"

"If they kick me, it is."

"Anything I should know?"

"It's cold in here."

"Did the gauge do anything?"

"Not that I saw. I'm outta here."

"Hey, did the Army stop by?"

"Yup, earlier."

"Okay, goodnight."

Tall Paul left. I watched from the door as he started up his green Rambler, turned it around in the road and roared down the hill.

I'd done time in the pump house before. I had cleaned the inside and stored materials for the wooden building that Dave and others were constructing out front. I turned off the space heater. I listened. The only noise was the hum of the water machinery. Inside was about the size of a studio apartment. There was a folding chair. I couldn't imagine sitting on that for six hours. Or fifteen minutes. I closed the door to keep out the cold night, but the rock walls closed in fast, so I opened the door back up. I had a parka in the car if I needed it. There was a port-o-potty out on the road. And there was a clock. I compared it with my watch to make sure I was synchronized. Check. Okay, what was I going to need from the car? My Volkswagen was packed with almost everything I had at the cabin. I didn't know what I'd need and I wanted to be prepared.

I went light. A little cooler with Pepsi and pecan cookies, a big red sweatshirt that could go over the sweatshirt I was wearing, a blanket, a book and the parka, just in case.

I laid the blanket on the cement floor near the gauge and checked for comfort. Not so good. The parka could serve as a pillow. The book was *Ragtime* by Doctorow. I was an English major, so I felt obligated to keep up with the new literature. I knew that if I got through the first two chapters, I'd read straight through, preferring getting to the end to sleeping. Normally that was an annoying habit of mine, but it was going to be helpful on the pump house shift.

I put the book down at 5:30 a.m., packed up my gear and took it out to the car. Damn, I forgot to check out the sunrise. I was too busy reading about Coalhouse blowing up New York. Oh well, I'd have plenty more chances. I moved the folding chair next to the gauge.

Dan pushed through the door at six sharp. The nighttime shifts were his responsibility and he probably figured he'd find me snoring on the floor. I heard the Army guys talking outside, getting ready to take over.

"You look bright-eyed and bushy-tailed for someone who's been here since midnight."

"Didn't want to lose my hide, Dan."

"Smart-ass. You can come in at ten. Get out of here."

YES, I said to myself. "Thanks."

* *

At 9:45 the next night, I pulled up in back of Chris's blue Honda. I decided to wait in the car until a little after ten. I didn't want to bust in on anything private between Chris and Sally. They might not hear my car if the pump house door was closed.

I saw headlights coming up the road. Probably a ranger. No, it was a park service truck. Whoever it was pulled up behind my car. They seemed in no hurry to turn off their brights. Finally, someone got out.

"What are you doing here, Hunter?"

It was Frank.

"Chris and I are keeping Sally company. He's in the pump house now. I was just about to go in."

"Everything should be fine, then. I was doing a spot check to make sure you people were awake." He never did turn off his lights. He got back in, closed the door and backed out on the road. Then he was gone.

"Hey, what's going on out there Sam?" yelled Chris from the pump house.

"Oh, just management checking to make sure the pump house is covered." I walked down the trail and into the pump house.

"Who was in the truck?" asked Chris.

"It was Dan. I told him we had three people on the job. He thought that should be enough. Hey, how many seasonals does it take to watch a chlorine gauge? Never mind, I'm still working on a punch line. How ya doing Sally?"

"Feeling like an idiot. I'm sorry, Samuel. I didn't know you had been roped into babysitting me until just now." She punched Chris in the shoulder and he pretended to stagger back a few feet.

"YOU feel like an idiot? I thought this was my shift. Dang it. Might as well stick around for a while."

"You're such a liar."

"Am not."

"Okay," interrupted Chris as he pulled on his coat. "I'm going now before I get yelled at some more. My roomies were having a barbecue tonight. I better go see if the cabin is still standing. Thanks, Sam. See you tomorrow, Sally."

"Bye."

Sally frowned. I guess she didn't like how this was working out.

"I could have stayed here by myself. You two are jerks."

"Well, that may be. But at no time was Chris going to let you stay here by yourself. He was afraid you'd get some unwelcome visitors. I hope you thanked him."

"I did. I gave him credit for being romantic. Then you showed up," she said laughing. "Kidding, kidding, kidding!"

"Wow. You ARE welcome."

She bumped her shoulder into mine and then walked over to her cooler and opened it up. "C'mon. Can't you take a joke? How 'bout a drink? Pepsi? I have one Orange Crush."

I took a position leaning against a coal-black box that held pieces of pipe. "Anything to eat?" I asked.

"Carrot sticks, celery."

"Are you kidding? That's it? No cookies?"

"My stomach still isn't feeling that great. I'm not throwing up or anything, just blah. I get a cramp every now and then."

"Maybe you should go see the nurse."

"Nah, I've got all the Pepto Bismol and Kaopectate I can use. It's not bad at all. If it gets worse, I can go see a doctor. What's new with you?"

Sally handed me a Pepsi.

"New? Hmm. I guess my main source of entertainment these days is reading the Oregonian. I can't believe what the Park Service and Haswell are willing to say to reporters. A headline a few days ago said that park service management thinks it's very possible that vandals stuffed that rock in the sewer line. If it hadn't been for vandals, there wouldn't have been a water problem. Can you believe it?"

Sally shook her head. She took a drink of her Pepsi. "It's scary how isolated we are. People can say anything up here and people will believe it. It's such a weird place.

"When I talk to my parents on the phone, they try to fill me in on world events or what's happening at home. That doesn't seem real anymore. All that's real is what happened walking to work, at work, and after work. No newspapers, no TV, no phones. If people from outside hadn't finally intervened in this mess, who knows what could of happened. How nobody died is beyond me. The people we work with were pissed, but it's like they were pissed at the inconvenience. Now it's all as good as new. Let's go play some softball."

"You're starting to sound like me, Sally. That's not good for your social life."

"What if we turned it into a drinking game? Maybe they'd listen to the news then. There are some girls in the dorm back at school that have a drinking game when *Kung Fu*'s on. Every time the old guy says 'Grasshopper' they gulp a shot of tequila. Maybe we can do that. We have a party and you stand up and read the Crater Lake–related newspaper articles. Every time you read a crazy quote or a lie, we'd salute and down the hatch."

"That's more likely to get me arrested. You know I don't think there are enough undisputed lies being told. Most are half-truths. I don't think we'd be able to keep our party animals happy."

We sat quietly for a couple minutes. She opened up her cooler and pulled out a baggie of carrot sticks. In the background was the ever present *hummmmm* of the machinery. While Sally crunched on a carrot, she turned to look at the gauge. It was fine.

"You know, Sally, when I was parking my car a truck pulled up behind me."

"I know. You said it was Dan, right?

"Yeah, that's what I said, but it wasn't Dan, it was Frank. And he was obviously taken by surprise that I was here."

Sally leaned back in her chair, looked straight in front of her and didn't say a thing.

"I don't know what's going on, Sally. But it seems strange that Frank stopped by. The water pump is Dan's problem. Maybe it meant nothing. Except the look on your face the couple of times I've mentioned Frank, makes me think otherwise. I could be much more help to you if you would just tell me what's wrong."

Sally's face remained flat and expressionless. "There isn't anything wrong. I just don't like the guy. That's it. Stop trying to build another conspiracy."

"Hold on, you've already admitted to me that's something is wrong. You just won't tell me what."

"Well, it doesn't have to involve Frank, does it? Get off the Frank thing. PLEASE. It's none of your business." Sally wrapped her arms around her stomach. "You're making my stomach hurt. If I throw up, you'll have to clean it up."

I let everything settle down for a few minutes. I got up and walked over to the gauge. No problems there.

"Can I have a carrot stick?" I asked.

"No."

"Man, pump house hospitality has gone completely out the window."

"Shut up," she said. Then she giggled.

"Does that mean I can have a carrot stick?"

"No."

"Fine."

"Do you want to play cards?" she asked. "I've got some cards right here."

"Can I have a carrot?"

"If you win."

"All right, what's the game?"

She pulled the blue-backed cards out of the box and started shuffling. "Go Fish," she said.

"What! You're in college now, you can't play Go Fish anymore."

"Do you want a carrot or not?"

"Fine."

For the record, I won three carrots before it was time to go. My roommate, Tom, staggered through the door at 12:10. He was sorry he was late. He'd been at the party at Chris's cabin. There was plenty of alcohol on Tom's breath. I warned him that management visited occasionally and that he better be careful. He pulled a pack of Dentyne out of his pocket and put a piece in his mouth.

"See? All taken care of. Hey, what do you think Chris is going to say when he hears you two were alone in the pump house?"

Sally and I didn't say a thing as we walked out into the cold night air.

I drove Sally to the Stone House. As she started to open the car door I stopped her. "Wait a minute. I almost forgot to give you something."

I reached in the pocket of my parka and pulled out my copy of *Sometimes A Great Notion*.

"Here. You said you were looking for some good books. Do you know Kesey? He's a Eugene boy."

"He wrote *One Flew Over the Cuckoo's Nest*. Right? I haven't read that yet."

"*Cuckoo's Nest* is good. This one is better. You'll like it."

She took the book from me and squeezed my arm.

*   *   *

The blissful, tourist-free days in the park went by fast. Scuttlebutt said the park would reopen bright and early Friday morning, August 1. Just two more days. If that held true, the park would have been closed an even three weeks.

A civilian crew from outside worked feverishly putting in pipe to connect Annie Springs and the park water system. Dan said they were still a month away from being done.

It took the R & T boys seven full days to figure out that B & U had opportunities they didn't—namely the overtime shifts at the pump house. They told Frank. Frank told Dan that wouldn't fly and they made a new schedule. My bitterness was short-lived. Turned out there was still plenty of overtime money to be made.

After that first night—to Chris's relief—Sally took her name off the schedule. A couple nights later, Tom, the Crater Lake Rock Star, drove a park service pickup off the road on his way to relieve Tall Paul at the pump house. Paul flagged down a ranger to drive him down to the cabin to see if I would take Tom's shift. Sure I would. Apparently Tom had been plastered. Luckily, he didn't go off at a place with a big drop, so he only got scratches, according to Paul. But by the time I got home the next morning, Tom and all his gear were gone. His Rock Star status didn't save him, he was gone for good.

Then someone in R & T did the math and discovered pump house duty wasn't quite the bonanza they had thought it was. After taxes, they might make just over forty-five dollars, net. They weren't sure if that was worth it, especially on weekend nights. I let it be known that I would pull anybody's shift for forty-two dollars in cash, in advance, during the week and forty-five on the weekend. I already had my first job this Saturday night. It seemed at least one person would rather pay me than tell Frank to pull him off the schedule, after the stink Frank made about the whole deal.

The Oregonian ran a story about the park almost every day. I thought I'd be reading lies of grand proportions after the headline in the paper on the first Tuesday after we closed:

"Blocked park sewer line believed work of vandals."

Somebody must have called from Washington D.C. about that beauty because I never read another word about vandals again.

Next came a barrage from unnamed sources spilling their guts. The number one target was George Haswell. Senator Hatfield's office said they had a lot of information about the concessionaire pressuring the Park Service to keep the park—and his business—open, no matter what. A

Senate subcommittee investigation was scheduled and Mr. Haswell was asked to attend.

Some of the couple hundred college kids Haswell abused up at Rim Village likely played Deep Throat this time. I didn't think anybody from the Park Service would say anything because, ultimately, they would be found at fault somewhere along the line. I did think there might be a couple seasonal rangers and naturalists that might give him up. And the state people Haswell had yelled at early on could be added to the prime suspect list.

By the eighteenth, it looked as if Haswell and the superintendent were being sacrificed to appease the gods. They were being allowed to say things in the newspaper that eventually would make them the fall guys.

The superintendent said, in print, that when the Fourth of July rolled around, "It looked like the Crud was on the wane. There didn't seem to be very many cases then. People were feeling better. Only one or two employees were sick."

Now that was a whopper. Haswell backed him up. Then other problems popped up for both of them. The Park Service started to receive threats of lawsuits. The State also came after Haswell for irregularities in how he paid, or didn't pay, his employees. And that's about the time the Rim Village college kids really started hacking away at their former boss.

The Oregonian quoted their horror stories in depth. Everything from throwing up in the dorm hallways because the lines to the bathrooms were too long, to being forced by their supervisors to work on the food lines while sick with diarrhea, and how the lodge employees were told not to say anything about being sick, while supervisors tore down signs warning them of problems with the water.

I didn't know how George Haswell would manage to stay out of jail. But that might be one of those things I didn't know that I didn't know. After that subject came up at Dave's the other night, he and I decided we should barbeque at least once a week. Then, after dinner, he could lecture on things I was clueless about. He told me he was having trouble narrowing it down.

But not tomorrow night—that was going to be a special barbeque to celebrate the next day's reopening of the Park AND a planned honey run to Cleetwood Cove. Sally was invited. Dan had given Dave the word that Friday was the day. Dan wanted Dave, Sally and me to go down on the first day tourists returned to the park, to investigate whether those port-o-potties needed to be emptied. They were generally emptied twice a season, but this had been a crazy summer. Apparently, if they needed emptying, we were the correct people for the job.

The honey run made a popular topic of conversation at Dave's barbecue. "Dave, I've asked this before, but you've never really answered—only laughed," I said. "How do you empty those port-o-potties at the bottom of that trail, and where do you put it?"

I was a newbie when it came to the special port-o-potties located lakeside at the bottom of Cleetwood Trail. Sally knew about them as she had to clean them once a week. Dave, of course, had been team leader for the honey run for the last couple years.

"You have a lot to learn about doing the honey run," he said. "You just don't know what you don't know." Then he started laughing.

"Sally, do you know?" I asked.

"I have absolutely no idea," she said. "There are two big ones and they sit at the end of the trail around the corner from the boat dock. You can't see them until you walk around that corner. I clean 'em, but I can't imagine how you empty 'em. You can't carry the stuff up. The trail is way too steep."

"C'mon, Dave," I begged.

"Sam, my boy, some things just have to be seen to be understood. The important thing is not to get any in the lake, because Crater Lake is 99.99999 percent pure. There would be another Senate investigation."

"Why would we get any in the lake?"

"Anybody want pie?" yelled Betty from inside the trailer. There were yeses all around.

"I got this pie at a bakery in Klamath Falls today, so it should be good," she said. "Dave, are you torturing these poor children?"

"I'm trying not to spoil the honey run experience for them, Betty. In everyone's life there should fall a little honey," he said. He chuckled and shook his head like he couldn't believe he was fifty-three years of age, a college professor and still emptying port-o-potties to earn a summer paycheck.

CHAPTER 14

SALLY LOOKED PALE THE NEXT MORNING when she met up with Dave and me at the maintenance office. She said she was having trouble getting rid of the cramps from her latest round of the Crud. But she perked up after we got in the truck and started driving the ten miles around the rim road to the top of Cleetwood Trail.

The parking lot across from the entrance to the trail was the last chance to turn around and head back to Rim Village. If you drove any further, it was a one-way trip all the way around the rim to where the road poured out near park headquarters. When we pulled in, there were already several cars scattered around the lot. Actually, I had been surprised at the number of tourists we'd already seen on the road. The park had reopened that morning with little fanfare. The rangers simply took down the closed signs and started taking money, waving visitors through with a smile and a wave.

Cleetwood Trail is the only way a tourist can get to lake level. The only safe or legal way, that is. Every couple of years the Park Service Rescue Team has to pull out someone who thought they could make their own way down in another spot—sometimes alive, most times dead.

The trail itself is a series of switchbacks that add up to a one-mile trek. The big issue for tourists is the grade. The trail drops seven hundred feet in that one mile. The Park Service theorizes that walking from lakeshore to the top of the trail equals sixty-five flights of stairs.

According to Ranger Bob, the trail is a heart attack waiting to happen. The brochure the park hands out does not recommend the trail for visitors not in good physical condition or those with heart, breathing, or leg difficulties. There's a big sign at the top of the trail for those who don't read the brochure. But everyone wants to see the water up close, so every year there are emergencies.

A small boat dock at Cleetwood Cove, at the bottom of the trail, was home to four plain boats that were specially built to limit any pollution of the water. George Haswell's company gave tourists boat rides to Wizard Island and around the Lake. Park naturalists rode in the boats to tell the Crater Lake story.

Both Sally and Dave said the hike down was deceiving.

"Going down it's pretty easy and doesn't feel too steep," Dave said. "But you notice that ten to twelve percent grade right away coming back and then add in the elevation. It's not fun. You'll be happy to see every one of those damn benches they put at each turn. Sally, you were coming down regularly before we closed shop. I bet you just jog up now."

Sally gave Dave a big smile. "Yeah, right, I jog. Usually backwards! No, I had gotten where I could pace myself and make it up okay with only a stop or two. But I remember my first time. It was awful. The boat drivers say by the end of the summer they can jog almost all the way up the trail."

"How long does it take to make the hike out?" I asked.

"You mean, how long will it take US? Well, let's see. Since this'll be your first time, Samuel, you'll probably slow us down a lot. It'll probably take us about forty minutes. That's a pretty leisurely pace. The boat drivers do it in under twenty minutes."

"Show-offs," I said.

We walked across the road to the trailhead. There was no need to take any equipment, because everything we needed was in a small storage shed near the port-o-potties. We each had sweatshirts tied around our waists because it often got cold at the bottom and the wind could whip. All three of us had disposable plastic bottles filled with water because there was none at Cleetwood Cove. We left sack lunches in the truck. We had agreed to eat after we hiked back up.

The hike down was uneventful. There were switch-backs and a lot of big Hemlocks and Shasta Red Firs. Once I caught myself picking up speed on a long downward stretch, because of the steepness, and had to purposely slow down, which my thighs thought was a stupid thing to do. The views of the lake were glorious. There were no clouds in the sky, but it got cooler the farther down we went. About two-thirds of the way down, we stopped for a quick break and looked out at the lake.

Dave was quiet. I hadn't hiked anywhere with him before, but I could see he was out of breath. Not that long ago, he had spent a week in bed with the Crud. He still hadn't gained back the weight. Sally hadn't complained since we met up at the truck, but she didn't look that great, either.

"That's going to be some hike back up," I said. "But look at the bright side. We have all summer to get back to the top. It doesn't snow real hard until October. We can camp each night along the trail. We can beg for food from the tourists walking by. There's plenty of firewood."

Sally got up from the bench. "Don't you men worry," she said. "I'm in shape. I can hook a line to you and pull you both up the trail."

"Great, Sally, I have nothing to worry about then," said Dave. "Except for the honey." He worked up the energy to crack a smile. "Let's get going, I'm ready to dive in."

We reached the final switchback that dumped us on the last downward straightaway to the boat dock. For some reason I had been thinking that there would be a quaint, yet picturesque little boating village or something at the bottom. Wrong. This wasn't Lake Tahoe. The trail ran right to a bleached shed where I supposed tourists bought their boat tickets. There were four or five people milling around. The boat dock area had been rudely gouged out of the natural slope. The L-shaped wooden dock had enough mooring space to handle the boats. A blue boat that looked like a cabin cruiser convertible was tied up there now. That was it—a wooden shed, a small wooden dock, boats, and a lot of rocks.

Past the ticket shed, the narrow trail hugged the rim wall and disappeared around the corner. I bet they had to dig that

trail out a lot because its sits right against a slide area. I figured the port-o-potties must be around the corner.

When we reached the ticket shed, someone on the dock
shouted out, "Hey, Sally, how you doing?" She smiled and
waved.

"That's one of the boat drivers," she said. "They're
pretty friendly."

"I dunno. I didn't hear them say anything to me or Dave.
Did you, Dave?"

Dave didn't stop. He kept moving down the trail. As we
turned the corner, I could see the two tall, beautiful beige
port-o-potties. They sat on a redwood deck. Off to the right
another little trail led to the storage shed. A sign saying 'No
Entry' hung on a chain stretched across the trail. It was held
up by two short posts. You could walk around the posts if
you really wanted to get to the shed.

"Why don't you two rest here a minute? Let Sam play
tourist and take in the sights. I'll go check out the shed to
make sure we have everything we need," Dave said.

"Do you need my key, Dave?" asked Sally.

"Nope, got my own."

Large rocks covered the shoreline. I was certain that
every one of them had rolled down from the slope behind
us. Now that I think of it, I remember Chris saying his crew
had been down here for a week clearing this trail. Sally
and I walked over to the rocks near the water and took a
seat. The breeze was strong and cold, so we both pulled our
sweatshirts on.

"I take my break right here after cleaning the toilets,"
said Sally. "If I face Wizard Island, and there isn't a boat

coming in or going out, it feels like I'm down here all by myself."

"I hate to say it, Sally, but from this vantage point the lake doesn't look so special. From above it's like, unbelievable, but down here it's just a lake."

"Yeah, I know what you mean. You really need to get out in the boat. Then you see the rim walls rise up all around you. It makes you feel real small, in kind of a comfortable way. And Wizard Island is incredible. Did you know there is a log—a mountain hemlock, I think—that's been floating around upright out there for over a hundred years? They call it the Old Man. The wind currents push it all around the lake. You never know where you're going to see it. Sometimes I think about what it would be like to ride on the log and just bob around. Wouldn't it be unbelievable to be down here at night, looking up with the rim framing the stars?"

"What are those?" I said, pointing to the water.

"Kokanee Salmon."

"Wow, look at them all."

"The water is so clear. Sometimes when I sit here they go by in big schools. Now this is the truth: I sat here one day for twenty minutes, watching a school of those salmon swimming by. When I had to leave, they were still swimming by. They're just itty bitty, but there are millions of them."

Dave shouted for us. "We're ready, guys, let's get this over with."

Sally and I walked over. The deck the port-o-potties sat on spanned a miniature ravine that tilted down toward the lake. The ravine looked like a dry riverbed emptying into the ocean. A wooden catwalk ran behind and below the port-o-potties.

Dave waited for us at the catwalk. He had two sticks that looked like yardsticks, but they were stained green like they had been used to check the oil. He also had a twenty-five-gallon can of some chemical and two empty cans about the same size.

Turned out the port-o-potties were flush toilets. What would they think of next? You did your business, then you flushed the toilet and a green chemical dropped in just like water does in the toilet in your bathroom.

"Are you ready?" asked Dave. "Oh Sally, I need you to go put out the sign at the corner that says the restrooms are closed for cleaning. Thanks."

Dave looked at me. I was getting a bad feeling about this. Dave chuckled and shook his head. He tried not to laugh, but he just couldn't help himself. He was still laughing when he turned toward the back of the closest port-o-potty and pointed to a rectangular panel. It opened in a way that you could see everything that had been flushed down the toilet. Fortunately, whatever the green chemical was, it pulverized the human deposits because it just looked like green liquid inside. Unfortunately, it didn't pulverize the smell.

"Oh geez, Dave."

He stood up straight with his back leaning against the port-o-pottie and made a face. "I know," he said. He grabbed one of the sticks, stuck it through the hole and started stirring.

"The theory is, if we give it a stir, most of it will empty out smoothly, without plugging up," he said, pointing to what looked like a simple plastic spigot. "Otherwise we'll just be back here again in a couple weeks. We also need to do this fast for obvious reasons. Bring the empty bucket down here.

"Okay, Sam, you and I are both going to hang onto the handle while I open this valve just a little bit. Easy does it."

Out poured the green sludgy liquid. The bucket filled up quickly. Dave closed the valve. I stepped up off the catwalk and lifted the bucket up onto the ground. Dave told me to follow him. I picked up the bucket. What an ugly smell. We went up the trail to the path to the storage shed. I followed Dave around the no-entry sign to the back of the shed. There he opened a hatch that had a lock hanging off it.

"Pour it in and let's go get some more." It was a deep pit. It smelled just like what I had in the bucket.

We filled up two more buckets and I took them to the pit. *This is the stone age*, I thought. And how did that pit affect the purity of the lake? *Sam, you don't know what you don't know. Just hurry up.* While I dumped green slime, Dave worked on the other toilet. To satisfy her curiosity, Sally had taken a look at what we were doing, then started cleaning the insides of the port-o-potties and filling the chemical reservoirs.

As I stepped up on the deck with my empty bucket, I saw Dave open the valve of the second toilet. But instead of opening just a little bit, the valve flew open all the way and green liquid started rushing into the bucket. Dave tried to hold onto the handle and shut the valve at the same time. The bucket was already more than half-full as I jumped down on the catwalk to help. I grabbed the handle as the stinking liquid flooded the bucket.

"Dave, I've got the bucket. Close that thing!"

It wouldn't budge. While we watched helplessly, the bucket overflowed onto our pants and boots, off the catwalk and down into the ravine.

"SALLY!" I yelled.

Sally came rushing around the port-o-potty.

"SALLY, HAND ME THAT BUCKET OVER THERE." I had left the other bucket on the deck when I jumped in to help Dave.

The nasty green stuff was still overflowing the first bucket. The sight of Dave standing there helpless, green honey splashing on him, pouring onto his boots was a sight I never wanted to see again. Of course, the same thing was happening to me. All Dave could do was laugh. I laughed right along with him.

After Sally tossed down the bucket, Dave moved the full one aside and I put the empty one under the spigot.

"Sam?"

"Yeah?"

"What are we going to do when this one starts over-flowing?"

"Go dump the other one, I'll stay here with this one." But just as he dragged the bucket off the catwalk the gusher turned into a trickle, then stopped. I looked through the hole and saw there was still plenty of green liquid. Maybe God intervened—we'd been punished enough.

"It stopped, Dave; it got clogged up. Maybe you can find some tools in the shed to fix this thing."

Dave went to dump his bucket. I took a chance it wouldn't start flowing again and went out in front of the toilets to see what damage we had done. Just as I got to the railing I saw a rivulet of green trickle into the lake. I felt sick. Most of the overflow had been soaked up by the dry, porous dirt and rock, but not all of it. The green was still flowing. I jumped off the deck and skidded down the bank to the spill. I picked up handfuls of dirt and threw them on the spill as fast I could. I scraped together a dirt berm next to the lake to block whatever was still moving. No more would get in the lake from the first spill, but my landscaping wouldn't stop another flood. I guess I could throw myself in front of the green sludge if I had to. Anything to stop it from getting in the lake. Oh man, how could it get any worse?

"I think I got it," yelled Dave.

"Are you ready to empty more?"

"No way I'm emptying any more today. I don't care. Let's clean this up and get out of here."

"Okay, Dave." I kept staring at the place where the lake had been violated.

"Hey, Sam, where's Sally?"

I looked around, then climbed out of the ravine. I didn't see her. Then I spotted her up the trail. She was on her knees. It looked like she was throwing up. The smell and everything must have gotten to her. I walked over and saw she was definitely throwing up. I knelt down beside her.

I pulled her long hair back away from her face. "Sally, is there anything I can do?"

She looked up and wiped her mouth with the back of her hand. Her eyes closed. She was pale, sweat rolling down her face. I put my hand on her forehead. It felt hot.

"Samuel, this isn't just the Crud. It's something worse."

"You sure it's not just another Crud attack?"

She turned her face toward me. Tears were rolling down her face.

"I'm pregnant, Samuel," she said quietly. "The cramps have gotten bad. And I'm bleeding, I can feel it. Something's really wrong. I need to get to a hospital." She kept looking at me. "You can't tell anyone, okay? Just get me to the hospital. Please." We looked at each other for about fifteen seconds without saying a word.

"Sally, I'll be right back. I'm going over to see if I can get some help from the boat crew. Okay?" She nodded and turned away. She leaned over, staring at the ground in front of her.

The ticket shed was about seventy-five yards away. When I got there, I found a tall blond kid, a little older than me, looking at a schedule nailed to the door.

I was out of breath. I blurted out, "Hey, man, I've got an emergency."

He turned to look at me.

"You know Sally, right? The girl who cleans the toilets."

"Yeah. What's wrong?"

"She's collapsed on the trail around the corner. She says it isn't the Crud, it's something worse. Her insides are burning up. She thinks she needs to get to a hospital fast."

"I'll radio to base. They'll call the rangers and tell them there's an emergency down here. We do that all the time. The rangers almost always say the person needs to stay put, relax, get comfortable, and wait for them."

"We can't wait. Listen, my name is Sam Hunter. Sally is a good friend of mine. I know it's serious. We've got to carry her out of here and get her to a hospital. Now."

I was rushing my words. I needed to slow down so I could communicate. Look rational, but serious. I was not convincing this guy. He kept trying to keep track of the boat that was arriving as he talked to me.

"Glad to meet you, Sam, I'm Steven Haswell." He looked around at the incoming boat.

"That Haswell?" I asked.

He nodded. "I have training in this stuff, Sam. The best thing is to get her stable and not move her."

A scraping noise diverted our attention. Sally staggered toward us on the trail, one step at a time, her arms wrapped around her stomach. Then, without a sound, she slowly crumpled to the ground. We could see Dave running toward her. Steven reached into the shed and pulled out a litter and pushed it against my chest.

"Take this and get her started this way. I've got to call in to base and I'll see if there is anyone on the boat coming in that can help. I'll bring the first aid kit. That's all going to take about ten minutes." He looked over at Dave kneeling beside Sally. "It's going to be hell getting her out of here, you know. I hope we're doing the right thing."

I quickly put my hand on his shoulder and said, "Thanks, man," and turned and ran down the trail.

I slid into a space next to Dave and Sally. He had his hand on her forehead.

"Dave, you need to help me get her over to the ticket shed with this." I spread out the litter.

"Sam, do you think this is the right thing? Moving her, I mean."

Before I could answer Sally put her hand on Dave's arm. She whispered, "I've got to get to a hospital, Dave. This feels really bad. I'm sorry." She crawled onto the litter. I took the front handles and we started walking. I could feel Dave struggling behind me. I hoped he could make it. I had average strength and this short trip was taking every bit of energy I had.

Ahead I could see the boat tying up at the dock. There were about ten people on board, most of them older. Steven stood by, ready to help everyone off. Steven Haswell. I couldn't believe it. He was tall, like his dad, and had long, curly blond hair. This must have been a hell of a summer for him.

"Dave, you all right?"

"Yes. I can make it."

"How's Sally look?"

"She looks great, just like always." I bet Sally was smiling.

We set Sally down next to the ticket shed. I took off my sweatshirt, wadded it up and pushed it under her head. With just a t-shirt I was instantly cold. The wind was brisk. I was sure I wouldn't notice it as we went up the trail. Dave leaned against the shed, breathing hard. Sweat poured down his face.

Steven jogged over. Four people followed behind him—two men, a woman, and a female ranger naturalist. He pulled a first aid kit out of the shed then knelt down next to Sally.

"Hey, Sally. What's going on?"

She tried to smile.

"Unfortunately, there wasn't any medical experience on the boat that just came in. But we did get some helpers. You're pretty darn pale, kid. I'm sure you're dehydrated, too. You have to keep drinking water. Here's a bottle. Keep it with you. I'm thinking the only thing in this kit that might help at all is aspirin. You want to try it?"

She nodded. Steven took off the cap and handed her two aspirin and then the bottle of water. He turned to us. He looked over his shoulder and waved over the four helpers.

"Sam, meet Teddy, William, Meghan, and Mary. They're going to help us get Sally out of here. And he's...."

Steven was pointing to Dave. "Dave," I said. "Sorry."

"This is going to be really tough. Just walking yourself up this trail is hard. I just don't know how well we're going to do. I'm up and down this trail every day, so hopefully that will help. The good news is the rangers will definitely be on the trail before we get to the top. It's only a fifteen-minute drive from Rim Village and they're already on their way. So we won't have to carry her all the way by ourselves.

"One person per handle. We can stop as much as we need. Let's put Teddy and Sam up front. I'll be on the back with William. Dave and Meghan, you're in reserve. Mary, would you go up the trail ahead of us and see if you can find anyone who can help us carry her? The more people, the better. Keep going until you hit the switchbacks near the top. If you haven't found anybody by then, come back and help. All right?"

She nodded. Then we all reached down and picked up a litter handle and started up the first slope.

Teddy was BIG, maybe six-foot-two and wide, most likely in his forties. His flat top gave him the ex-military look. He had gigantic calves that rippled when he walked. He was carrying a lot of weight, but he looked tough. I also sensed that he would rather be giving orders than receiving them.

William and Meghan, the couple, looked like professional hikers. William had a brown ponytail and fancy hiking boots. Like William, Meghan was slim and tan, but had the streamlined look of an athlete. She had straight, blond hair.

Mary was one of Sally's roommates at the Stone House. She was tiny. She wore a brown ranger hat wider than she was. I'm guessing she was five-foot nothing. But she climbed the trail regularly, so she was a good candidate to go up ahead. She held Sally's hand for a second before she took off.

My lungs burned before we even made the first switchback. We'd carried Sally maybe a hundred yards. Next to me, Big Teddy had no problems. I was probably holding him back. We could only go as fast as the weakest member of the team. But there was no way I was going to be the person to ask for a breather. With the four of us carrying the litter, I'd say we were moving at about three-quarters of a casual walking pace.

One foot at a time, Sam. One foot at a time. Blood pounded in my head. My calves gave me a heads-up that they'd be throbbing real soon. I was drenched in sweat. The only good thing was we were still low enough to get some breeze from the lake. I could see Mary had already gotten to the switch-back and was heading the other way above us.

"Sam, let Meghan take your spot for awhile."

Damn, I said to myself. Out loud I said "Let me get to the first switchback."

Nothing.

Steven said it again. "Sam, let Meghan take your spot. C'mon. We'll take a rest at the end of the next short switch-back. You'll be needed then."

I turned my head to look over my right shoulder. Meghan was walking right next to me. She smiled, then grabbed the handle effortlessly and I moved aside. I'm sure I had anguish on my face as I looked back at Dave who was trailing the pack.

When he caught up with me, Dave said, "At least a girl wasn't picked ahead of you." He chuckled and patted me on the back. "Let's go, big guy."

The litter bearers powered right through the first switch-back and the forty yards or so to the next one.

"Okay, let's stop for two minutes. Sam, you take over for Teddy. Meghan, you okay?"

"I'm fine," she said.

Steven looked over at William. William nodded. Teddy, Dave and Meghan sat down on a trailside bench. I knelt next to Sally and asked her how she was doing. All she could do was grimace and pat my arm. William and Steven stretched out on the cool dirt. Teddy looked beat. Every inch of his shirt and shorts were wet. He had his hands on the back of his head trying to let more air in. But he was the first one to say, "Let's go."

Just then Mary hollered down from way above us. "I've got two coming down to you. They're about a third of the way down the long stretch."

"Thanks, Mary," Steven yelled back.

Mary said that was probably all we'd get, but she expected to see the rangers any minute. She didn't have to yell the second time because she was straight above us and her voice carried easily.

We set out again. Two people walked down the trail toward us, but they weren't the help because they looked to be about sixty years old. They stepped off to the side to let us pass. Walking two abreast on this trail was problematic in some of the narrower spots. It could be tricky on the corners, but we passed them in a wide place so we had plenty of clearance.

Steven Haswell and William were awesome. When I walked behind them, I could see them adjust to whatever speed the front people were going. They kept their eyes on the front people. They were sweating and obviously laboring, but they stayed focused. They didn't make a sound as they moved up the trail. This next stretch was a little shorter than the first, so I expected to make it to at least the next switchback. Teddy took over for Meghan.

Through the trees, we could see two men coming down the path. We were getting close to the switchback. My calves were screaming at me now. I couldn't breathe, but I wasn't stopping. *One step, one step.* I think I wasn't being replaced yet because Steven and William were slowing down. *One step, one step.* Finally, we made the switchback, just as a man about forty and his teenage son got there. Thankfully, both were husky and looked in great shape. They announced that they were ready to help.

Mary yelled that she could hear the rangers at the top the trail. We put the litter down. Steven knelt down next to Sally. He told her to finish the water. The rangers would have more. She nodded and then grimaced. Then Teddy took charge.

"You two have to fall out. You'll kill yourselves." Steven and William nodded. They lay back flat on the trail. "I'll take the back, with you." He pointed to the father. "What's your name? Tony? Great. What's your son's name? Randy? Great. You take the front with Meghan. Sam, you relieve the first one that needs it."

"The rangers should meet you at the top end of this stretch," Haswell said. "It's a long stretch, though. Sam, I think you have all the help you need now. I should really get back to the boats. I'm responsible for those expensive toys."

"No problem. I'll be able to back them up," William said.

Teddy said, "Let's go."

I walked over to Steven. I grabbed his hand and pulled him up.

"Thanks, man," I said. "You were great. Obviously we couldn't have done this without you. I appreciate it."

"I'm sure everything will work out fine." He said, "Tell Sally I'll be thinking about her."

I shook his hand. "Thanks again." He grinned. "Anytime." He pulled off his shirt and hustled down the trail.

The rest of the trip went as smoothly as possible. Ranger Bob, another Ranger—Larry Smith—and Andrew the carpenter met us halfway up the long slope. Those three teamed with William to hurry Sally right up the trail. I said thanks to everyone who was no longer needed. I shook everyone's hand.

Then I rushed as best I could up the steep slope after the fast-moving litter carriers. I didn't want to let Sally out of my sight.

CHAPTER 15

"WHAT HAPPENED DOWN THERE, SAM?" asked Andrew. We had reached the trailhead and he stood next to me, looking down at Sally. The two rangers leaned over her. Ranger Bob was taking her pulse. Larry Smith was feeling around her stomach. Before that he made her drink more water.

"She started throwing up and cramping really bad," I said. "She said her insides were on fire and she needed to get to a hospital because it felt really serious. How did you get here?"

"The rangers called the maintenance office and I figured I might be able to help."

Dave made it up the trail. Teddy, William and Meghan were all standing around, waiting to see if they were needed. I had told them they weren't, but they stuck around anyway.

It felt like the rangers were checking Sally in slow motion. "We need to get going, Bob. We've got to get her to the hospital." Luckily, it was on this side of Klamath Falls.

"We're just looking for something obvious, Sam," he said patiently. "But I don't see anything. It's not an appendix. We'll get her in the car and take her to get some help."

I took a second to get control of my emotions. I wanted to start yelling, but I knew that wouldn't help.

"Bob, I'm going with you."

Bob frowned, but Dave intervened. "You should take Sam. He was with her at the bottom and he's talked with her. He has the information. And she'll feel better having a friend along, don't you think?"

I nodded while I watched Dave explain to Bob.

"Okay, let's get her in the car," Ranger Bob said. "She can lie in the backseat. It's pretty roomy back there. The three of us will sit in the front. Let's carry her over on the litter."

The rangers had parked their green park service station wagon right on the trailhead because of the emergency. William and Teddy stepped in to help Bill and Larry carry her over. Ranger Bob and I moved things around in the backseat to make it more comfortable. It was tricky, but Sally was able to crawl into the backseat.

"Bob, I'm going to sit in the back with her. I think there's room. Let's go, okay?"

The rangers got in the car. They turned on the flashing lights. We did a U-turn and headed back toward Rim Village.

Ranger Bob made good time. He was obviously experienced on the narrow, winding rim road. Sally started shaking a little, so I pulled a blanket from the back and put it over her. She lay with her head on a pillow on the other side of the seat from me, her feet up on my lap.

"Sam, there's a new park service policy that any park service employee that gets hurt or is sick enough that they may need to be hospitalized has to first be checked out by the nurse. So we're going to have to make a stop at headquarters before we get the okay to go to the hospital."

Bob looked in the rearview mirror at me.

"Even in a life or death situation, Bob?"

"I don't think we can say this is life or death."

Sally was looking at me. *Don't get mad, Sam.*

"I think I have some good points if anyone challenges us."

"Let's hear 'em."

"Sally is a political appointee. She's a family friend of the senior senator from the State of Pennsylvania, Robert Mills. He personally got her this job. She's asked that she get taken to a hospital immediately because she thinks her condition is serious. If you don't take her to the hospital, she'll get out of the car and have a maintenance worker drive her to the hospital in his beat-up Volkswagen."

Larry looked back at us. "Is that what you want, Sally?"

"Yes," she whispered.

Larry nodded at me. "Okay, I'll give it a try, Sam."

He picked up the radio mike. "Dispatch, this is Ranger Patrol 4. Be advised that we're taking the sick female maintenance worker straight to the hospital in Klamath Falls. Out."

"Patrol 4. Stop by the nurse's office at the Community Center in Steel Circle to get medical permission. Out."

"Headquarters, be advised, the female maintenance worker has requested she be taken to the hospital immediately. We checked her out at the trailhead. I don't believe there's anything the nurse can do to help her. Everyone involved in the rescue believes she's seriously ill and should get to the hospital right away. I also suggest you check out her political appointee status. Out."

"Patrol 4. I'll be back to you in five. I have to check on this with the chief ranger. Out."

"10-4."

Ranger Bob said, "We'll see if that works. Never tried anything like that." He turned right to go down the mountain toward headquarters instead of straight, which would have taken us to Rim Village. About three-quarters of the way to headquarters the dispatcher radioed saying we could proceed to the Klamath Falls hospital.

"When we reach headquarters, stop and let me out at the parking lot," said Larry. "I think I should go in and contact the hospital and round up a paramedic or an ambulance. Maybe they can meet you at the 62—97 junction. I'd feel better if someone saw her sooner rather than later."

Larry was looking at Sally when he said that. Her eyes were squeezed shut. Her jaw was tense and she was obviously in pain.

"Great idea, Larry. You'll be able to keep in touch by radio, right?"

"Yes. I should be able to work with their dispatcher to get you both to the same spot at the same time."

We turned into the headquarters parking lot and dropped Larry at the front of the building. We pulled back out on the main road toward Annie Springs. Ranger Bob asked me if I wanted to move to the front seat. I told him no. I could keep better watch on Sally from where I was. She wasn't saying anything. We'd exchange looks, but there wasn't much to talk about now. She clutched the water bottle tight.

We passed through the Annie Springs entrance, turned left and headed down what I called "Deer Alley" toward the east boundary of the park, and then Fort Klamath. Larry radioed to tell us the hospital had dispatched paramedics and they thought Modoc Point would be a good meeting place. Modoc Point, where Highway 97 first touched Klamath Lake, was about twenty-five miles from the hospital, and about twenty miles away from us.

Bob had his flashing lights on, but not the siren. Midday there wasn't any traffic going our way. All the tourists were headed the opposite direction—toward the park. But once we hit 97, there could be all kinds of truck traffic. Hopefully we wouldn't get stuck behind anyone.

Before now there hadn't been a single second to think about the bombshell—Sally being pregnant. Chris was the most likely father, but clearly she hadn't told him. Which seemed odd, as they were both reasonable people. Even if she didn't want the baby, I think they would definitely talk it out. But if it wasn't Chris, the only thing left was the nightmare scenario—the Frank conspiracy. I just couldn't picture how that could have happened.

The radio crackled. Larry reported that the paramedics would be arriving at Modoc Point in five minutes. They would be parked on our side of the road at a turnout. We were just turning onto Highway 97, so we were just minutes away, too.

A few minutes later, the paramedics saw our flashing lights and switched their flashing lights on. We were almost there.

"Bob, please make sure they know I'm going with them to the hospital."

"Sam, I'm pretty sure that you'd throw yourself in front of the truck before you'd let them go without you. Take it easy when we get there. I'll talk to them. Okay?"

"Okay."

Bob slowed down and turned his blinker on. Then we were bumping around on the gravel. Sally winced and twisted in the seat. The two paramedics stood out in front of their truck. The rear door hung open. It got a little dusty as we came to a stop. Bob got out.

"Sally, how are you doing?" I asked. She was bleached white and her breathing had gotten ragged. "My back really hurts." She gave off a tiny moan.

"Hang on, Sally, the paramedics are here."

The door opposite me opened and the paramedics leaned in. One of them motioned at me to get out. *All right, I hope I can.* I was stiff and sore. I eased out, trying not to bump Sally as I laid her feet back on the seat. Then my right leg started to cramp up. *Stretch it, Sam.* The paramedics were taking Sally's vitals as best they could, given her position in the backseat.

I hopped around the front of the ranger car to where Bob was watching Sally. One of the paramedics leaned close to Sally and put his ear by her mouth. I guessed he was about to hear the bad news.

"How you holding up, Sam?" asked Bob. "Must have been a hell of a climb up that trail."

"I'm a lot better off than Sally. But I'm cramping up."

"Bob, can you help us get Sally out of the car?" asked one of the paramedics. The other jogged to their truck and pulled out some sort of litter bed.

"Hey, you guys just let me carry her over there," said Bob, his voice rising. The two of them helped her maneuver to the end of the seat. Then Bob reached down with his big forearms and gently picked her up and carried her to the back of the paramedic's truck. She disappeared. I opened the passenger door and got into the truck before anyone could tell me I couldn't go.

I looked back and could see they were securing her into a bed. One of them was setting up an IV.

Bob knocked on the window. I rolled it down.

"Later this afternoon call headquarters and give us a report," he said. "Here's a card with the number on it. And you try to get some rest too, Sam. You did good today."

I was about to thank him when one of the paramedics got in the driver's seat and asked if I was ready. I nodded. I looked back at Bob and gave a little wave. He mouthed the words, "Good luck." The paramedic started the engine, then turned on the siren and flashing lights. I looked back and saw that Sally now had the IV in her right arm. The paramedic was leaning down, listening to her. Asking a question. Then listening again.

I turned back toward the front and closed my eyes. For the first time in what seemed like hours, I felt like I could relax. I stretched my right leg out as far as I could, hoping it would slow down the cramp.

I felt the driver looking at me, probably wondering why I looked so beat up. Or maybe it was the smell of my boots. I kept my eyes closed. Vegging out seemed appropriate. I fell into daydreams of water skiing at Klamath Lake out the window to my right. I didn't like skiing on a single ski, but my friends in the boat would laugh all the way to Rocky Point on the far side of lake if I put on two skis or training wheels, as they called them. All I could do on a single ski was get up out of the water and hold on. Couldn't jump any wakes or do any big looping turns. I could do that on two skis. It was fun. But it wasn't worth the non-stop teasing.

Tap, tap, tap. Huh? Oh. A paramedic was tapping on the window. We were at the hospital and I could see the wheeled gurney Sally was strapped to disappearing through the doors. I opened the truck door, almost hitting the paramedic.

"It's all right, buddy, she'll be taken care of," he said. "How are you doing? Do we need to check you out?"

"No, nothing wrong with me but my stinking clothes." I grabbed his hand, shook it. I thanked him, then double-timed it into the hospital.

I saw Sally being taken behind a curtain. I headed in that direction. A nurse in a bright white uniform cut me off. "We'll take care of her now, son. We know the story." The nurse patted me on the shoulder. "You wait over there. I'll come find you later."

She pointed toward a line of chairs by the window. I gave up without a fight, turned around, went over and sat down. I leaned back. *Concentrate, Sam. What's next on the agenda? That's easy. Clothes.* I went to the pay phone, called my mother at her office and told her I needed someone to bring me a new set of work clothes because I was at the hospital and couldn't leave. I was the only person here with this girl who was hurt. And I also mentioned that it was sort of an emergency because I had sewer sludge on my boots and pants. That got her worked up. She said she didn't know who, but someone would bring me clothes right away. "A little food would be great, too, Mom."

A frustrated administrative lady with a lot of questions sat down next to me. She needed forms filled out so Sally could be admitted. She and I both knew Sally was being admitted, no matter what, but she just couldn't help herself. I kept telling her that she could get all the info she needed if she would just call the Park Service Regional Headquarters. It was only about a mile away. I'm sure they're in the book, I kept saying. This went on for about twenty minutes before she saw she was getting nowhere with me.

It wasn't long before my father came walking through the double doors, about forty-five minutes after I called Mom. He had on a brown suit and striped tie—military investigators don't wear uniforms. He had the wingtips on and the tinted glasses. He was all business, except for the ball of clothes he held under one arm. I hoped he brought shoes. Yes, he did. I could see part of a tennis shoe sticking out from the bundle. I got up and walked toward my dad.

"What's this all about?" he asked with a quizzical look on his face.

"It's such a long story, can I go change first?"

He stared down at my boots and agreed that was probably the best course of action. He said he had some McDonald's hamburgers and fries back in the car. He'd wait for me at a bench outside.

I washed my face. I took a long, deep breath. The hospital restroom was cool and quiet. I put my hands on the front of the sink and stretched out my back. I'd heaped the disgusting clothes in a pile across the room. My first thought was just to leave them there, but that wasn't right, so I squashed them into a tight bundle. With the clothes under one arm and the boots dangling from one hand, I pushed through the door and headed for the ER entrance.

My father saw me and pointed to the trash bin across the driveway. I took the detour and deposited all of it down the chute. I looked up at the sun. It was hot—ninety-five, at least. Get me back to that mountain air. My father handed me a Big Mac as I sat down next to him. We were sitting on a wooden bench in the shade outside the hospital. My dad said it was about two-thirty.

I wolfed the Big Mac. The large Coke sitting next to me was next. I downed half of it in a few big gulps. I guess I forgot to get thirsty. Big sigh. Now I wanted a nap.

"So what's the story here?" Dad asked.

I took another long swallow of Coke, then proceeded to tell him what happened, starting with Sally collapsing at Cleetwood Cove. I didn't give many details. Just the bare facts. He didn't interrupt, which kind of surprised me. He just listened. When I was done, I looked in the McDonald's bag to see what else was in there.

"You've had quite a day," he said.

I nodded as I pulled another hamburger out of the bag. I couldn't handle another Big Mac, but this small burger would be no problem. Eight or nine bites and it was gone.

"Don't you have to go back to work?" I asked as I swallowed the last little bit of the burger.

"No. I'm flexible today," he said.

I know he wanted to ask me a bunch of questions. My mother tried to counsel him against interrogating me. That was our major impasse. If either one of us pushed the other things got worse. Neither of us said anything as I chomped through a bag of fries.

I took another swig of Coke.

"I wanted to ask you about those life lessons you were explaining to me the other day."

He didn't say anything. This was a new strategy.

"If it's certain doom to go outside the chain of command about something that's really wrong, how do you get rid of an abusive, stupid, idiotic kind of boss?"

He didn't say anything for about thirty seconds. He looked straight ahead.

"Those kind of people usually hang themselves," he said in a low, steady voice. "The problem is that sometimes it takes a while. So you have to be patient and remember what you have that you wouldn't want to lose."

"What if you don't have anything to lose?"

He sighed. He turned and grabbed the McDonald's bag. Digging around, he came up with a couple french fries.

"You're going to learn someday that everyone has something to lose. Young people don't recognize that they have things that are very important. And, more importantly, that you can lose them. Your life. Your health. Your job. Your chances for a job. A year of your life. It goes on and on. Even you, my friend, have a lot to lose. It just won't occur to you until it's too late. That's why parents are always worrying about their children."

I was sweating even though we were sitting in the shade. The heat seemed like it was percolating off the asphalt. Not much action at the ER. Since we'd been sitting here, there had only been two new customers. Both were mothers with sons. One might have been a broken arm; the other looked like stitches.

"So what's the plan—are you coming home or do you need a ride back to the park?" he asked.

"I have to go back to the park. But I don't think I'll need a ride. I'm guessing her boyfriend will be down after work, which gets him here probably sometime shortly after six. I doubt they'll let him stay long, so I can go back to the lake with him. I'm doing a pump house nightshift tomorrow night and I'll be sleeping it off Sunday, so I won't be home till next weekend."

"It's a long time between now and after six," he said. "You could go home, relax, have dinner, and I could bring you back at six, if you wanted."

"I don't think so. I think I should stay. But thanks."

Silence. He was looking straight ahead again.

"Is this girl something special to you?" he asked.

Easy question. But how to answer was tough. I liked Sally. Deep down, I probably wished she had walked to the stream with me way back at the Stone House party.

"She's a nice girl. And she's a good friend. Her family's in Pennsylvania and I don't want to leave her here alone. I guess I wouldn't feel right about leaving anybody alone at a hospital."

He patted my knee, then stood up. He told me to call if anything changed and that it was likely that mom would want to bring me a care package for dinner, so don't go wandering off.

"Thanks, Dad. I'll call home a little after five to give you an update."

I watched him as he walked across the driveway to the parking lot. The bald spot on the top of his head lit up in the sun. He was right. I needed to think things through more. I'd been getting that message from different people all summer.

Around 4:00, a nurse came to talk to me. She was a different nurse from the one that had patted my shoulder before. She was a lot less starchy. Maybe that was because it was the end of her shift. Anyway, she told me that the bacteria from the crud had caused Sally to miscarry. Sally was going to be okay. No lasting physical problems. She just needed a few days in the hospital. She had been admitted and moved to a private room. She said Sally was asleep, but I could go into her room now, and wait there if I wanted.

At the doorway, she stopped me. They all must have been assuming Sally and I were a couple, because she said,

"I'm sorry about your baby." I couldn't think of a thing to say back to her except thank you.

Even with the lights low, I still could see how white Sally was. She blended in with her sheets and pile of pillows. An IV tube ran out of her right arm and snaked up to a big bag of clear, dripping liquid suspended from its metal stand.

I sat down in the chair at the foot of the bed and watched her as she slept. I thought about everything that had happened, and then about what my father had said. He'd figured Sally must be a girlfriend. Why else would I have gone to all that trouble and then insisted on staying here? There had been plenty of better-qualified people around all day to handle the situation. It made me wonder what everyone back in the park was thinking. They probably thought they had it all figured out, too. But it wasn't so obvious to me. I couldn't say exactly why I had done what I had done. All I was sure of was that she had needed me. She'd asked for my help. Wasn't that enough?

It wasn't quite five when Sally started waking up. She smiled weakly when she saw me. I smiled right back.

I dragged my chair up from the foot of the bed and sat down beside Sally. She just kept looking at me, but I could tell it was an effort to keep the smile in place. She reached out with her free hand and rested it lightly on my arm. "You don't have to stay, Samuel. I'm fine now. They say in a couple days I'll be as good as new. No more hugging trash cans or running to the bathroom. Go back to the park. Or go home. You look tired."

"I'm fine, Sally. My dad brought me some clean clothes and I'm a new man. I think I'll just wait around awhile."

"Okay." We were both quiet.

But I couldn't just ignore what I knew. It was too big a thing to just ignore.

"Sally, they told me about the baby."

She flinched. She moved her hand back to the bed.

"You know, I didn't even know for sure I was pregnant until they told me here a few hours ago. I mean, I'd been worried for a while that I was. But I kept telling myself that it was just being sick from the water like everybody else. But then at Cleetwood Cove, I just knew. The cramps were different. They were so low in my back. And I could feel myself bleeding. And I just knew. I was scared. That's when I told you."

"I'm glad you told me, Sally."

"Samuel, it wasn't Chris. He didn't know, or even suspect anything was wrong."

Then she looked straight back at me, not even trying to smile anymore. "Something happened, and I wanted to tell you. I wanted to tell you that time when you found me at *The Lady of the Woods*. But I was afraid of what you'd think."

"We're friends, Sally. You can tell me now."

She kept staring at me, but she didn't say anything. I was pretty sure I knew what she had to say anyway. "Was it Frank? Did he do something?"

She stared at me, tears rising in her eyes.

"What happened, Sally?"

She fixed her eyes on the ceiling and took a deep breath. "Remember that cookout at the beginning of the summer? It was really beautiful that night and, after we ate, Chris and I took a walk along the creek. I pulled my shoes off and waded in and I couldn't believe how cold it was. Everybody stayed pretty late. Except for you, of course. And Frank stayed on, even after Chris finally left. He said he wanted to help us clean up. But what he mainly did was keep drinking beer. He joked and flirted while Marcy and I washed the dishes. She didn't seem to think he was too funny and at some point she disappeared and Frank said to me, 'Could you please help me take my stuff back to the house?'

"I should have made some excuse and said no. But I didn't know how I could. He needed some help and he was drunk and I was the only one there. Plus, I thought it would get him out of the house faster. Maybe I was a little flattered he was talking to me instead of Marcy. I don't know. So I went. We pulled into Steel Circle and stopped in front of his place. He got out and grabbed one of the boxes of beer and sodas from the back of his truck. I picked up the barbecue tongs, lighter fluid and his guitar and followed him.

"But inside, everything was all wrong and I knew I had made a huge mistake. He just started kissing me, really hard. He pushed me down on the sofa and I couldn't move.

"Samuel, I said no. I really did. And I tried to push him away. But he wouldn't listen. He wouldn't stop. He said, 'What did you think we were going to do?'

"And I guess he was right. I should have known. I should have yelled. Maybe someone in that circle would have heard me. But I think I was afraid of being heard. I didn't want to face anyone finding us like that. And so, finally, I just turned my face away from him and let him do what he was doing until he was finished. I tried to think about how good and cold the creek water had felt earlier. I just tried not to feel anything that was happening on that sofa.

"Then he rolled off me and headed into the bathroom. While he was peeing he said I could come into his room, or stay out there. He said either way was fine with him. All of a sudden he didn't seem that drunk.

"I lay there a long time. Until Frank was quiet. Then I put on my clothes and left. But I didn't get far. The road was so dark. And I was shaking. And I kept tripping and falling. I was so cold I went back into Frank's house and I sat on a chair by the window waiting for light.

"At dawn, when I headed up the hill, I remember thinking how quiet and peaceful everything was. And I felt like I didn't belong there. And before I went into the house, I stopped at the creek and put my feet in that cold, clean water just like I had done the night before.

"I'm so dumb. It was two days before it even occurred to me that I might have gotten pregnant. You can't tell anybody. Please."

Sally stopped talking. She wouldn't look at me. I was stunned. I couldn't put enough thoughts together to figure out how to react.

"I'm so sorry, Sally."

"Do you hate me, Samuel?"

"No, I don't hate you."

Sally sank deeper into her pillows. She started crying. I got up from my chair and sat next to her on the edge of the bed. I leaned down, kissed her forehead and then her hair. I whispered, "It wasn't your fault." I whispered it over and over.

She finally stopped crying, but she still was trembling. "Samuel," she said, "I didn't want this baby. Part of me is glad it is gone. So why do I feel so empty?"

I had no answer for her.

"Sally, if you don't want anybody to know, you need to tell the nurse you want to keep this private. Okay?"

She nodded.

"I've got to go call my parents. On my way out I'll tell the nurse you need to talk with her right away." She nodded again.

Before I made any phone calls I had to sit down. The blood pounded in my head like it did when we were carrying Sally up the trail. I couldn't breathe. I had to call home and I had to call park headquarters, but, before I did that, I had to calm down. That took a full fifteen minutes. I made the calls. When I went back to see Sally, the nurse stopped me and said she needed her rest. I told her that at least one other person was en route and would probably arrive after six some time. She said that was fine and I could have another thirty minutes then.

My parents dropped off a couple roast beef sandwiches and a Dr. Pepper at about 5:45. Chris arrived at 6:15. I took him down to her room and then went back to the waiting room. About twenty minutes later, he came back and told me he was being kicked out by the nurses, but Sally wanted to thank me for everything. He'd wait at the front of the hospital.

"Have a good visit?" I asked Sally.

"It went fine. Chris is very sweet. He's going to be back tomorrow, how about you?"

I told her about the pump house late shift I was taking. I had tomorrow night for the R & T guy and I had my own shift Monday. So I told her I might have to wait to see her until she came back to the lake.

"I may not be going back," she said. "I think I should go home."

"I know," I said.

She held out her arms so I would come closer. She pulled me down and we hugged each other tight. As I walked out the door I could hear her crying.

Of course, Chris wanted all the details about what happened to Sally down at Cleetwood. As we drove toward the park, I gave him the blow-by-blow account, trying to downplay my role in events. I didn't want things getting all blown out of proportion. Then I told him I was tired and that I was going to try and take a nap. I pretended I fell asleep. There was no way I could sleep. I kept thinking about Frank Noble.

CHAPTER 16

A S LONG AS I HAD A GOOD BOOK, I didn't mind pump house duty. It wasn't working this time. My body ached and I had to change positions every ten minutes. I started on the folding chair. I lay down on the blanket. I sat on the floor leaning up against some machinery. I paced. I put on my parka, found a rock to sit on and watched Munson Creek splash down the hill.

I couldn't get Frank out of my mind. I had visions of beating him to a bloody pulp. I saw myself slipping a note under the superintendent's door and hearing about him getting fired the next day. I imagined an unfortunate accident with a baseball bat. Maybe the other park service permanents would rise up against him and toss him out of the park once and for all.

I came up with more than forty plans to bring retribution down on Frank's head. Unfortunately, all forty crossed two lines that couldn't be crossed. I wasn't willing to go to jail. That would make me just another one of Frank's victims. And I would not tell anyone what had happened to Sally.

I weighed what I stood to lose if I went after Frank. My dad had pointed out in great detail that everyone risks something in a fight. Even me. Frank could get me fired. Which meant no chance of being hired back next summer. That would hurt. This job paid well and I needed every penny. Getting fired would be a big financial blow, but I figured I could recover.

Was there anything else Frank could do to me? If he felt threatened, he might get physical. He could hurt me himself or arrange for some accident. If I survived an attack, I couldn't complain without bringing Sally into it. The real question was, WOULD he really hurt me? If he felt backed into a corner with no options, the answer was a definite yes. If I talked, Frank stood to lose his job, his career. He might even go to jail. I figured I could count on Frank being ruthless if things hit the fan.

One more thing: Frank was a pro at infighting. The Crater Lake bureaucracy would be behind him until the bitter end. I had nothing. I was an outsider. I was a babe in the woods. I didn't know what I didn't know.

I felt nauseous.

* * *

Chris dropped by Sunday evening with an update from the hospital.

I hadn't seen him since he drove me back to the park Friday night. I'd slept most of Saturday and assumed he'd gone back to Klamath Falls to see Sally. Chris and the rangers had apparently done a good job of getting the story out, because the few people I ran into seemed up on what had happened. I was glad. I'd been dreading talking about it.

I was sitting on the cabin porch with my legs up on another chair. Every bone in my body still ached from the march up the trail.

"Sally says hi," Chris said.

"How's she doing?" I pulled my feet off the chair and offered it to Chris. He waved it off. He wasn't staying long.

"She looks a lot better today. She was out of bed walking while I was there. They did some testing yesterday and everything checked out fine. Now she just needs rest. Her mom flew in today. I think that's helped a lot."

"Did they say what the problem was?" I asked.

Just then Dave came around the corner and walked up the steps. "Hey, men."

"You're just in time. Chris was giving me the latest on Sally."

Chris took a minute to get Dave caught up. I felt guilty because I hadn't talked with Dave since we'd brought Sally up the trail. Once I even started the walk down to his trailer, but I'd turned around halfway because I was afraid once I started talking I would tell him everything. I couldn't do that. I had no solutions anyway. He'd have told me there was nothing I could do and I wouldn't have liked hearing that. So I just didn't go. I felt bad about it.

"No, I don't know exactly what the problem was, Dave," Chris said. "All they would tell me was that her body had a hard time fighting the bacteria from the Crud. When I asked for more specifics, they said to ask Sally. And Sally says she's just tired of talking about it. The nurses did say getting her to the hospital fast was a good thing. She was in really bad shape when she got there and was getting worse. I guess the important thing is she's getting better. In fact, she's leaving tomorrow."

"Leaving the hospital?" Dave asked.

"Yes—well, no, going home, all the way home," Chris said. "The doctor is going to give her a final check up tomorrow morning, first thing, but they expect her to be able to leave right after that. I'm taking the day off. I'm going to pick up Sally and her mother and bring them here for her stuff, and then take them to Medford to catch an early evening flight. Sally seems real ready to get home."

"I bet she is," Dave said.

"We talked about that Friday," I said. "She all but said she was leaving as soon as she got out of the hospital, so we said our goodbyes then, just in case. I think she's had enough of being sick and this put her way over the edge."

I felt bad for Chris. He looked beat, but I could tell he was also disappointed about how this was turning out. I knew he really liked Sally and now their summer was being cut short. Pennsylvania was a long way away. This might be the end of it.

"Chris, you've done a great job sticking by her," I said.

"Yeah," he said. "Thanks." He looked straight at me. "You were a tough act to follow, though." He stuck out his hand and we shook. "I guess I should get back to the cabin and get some rest. See ya, guys."

Chris turned and headed home. We could hear his steps in the gravel for thirty seconds or so.

Dave took the chair I had offered Chris. He seemed tense. "So, how you doing, Sam?" he asked.

"I am SO sore, Dave. Every bone, every muscle. Even my fat hurts. It was everything I could do to get in the car and drive up to the pump house last night for my shift."

"I expected you to track me down and give me a report."

"Sorry," I said. I quickly picked up the story from us driving away from the trail in the ranger car. I gave him complete details, except for the secret one. I told him how the rangers had helped and how serious the nurses looked after Sally arrived. I told him about throwing my boots, pants and shirt in the trash can. About my parents bringing food and the very last thing—saying goodbye to Sally.

Dave took it all in without saying anything. He just listened.

"You know, Sam, there are more important things to be good at than using a hammer or climbing a ladder," he said. "You did real good in a tough situation."

I was struck dumb for a moment. I quickly flipped through the card file in my brain looking for help on how to accept a real important compliment. Nope, I had no previous experience.

"But there's one thing you need to get better at," Dave said.

"What's that?" I asked.

"Lying. If you intend to tell a really big lie in the future, then you have to get a whole lot better at it," he said. "You know what was wrong with Sally, don't you? You knew down at the bottom of the trail."

Oh, God. Now what do I do? I let out a big breath. Where was my Dr. Pepper? I needed a drink. Leaning back on the chair reaching for the soda, I crashed in a heap, sticky Dr. Pepper flying all over me. My body lit up with pain.

"Okay, okay, you don't have to tell me now. I don't want you to get hurt," Dave said as he helped me up. He was laughing at me. "We're barbecuing Thursday. You're coming, right?"

"If I survive the next few days," I said. I wasn't joking.

* * *

Monday morning was miserable.

First, I had to watch Frank yukking it up with his boys as I walked in the maintenance office. He was describing some softball exploit. He leaned down, re-enacting a backhand stab at a ball. His sunglasses—attached to a chain around his neck—bobbed below his head as he reached way out. As usual, Frank was basking in being Frank Noble, Prince of Crater Lake. Bastard.

Then I had to explain the Sally story to the few people who didn't know the details. It was an ordeal. But I did get to practice my lying. I got a few congratulatory slaps on the back. There was also a, "I guess Sally was lucky you were around." I got the feeling that some people doubted my intentions and were wondering what exactly was going on with me and Sally. Fortunately, they didn't ask out loud.

The worst part was knowing that Sally would be in the park today and I wouldn't be able to see her. We had said our goodbyes and she'd probably already started trying to forget what happened to her. Seeing me again wouldn't help that. I just wished I could tell her again that it wasn't her fault.

Tall Paul and I spent most of the morning painting at the Community Center in Steel Circle. The two-story build-ing looked naked without the big milk truck and herd of port-o-potties out front. Beige was the color of the day. Putting paint on walls turned out to be something I could do. Rolling coat after coat took my mind off Sally and Frank for minutes at a time. Paul did the trim and places close to the trim. No need to press my luck.

When time for lunch came, we hopped in the truck and drove back to the cabin. I couldn't help looking around as we drove, in case I saw Sally driving by. When we got to the cabin I could see something on the front door. It was a light blue envelope with my name on it. I pulled the thumbtack out and hurried inside the door to my room.

Dear Samuel,

We said goodbye at the hospital, but I didn't thank you for what you did for me. You've been my friend all summer. And yesterday, you were my hero. I couldn't leave without telling you that.

Crater Lake is a beautiful place and I found so many good things here. And you were one of them.

I never returned *Sometimes A Great Notion* to you. I think I'd like to keep it. I wish we'd had a chance to talk about it.

Thank you for taking care of me, Samuel. Please take care of yourself.

Love, Sally

I read it nine or ten times before putting it away. I lay down on the bed. I had nothing left. I'd hit the wall, run out of gas, whatever you want to call it. There was going to be a big argument between my heart and brain over whether I was getting out of this bed for an afternoon of painting.

"Sam, it's time to go. What are you doing in there?"

"JUST A MINUTE."

Sam, you've got to get out of this bed and get to work. But I didn't want to go. *Sam, you've got to go.* Okay. *Now.* Okay.

* * *

The Lady of the Woods was sadder than usual, her head buried deeper in her arms. The wind in the trees made a crying sound.

My little hideaway didn't have the soothing effect I'd come for. The air was cool in the twilight and I could hear Munson Creek gurgling, but it didn't matter. Nothing helped.

Man, this had been a long day and it wasn't over yet. I still had the pump house in a few hours. I didn't know how I was going to get through that without my head blowing apart.

I sat down and leaned back against *The Lady.* I went through my options for the hundredth time.

I could just keep quiet. Keep working like I didn't know anything. But did I really think I could work here with Frank around and never say or do anything? Go another couple summers face-to-face with a smirking Frank?

No. I couldn't do that.

I could keep trying to find a way to go after Frank. Okay now, what did I have to lose going down that path? My paycheck—the money I needed to get through college without my dad's help. What else? I could get beat up. A few broken bones. I guess he could kill me. Or try a little mental abuse. Frank could try and drive me crazy. It'd be a short trip. Ha, ha. He could make it so uncomfortable for me that I would leave on my own.

Now that was a likely strategy.

But remember, Sam, he will only be able to push you so far, because if he takes all your options away, you'll have nothing to lose by turning him in. And no matter what he says, he'll want to avoid that. But you're in the same boat. You're going to do everything you can to avoid Sally's name being officially brought up. So you can't take all his options away, either.

I looked at *The Lady of the Woods.* "Thank you," I said out loud. I got up and started my walk back to the cabin. The night air felt a lot better all of a sudden.

* * *

Surprisingly, even at three in the morning, I had no problem staying awake as I guarded the chlorine gauge up at the pump house. I sank deep into strategic thinking. I'd gone from an absolutely hopeless feeling to thinking I had a chance to get Frank. It wasn't likely, but hope made it easier to run headlong into a brick wall.

I now felt comfortable with the possible negative outcomes. I was ready to weather all the storms except for the big one. Being killed. At this point, that didn't seem like a possibility. I felt sure of that. So what could I do that wouldn't cross the two big lines—Sally and jail?

My sudden euphoria disappeared when I came to the same conclusion I had reached before. There wasn't anything I could do, even if I was willing to give up something important.

C'mon, Sam, THINK.

At 4:45 a.m., I took a new direction. *What would Frank do in your situation, Sam?* I shuddered. Did I really want to get into Frank's head? *Well, your head's got no ideas, so what can it hurt?*

By 5:37 a.m., I had a plan. Well, not really a plan. But something. Definitely a Hail Mary. I wasn't likely to survive the counterattack, but I didn't care. That asshole needed to get rocked, even if it was just a jab.

I packed up my gear and loaded up the Volkswagen. Two Army guys arrived with rags, solvent, and oil. The generator was getting spruced up.

"Good morning, sir. Everything okay in the pump house?"

"Everything is just excellent in the pump house. Have a good day."

* * *

I didn't take a shower when I got back to the cabin because I didn't want to wake Paul up. I set my alarm clock for 7:15 a.m. and tried to get a quick nap. Nothing doing. I was likely to collapse from sleep deprivation soon, but for now I was wide awake.

I went over my plan. My confidence had ebbed a little since I left the pump house, but I still was willing to go through with it. I had to get out and walk.

Not much happening at park headquarters at 7:00 a.m. Here came a ranger. He raised the flag. He asked me what I was doing up so early. Just getting a morning walk in before work, I told him. I turned and walked back toward the maintenance yard.

As I crossed over Munson Creek and went around the corner, I could see Frank's park service stud truck parked all alone in front of the maintenance office. This was good and bad. Good because I needed Frank by himself. Bad because I wasn't mentally ready. I took several deep breaths. *Now or never, Sam.*

I took one last deep breath and started walking, my fists clenched. I opened the door to the maintenance office, walked the few steps to Frank and Dan's office. I could see him through the glass. He must have looked up when he heard my footsteps, but now he was staring down at the paperwork in front of him.

I opened the office door.

He still didn't look up. "What are you doing here, Hunter?"

I didn't say anything, I just closed the door behind me. Inside my head I was yelling, *BE CALM, Sam. Don't let him see you sweat. Keep your voice under control. Don't sound like a little girl.*

Louder he said, "What do you want, Hunter?"

When I finally spoke, my hard tone surprised me. "I came to tell you, Frank, that I know about Sally."

His head shot up. "WHAT?"

I looked straight at him. "I know what you did to Sally."

"I don't know what the hell you're talking about. Get out of here before I throw you out."

"I came to tell you, Frank, that I know about Sally, but I haven't decided what I'm going to do about it yet." I paused. "I'm still thinking." I turned around, opened the office door and walked out.

I wondered if he would follow me out. I opened the door of the maintenance office and walked out onto the blacktop. No Frank. I tried to stand as tall as I could, but walk casually back to the cabin. I'm sure he was looking out the window. No matter how confident he felt about his position in the Park Service, he had to be sweating at least a little. Even if this was all I got, it was much better than nothing. I hoped I was ready for the consequences.

CHAPTER 17

FRANK'S FIRST MOVE SURPRISED ME. I'd be lying if I said it didn't scare me.

After work Tuesday, Dan pulled me aside. He told me he remembered that, earlier in the season, I had lobbied to work Roads and Trails. Now's your chance, he said. I thought he was kind not to mention how useless I'd been in B & U.

"You proved yourself digging that trench at Rim Village," he said. Dan wasn't a naturally funny man, so I didn't suspect he was making fun of me. "Frank's got some more trench work he needs done and he wants you to help. That okay with you, Hunter?"

For obvious reasons, it wasn't, but all I could say was, "Sure, Dan."

Wednesday morning I waited in the maintenance office coffee room after everyone else had gone off to their jobs. I had the gray metal lunch box that my mom had given me, which had sat under my bed all summer. Today it held two peanut butter and jelly sandwiches, pecan cookies, and a thermos of cold orange juice. It was just me and my lunch pail, wondering what was going to happen next.

From down the hall I heard what I had been dreading, "Let's go, Hunter." Frank reached the maintenance office door as I got up and walked his way. "Go to the tool rack and grab a pick and shovel and put them in the back of my truck."

I followed him out the door without saying anything. I went next door, grabbed the tools and put them in the truck. Then I stood there like a bozo, holding my lunch pail and waiting for further instructions.

"Well, get in the truck, Hunter," Frank barked. He was in the driver seat, sunglasses already in place.

Not a word was said on the drive up to the rim. I knew from Dan that digging loomed in my future, but that's all I knew. Frank wasn't dropping any hints. I would have felt better if he had started yelling or something. He just stared straight ahead.

I wasn't going to be the one who said anything. I have a cousin Danny—about forty years old—who considers himself a wheeler-dealer. At family gatherings, you could bet that some of the men would go off to the garage or somewhere in the backyard to tell tall tales. When I was younger I tagged along. Sooner or later, Danny would give a play-by-play account of his latest business negotiation. It always ended with him being the big winner. Then, while everyone nodded, Danny shared his secrets for success: Don't be the first one to mention a number. Don't give up any important information until you know what the other guy is all about.

Get him to tell you what you need to know. First guy that mentions a number, loses.

You could make the argument that I'd already blown it by telling Frank that I knew something. Hard to say, since I didn't really have an endgame. Making Frank sweat was my only goal at the moment. And the best way to rattle him was to stay cool, calm, and collected. So I just sat there and waited for a Bolt from Heaven. Besides I was so nervous that, if I said anything, my voice might squeak.

We got to Rim Drive and Frank turned left. Still he said nothing. I had my window down and stared out like a tourist. It was so clear a morning that Wizard Island seemed just barely out of my reach as we passed Discovery Point, the first place I'd ever seen the lake. But there was no way I could enjoy the scenery today.

We slowed down as we approached the turnout just this side of Watchman—a mini-mountain peak with a fire lookout at the top. Visitors could get a great view of the lake here. The cleared area included a short rock wall that had been built back in the '30s, a sign that said don't go past this point, and a trail to Lightening Springs on the other side of the road.

Frank pulled off the road into the gravel parking area. As we slowed to a stop, I could see the beginnings of a trench next to the rock wall. The wall itself was crumbling in a couple different places and one end pulled down toward the lake.

Frank pulled the emergency brake, opened his door and got out.

"Grab your tools, Hunter."

I got the pick and shovel—and my lunch pail—and followed Frank to the rock wall. He stopped and examined the trench, then looked up and down the existing wall. I propped the tools up against some crumbling rocks.

Frank turned toward me and flipped a tape measure at me. I caught it and studied it for a second.

"You're going to need that tape measure for the trench. A new rock wall will be built here. To do that we need a trench dug, two-and-a-half-feet deep and eighteen inches wide. It needs to be three feet in from the rock wall all the way to the end of it up there." He pointed to the end of the rock wall about fifty yards toward the Watchman.

"The YCC started digging just before they left, but now the job is yours. You're going to be here every day digging this trench by yourself. I don't want any goofing off. If I drive by—and I will—and see you not digging, I'm going to write you up. If anybody else drives by and tells me you weren't working, I'm going to write you up. Don't take your shirt off while you're working. When you stop for lunch, go across the road over there out of sight. Don't be visiting with any tourists. Any questions?

"What do you want me to do with the rock and dirt that I dig out?"

"Just leave it between the trench and the rock wall. Anything else?"

I shook my head no.

"This is all you're going to be doing every day," said Frank. "If you can't hack it and you want to quit, just say the word. I'll be happy to fill out the paperwork. Got it?"

I just stared back at him.

Frank Noble tried to intimidate by acting tough and talking tough. He wasn't tall. He wasn't muscled up or anything. But his body language was menacing. He always looked like he was about to leap at you. I think he believed this worked for him, so, if you weren't one of his favorites, he combined his snarling attitude with verbal abuse to put you in your place. Nobody actually thought he was scary. His power came from the simple fact that he was the boss and could do what he wanted with you.

Frank took a little stroll down the rock wall. I got a quick peek over the edge of the rim and felt queasy. It was a long way down. I stepped down into the depression, soon to be a trench, in case Frank planned to push me over the side. I laughed at myself, but I still stepped down into the trench.

I took the tape measure and quickly measured what had already been dug. I heard Frank walk up behind me.

"So, Hunter, what was that crap about Sally the other day?" That wasn't very slick. Was he really going to pretend like me digging rock wasn't related to our brief discussion Tuesday? I wanted to say, "What crap are you talking about Frank?" but I didn't. I needed a matter-of-fact tone. Something that fell well short of smart-ass. Maybe he was trying to set up a deal.

"I thought I was pretty clear, Frank."

He walked past me to the truck, turned around and leaned back against the fender. When I looked up at him, I was staring straight into the sun. Was this a tactic? He was quiet for about sixty seconds.

"Yeah, you said something about me taking advantage of Sally. That's bullshit."

I leaned down and took a measurement. Then I looked up at him. "Well, Frank, I don't believe I actually said what you did when we talked." I paused. "But I know. She told me, Frank. She said you got drunk, tricked her into going back to your house and then forced yourself on her. Are you saying that didn't happen?"

He stood up straight. "I've never taken advantage of a woman in my life, you son of a bitch. If anything like that had happened, there would have been a complaint filed and I'd be up in front of the superintendent. This is the first I've heard of it. When was this supposed to have happened, anyway?"

"I'm not going to say anymore until I figure out what I'm going to do about it, Frank. I've got a couple ideas I'm working on."

Frank suddenly relaxed. "Are you thinking of black-mailing me, Hunter?" He laughed out loud. "You're not very good at this. The trail crew will pick you up at the end of your shift. We'll talk more later, you dumb-ass." He laughed some more. He got in the truck and peeled out kicking up as much dust as possible.

Clearly, I had lost the first round. Frank was laughing and I was breaking rocks. As usual, I had forgotten to study the gray area. Sally went with him into his house. She didn't scream out for help. She said she didn't really fight him physically. Even if I told the authorities, it would come down to Frank's word against hers. Frank would win by not losing, because there was no evidence that it wasn't consensual. And he knew this way before I figured it out.

I took a swing with the pick and yelped when it bounced off the rock. Anything short of a big power tool or jackhammer wasn't going to make a dent. Got to hand it to Frank, this was a good move. But still, I knew he was sweating.

The YCC hadn't accomplished much. They had dug out about six linear feet at a depth of maybe nine inches. I don't know how long it took them, but that in itself was pretty darn good. I decided that I would follow in the footsteps of my mentor, Dave. Instead of just digging, I would draw it out first. I didn't have anything to make marks on the ground, but I could use the tape to do the measurements and gouge out markers with the pick. I planned to be very precise, so it would take me all day.

Just before 4:00 p.m., the crack trail team rolled up in its crew cab truck. There were four of them, all longtime seasonals except for Chris. He was the junior partner. I walked over to the rock wall to collect my tools and lunch pail.

Ron the foreman leaned out his driver side window to survey the great trench project.

"Wooooweeeeee. What in the hell did you do to piss off Frank?" The other three, including Chris, laughed at that. "You're supposed to dig a ditch in that solid rock? Woooooweeeeeee. Better not make any plans for the next few summers, that looks like mission impossible to me. Even a crack trail crew like us would need a little time to get that done. Better squeeze in. Or do you want to jump off the cliff now and get it over with?"

That was pretty good. "No, I'll just get in the back of the truck and lay down, if you don't mind. I'm just an R & T trainee. I don't think I deserve to ride in the cab with you men just yet."

"Maybe you're right about that, Hunter. Get your stuff and let's go."

* * *

By all standards of measurement, day two in the rock pit was a giant pain in the back.

It started with the laughter I clearly heard emanating from the crew cab as it drove off down the road after dropping me at the trench. Actually, it started in the shower when I painfully discovered sunburn on my neck and arms from the day before. I had a long-sleeved work shirt, but I had no sun block or any other way to protect my neck today.

A cold wind blew, but that wouldn't stop my neck from being charbroiled. Wave patterns crisscrossed the lake. Tourists drove by. I was surprised that not a single car had stopped at my turnout yesterday. Maybe there was a sign back there that said not to talk to the inmate pounding rocks.

I stared at the ground. I had no way of getting around it now. I had to start digging. After steadily swinging the pickaxe at seven thousand feet for a few minutes, I knew I needed a new plan if I was going to last all day. So what did I come up with? Go real slow. I figured the best I could do was to take a short swing at the ground about once every minute and a half. Look for weak spots in the ground. If I found one, I'd work it with the shovel. I'd pretend like I was digging this trench underwater.

At break time, I walked across the road and sat behind a tall Hemlock. After one day I had to retire the lunch pail. It turned out to be woefully inadequate. Yesterday I had eaten everything I'd brought before lunchtime. I ended up rationing the orange juice. So today I had a clothes bag with four sandwiches, a box of cookies, a thermos of orange juice, a little cooler of ice water, and another frozen thermos of Pepsi. I was going to have to buy a backpack this weekend.

I stared at my hands. They'd toughened up a bit over the summer, but not nearly enough. Even with gloves, my soft hands would turn into a blister farm. Oh well, how much worse could it possibly get? I had said that before and it got plenty worse. It can always get worse. Remember that. I wondered what time Frank was going to show up.

The Prince of Crater Lake arrived at 11:05. I worked facing toward Rim Village so I could see him drive up. I caught sight of him out of the corner of my eye. I kept my head down and dug until he got out of the truck.

"This is all you've got done in two days, Hunter?" he yelled. I looked up at him without any expression. I continued poking at the ground. "I should have known a B & U pussy would dig about as much as a little girl."

He walked past me, then turned around and walked back toward the truck.

"If you can't get more done than this, I'm going to fire your ass. Jesus Christ, Hunter, you've done absolutely nothing. We shouldn't have to pay you a cent for this. What do you have to say for yourself?"

I didn't say anything. He was whipping up an intimidation storm. The subject would switch to Sally here in just a minute.

"Well, Hunter?" he barked.

"I've got nothing to say, Frank."

"Well, you better have something to say if you want to keep your job, you B & U pussy. And I'm tired of your bullshit about Sally. I don't want to hear another word about that. I've never forced a girl to do anything. I've never had to. Never. They all want to. And if Sally says I forced her to do anything, she's a liar."

Again, it was now or never. I stepped out of the small hole I had dug. I hung on to the shovel and looked right at Frank. Then I spoke very slowly.

"So you're saying that if I went to the superintendent or Senator Hatfield's staff and told them that a Crater Lake park service maintenance manager had sex with a political appointee seasonal maintenance worker, that that would be a good thing for you, FRANK?"

Frank yanked off his sunglasses. He looked in back of him to see if anyone was around. Then with his head down he walked the few steps to where I was standing. He put his face right in my face. He wanted to be nose to nose.

"Listen, you lightweight punk. You're bluffing. You know it and I know it, so what the hell are you doing? If she told you anything near the truth, you know there's no evidence of it being anything but consensual. And even if it wasn't, she's never going to want it out in the open. That's how these things work, Hunter. It's much worse for the woman if they say anything. Welcome to the real world. You're going to be sorry you ever said anything to me. I'm going to break you. And there's nothing you can do about it except quit and run away."

My hand instinctively tightened around the shovel handle. The movement caught his eye. He laughed in my face.

"Go ahead, Hunter. Take a swing. Please. I'll be happy to wrap that shovel around your neck so fast you won't know what happened. And if you accidentally get knocked over the side of the cliff, so much the better."

I didn't move or change expression. We stared at each other for about twenty seconds.

"Get back to work. And you better start doing a better job up here."

He turned around. Before he opened the door of his truck, he turned back around towards me. He zipped up his green park service jacket. "Getting cold up here. Too bad you don't have a jacket."

Then he was gone. *Nice job, Sam. See, it can always get worse.*

* * *

"Sam, you seem a little distracted," Dave said. "You're not your usual enthusiastically cynical self tonight."

"Don't start in on me, Dave. I've had a hard few days and my back is very, very sore."

"Dave, Debbie and I are going to take a walk," Betty said.

"Another great dinner, Betty. Thank you very much," I said. Betty waved it off like it was nothing. Dave watched his wife and daughter walk down the road toward the maintenance yard.

"So, tell me again how you got into the rock quarry business?"

"Just my big mouth again, Dave. I whined to Dan a couple times early on about being better suited for Roads and Trails. I guess they were trying to prove to me that I should be careful what I wish for, I just might get it.

"By the way, that's what I want on my headstone. 'All you people passing by, just remember, it can always get worse.'"

"There we go, that's the Sam I know," Dave said with a little laugh. "What's going on in the funny papers?"

"Well, I'm glad you asked that. But first, do you think Betty would mind if I stole another piece of pie?"

"Not at all, help yourself."

I got up and walked up the steps into the trailer and checked out the kitchen. I opened the refrigerator door and saw two pies. Gold mine. As I considered apple or cherry, I called out the latest news to Dave.

"Health inspectors for the state said in black-and-white that the Park Service was risking making everyone sick again because they were still making us use water from Munson Springs. They said that, even with all the cleaning and chlorine, it was unlikely that everything was killed off."

"What did the Park Service say about that?" asked Dave.

"They said everything is fine, thanks anyway. Now tell me, Dave, how can anyone in their right mind believe anything the Park Service says about water? Tell me. HOW?

"Do you want a piece of pie, Dave?"

"Nope, I've had enough pie, thanks. But you're forgetting what I've been trying to teach you. Look at the situation. Who needs the park open? The Park Service and concessionaire and businesses around the park, as well as the politicians. Who doesn't need the park open? Nobody. So, again, you have to stop asking if it's right or wrong. You have to evaluate whose interests are served and whose aren't."

"That's it. I'm killing myself. Death by pie."

"You're getting all worked up, Sam. I'm trying to teach you not to get so upset about all these things that really are how life goes most days. You need to accept life for what it is or you're likely to go crazy."

I sank back into my chair. "I'm feeling beaten down, Dave," I said in a serious tone. "How could that happen?"

"Just make sure you're not doing it to yourself," he said. "From over here it looks like you might be doing just that. Unless there are things I don't know."

I looked over at Dave. "I guess there's a few things I need to tell you."

It all poured out like a dam breaking. I began by telling him I'd known there was something wrong with Sally for quite a while. Then the revelation at the bottom of Cleetwood Trail and what she told me in the hospital. Even how I'd promised not to tell anyone. Dave looked straight ahead, not saying a word. I told him what had been going on up at the rim and exactly what Frank and I had said to each other so far.

"So what are you going to do, Sam?"

"I'm going to give Frank some sort of ultimatum next week. I'll let you know what kind when I have it figured out."

Dave looked annoyed. He slowly shook his head back and forth. He put his hand behind his head and rubbed his neck.

"Sam. Tell me the truth. Is that really what you call a plan?"

CHAPTER 18

DAVE SENT ME HOME SO HE COULD THINK. He reluctantly agreed that I had no choice but to continue with my Bolt from Heaven strategy. He didn't think it had much chance of working, but it was do or die now. We also agreed that if the plan had any chance of working I'd have to turn the heat way up on Frank.

But, as Dave pointed out, there was a big, gaping hole in the Bolt from Heaven strategy. There was no way the good guys could really win. Under no circumstances would Frank say, "Sam you're right, what do you want me to do?" Most likely, I would quit or be fired in return for giving Frank two or three weeks of heartburn.

Well, if that was the best I could do I'd start dropping firebombs on him when he showed up today. Maybe I could at least give him an ulcer.

But Frank didn't show up. It was Friday, so maybe he had bigger fish to fry. More likely it was just a tactic. Giving me time to stew. I had plenty of other visitors, though. The tourists came out in force and several stopped by to ask me why the lake was so blue and where the toilets were.

I happily leaned on my shovel and gave them the very longest version I could. I had a great visual aid right next door. There were shallows around the rocky coves and inlets that edged Wizard Island and, with the changes in depth, came a kaleidoscope of colors. Deep blues melting into emerald greens and creating brand new never-land hues.

I didn't care if Frank drove up. Was I supposed to be rude and blow off the tourists? He couldn't punish me for answering questions. What could he do? Have me pound rocks all day?

Ranger Bob also stopped for a visit. He walked up as I finished giving one of my soon-to-be-copyrighted nature lectures to a mesmerized family.

"Pretty good, Sam. You sound like you know what you're talking about. I guess you'll be after my job next."

"Not to worry. I can't imagine exchanging this cushy gig for riding around in a ranger-mobile."

Bob laughed. "So what happened? Did you lose a bet?"

"No, I heard you rangers wanted a new rock wall so I hustled up here and started digging," I said.

Bob took off his smokey hat and surveyed the situation. He took out a handkerchief and wiped his forehead. "Do you really believe you can dig a trench in solid rock with a pick and shovel?" Ranger Bob asked.

"No," I said. I looked up at him and leaned on the shovel.

"Well..."

"I've been a bad boy," I said.

"What did you do?"

"I think I looked cross-eyed at Frank."

"Oh, that would explain it. Frank. Now there's a real bad boy. I'm always a little surprised to see him here when I come back each year. I always expect the permanents to rise up and make him disappear during the winter. He's tougher than them, I guess. I heard he had some relative in the regional office. Something like that."

I picked at the rocks with my shovel. "I could use some dirt on Frank, if you got it," I said with a smile.

Ranger Bob shook his head and laughed. He turned and started to walk toward his ranger car. "No, no, my man. I see no evil, I hear no evil, etc. I'll see you later, Sam. Sorry about your troubles. You did a great job at Cleetwood Cove—too bad this is how you get rewarded."

"I'll pay good money," I yelled.

He waved before opening his car door.

The trail crew picked me up late, so, by the time we got to the maintenance office, Dave had already walked home. I hurried down to his trailer for a consultation.

"He's already left, Sam," Betty said. "He went down to Fort Klamath to get some things and make some phone calls. He said he'd be back about seven. I'll tell him you were looking for him."

"That's all right, Betty. I'm going to Klamath Falls now. But I'll be back for a shift at the pump house Saturday night. I'll catch him later."

Actually, I hoped I might catch Dave in Fort Klamath because it was on the way to my parents' house. But when I got there, I didn't see his station wagon anywhere. I couldn't have missed it, as downtown Fort Klamath is only about five buildings huddled on each side of the main road.

Maybe he was avoiding me. I would if I was him.

* * *

Damn it. I knocked the already beat-up alarm clock across the room. The alarm had rung at noon, but I had turned it off. It was now 1:00. I had finished my pump house shift at 6:00, but I wanted to get down to Cleetwood Cove in time to catch a boat and walk around Wizard Island. The longer the pump house shift dragged on early Sunday morning, the more I thought this might be my last week working at Crater Lake National Park.

I had planned to catch the 2:30 boat. No way that was going to happen now. But I could catch the 3:30 and still spend a few minutes looking around before the last return trip of the day. At least I could say I had been there.

As I walked down Cleetwood Trail, I relived the pain in my calves and lungs. We had carried Sally to the top just ten days ago. It seemed like months had gone by, except that my poor feeble body still ached.

When I got to the bottom, I saw Steve Haswell at the ticket shed.

"Hey man, remember me?" I said. I stuck out my hand.

He laughed. We shook hands, talked about that day, and how lucky we got with the people that helped. I updated him on Sally, but he knew most of the details. He knew she had left for the summer.

"Got room for me on the last boat going over, Steve?"

"Yup, plenty of room. And we only have a few people over on the island, so we're in good shape for the return. And, of course, your ticket is on us. Anything for our park service brothers, you know."

"Thank you very much. Will you carry me up the trail, too?"

"Get out of here!"

"Hey, I'd like to ask you. I mean, I hope it's all right to ask. How are you guys holding up with all the stuff in the papers?"

Steve was filling out some paperwork. He didn't seem to flinch or take exception. "You mean my dad, right? He's taking it pretty hard. You know, he's not as bad as everyone makes out. He's sixty-five years old. He's just an old man trying to hang on to his life, I guess. We've tried for years to get him to retire, but he's stockpiled fifty-odd years of pride, and it's tough. Thankfully, this will be it. It will be out of his hands. There's no way the Park Service will renew his contract.

"Hey, would you get of here? I've got work to do. But stay close so you don't miss the boat. We leave at 3:30 sharp."

"Okey-dokey," I said. I could go watch the salmon swim by until it's time to go.

Thirty minutes later, I sat on the back bench of the half-filled boat, out on the water, headed for Wizard Island. I tuned out the park naturalist spewing statistics and historic notes over the loudspeaker up front and tried to get a feel for the experience on my own. It was cold. And Sally was right: you feel very small down at the bottom of that two thousand foot deep bowl. It wasn't hard to imagine I had time-warped back to a prehistoric world. I was heading to an island that was really a volcanic cone rising seven hundred and fifty five feet out of the deepest lake in the U.S., and scientists predicted it would erupt one day. I half expected a pterodactyl to swoop off a rim cliff and ride the wind currents down to the lake's surface.

Sally said Wizard Island was one of the most beautiful places in the park. She had visited every few weeks to make sure the one port-o-potty on the island was clean and in good shape. And, once, she and Chris had gone over on a Saturday morning and spent the day. Chris had told me the details the day after he drove Sally and her mother to the airport in Medford. He'd shown up at my cabin after dinner with a six-pack. He was already missing Sally and he picked me to drown his sorrows with.

As he drank, he told me about a lot of the stuff he and Sally had done together—the trip to the coast over the Fourth, some hikes they'd taken, how they'd just sit around listening to music sometimes. They both liked Sinatra, but he made me swear not to tell any of his hard-rockin' R & T pals.

"But, Sam," he'd said. "The day on Wizard Island was the best. You know how some days are just perfect? Well, that day will always be one I remember."

It was still early in the season and after they climbed to the top of the cone, Sally had insisted they slide on their bottoms down the crusty snow that still lined the inside of the crater. They picnicked and then swam in a secluded emerald lagoon surrounded by volcanic rocks to cool off. And they'd fished for trout along the shore as they headed back to the boat dock.

"I couldn't believe it, Sam. She caught this gigantic trout and she just couldn't stop grinning. When we got back, we drove around Steel Circle showing it to everybody. Even Andrew the carpenter was impressed. He said it was the second biggest trout he'd seen come out of the lake. We grilled that fish on the barbecue at the Stone House and ate it outside on the picnic table."

After his third beer, Chris got quiet.

"You're really going to miss her, aren't you?" I asked.

He looked over at me with an expression I couldn't quite read. "Yeah. I already do. But I figure you're missing her too, right, Sam?"

"Sure, I do. Sally's a nice girl."

Chris popped the tab on one more beer.

He continued talking, slowly and carefully. "You know. I've been wanting to ask you for a while now. Do you love Sally? Sometimes it sure feels like you do." He paused to take a few swallows. "Did you know Sally and I never made love? Don't get me wrong. It's okay. But it just always felt like she was holding something back. And I couldn't help but wonder if that had anything to do with you. And then that heroic rescue...wow. I have to wonder, man."

I was having trouble breathing and I had no idea what to say. "Chris, I never did anything to try and come between you and Sally. Never. You know how hard I tried to not be a third wheel."

There was a long, unpleasant pause.

Chris pulled himself to his feet. "Nope. I can't think of a single thing either."

Out on the porch he turned and stuck out his hand. "Don't mind me, Sam. It was the beer talking tonight. Thanks again for what you did for Sally." And then he wobbled off to his cabin.

When the boat stopped, the naturalist informed us we had about fifteen minutes before the last boat would leave. We were told not to wander too far. Suddenly I didn't have any desire to explore the island. A headache was beginning at the base of my neck and I just lay back on the seat and let pain and worry wash over me in crashing waves. I never stepped foot on Wizard Island.

* * *

Frank's truck came roaring around the bend at 1:35 Monday afternoon. There had been tourists all morning, but the only people around now were on the other side of the road, heading down to Lightening Springs. I took several deep breaths and looked at the high clouds, the lake like glass in the sun. I wore a short-sleeved work shirt with sun block dripping off me.

He slammed the truck door shut. I was digging in a spot that was about a foot deep. He walked up close so he could look down at me.

"I'm surprised you're still here, Hunter. We've started a pool. Pick the hour Sam Hunter quits."

"Why would I quit, Frank?" I looked up at him, then back down at where I was digging.

"Because you're a lightweight B & U punk," he said. "Remember, we've been over this. Look at what you've been doing up here. Nothing. I don't see any difference in this trench from when you started. I'm going to bring the chief of maintenance up here and maybe he'll fire your ass before I do."

I stepped out of the trench. "Now who's talking bullshit, Frank? If you brought the chief of maintenance up here, you'd get fired for having someone working a job with a shovel when a jackhammer is required. SO GET OFF MY BACK."

"You're really asking for it, Hunter." He pushed me aside and walked toward the truck.

"Oh—there's one other thing, Frank. I've decided what I'm going to do."

He stopped and turned around.

"Ready?" Pause. "I want you out of this Park by September 8. Transferred, paperwork signed, and moving. Or I'm going to the authorities and tell them what you did."

Frank rushed at me, but stopped just before bowling me over. He looked like one of those drill sergeants exploding in a recruit's face. His eyes got big and crazy looking.

"WHAT AUTHORITIES, YOU ASSHOLE?" He stopped for an instant to catch his breath. "I told you what would happen if you did that. Have you talked to Sally about this, Hunter? She's going to end up being called a WHORE in public. Is that what you want? What's all this to you, anyway? I thought Sally was Chris's girlfriend. Were you screwing her too? Or did you just want to? Maybe she really is a whore."

I stepped back down into the trench and grabbed the pickaxe. I looked up at him and then took a swing down into the rock.

"I swear to God, I'm going to kick the shit out of you, Hunter. I'm leaving before I do it right here and now. We'll continue this discussion tomorrow." He stormed away cursing.

I waited for him to open the door to the truck.

"FRANK, SEPTEMBER 8TH. DON'T FORGET."

He slammed the door and drove off.

When Frank was out of sight I sank to the bottom of the trench, shaking from adrenaline overload. I decided to call that round even.

* * *

Dave stopped me after work and shoved a roll of quarters in my hand. "Keep these in your pocket at all times. Got it?"

I told Dave I got it, but what was IT all about? He said he was talking with colleagues back at the Jet Propulsion Lab and Cal Tech for advice on our little internal governmental problem. His colleagues were all pointing him in the same direction, but he still had a lot of calls to make to see if he could save my butt.

"At some point I may need you to talk with someone," he said, "So just keep those quarters in your pocket, okay?"

Okay. Then he walked off toward his trailer.

* * *

Tuesday brought more of the same with Frank up at the rock trench. He threatened. I smart assed him. He swore at me. I ignored him. Anyone watching would have expected a shooting war to start, but for the moment I felt pretty safe, which made it easier to stand up to his attempts at physical intimidation.

Actually it was like the Cold War—mutually assured destruction. The huffing and puffing lasted about fifteen minutes, at the most, but another spitting match was sure to erupt soon.

I had abandoned my after-work naps because my mind wouldn't stop racing. I would try, but just end up lying there, thinking about money, finding another job, moving back home for a month or so, letting Sally down. I didn't know what was going to happen. I didn't know what Dave was working on. All I could do was worry and eat my Beanie Weenies.

Tuesday night, after dinner, I sat out on the porch of the cabin waiting for my body and brain to shut down so I could get some sleep. I watched as Dave walked up the road out of the darkness. He looked as serious as I'd ever seen him. No hello or how ya doing. He just plunged right in.

"I need you to use that roll of quarters I gave you. Tomorrow morning at 6:00, you'll be calling Mr. Stewart from the pay phone at Mazama Campground. Here's his number. No mistakes. You have to make the call right at 6:00. Okay?"

"Sure, Dave. But why are you being so mysterious? What's going to happen?"

"Look, he's just going to ask you about what happened to Sally. He needs to verify what I've told him. He's doing this as a favor for me, so just answer his questions. Don't chat him up or ask what he's working on or anything. Just tell him what he asks for, then say goodbye. I mean it. Okay?"

"Okay, but we're not suppose to tell anybody what happened to Sally. I feel bad enough I told you. How far is this going to go?"

Dave stared up at the dark sky. "There are going to be some trade-offs, Sam. And there are no guarantees about what's going to happen. I'm just trying something, anything to get you out of this mess." He stepped off the porch. "I've got to go. Don't forget to set your alarm."

And then he was gone. Dave spent as little time with me as possible these days.

I reached into my back pocket and pulled out a blue envelope. After Dave had given me the roll of quarters Monday, I had checked for mail at park headquarters. There was a letter waiting, addressed to Samuel Hunter, General Delivery, Crater Lake National Park. Sally must have written it as soon as she got home. I could tell she was trying to sound cheerful, but mainly she sounded tired. And sad. She thanked me again for getting her to the hospital. She said knowing her secret was safe with me made her feel like she could get through this okay. She ended it with, "You're very special to me, Samuel. I hope we haven't really said goodbye." And, at the bottom, she had written her phone number and address. I knew I'd write back eventually, when I knew what to say.

I stuffed the letter back into my pocket. For the first time I started thinking maybe I should just quit and go home. I got up and headed for the refrigerator for a can of soda. *Too late, Sam. Dave is involved now. Whatever happens, you have to see it through. Ride it right into the ground if necessary.* I remembered when I was so excited about a peaceful summer living in a national park. Those were the good old days. *Set your alarm, NOW!*

Not many campers were up at 6:00 at Mazama Campground. I saw a couple folks walking around sleepily. There were a lot of campsites, packed in close, so a lot more people were here than you would think. It was wet and foggy. Just a couple more minutes and I could call Mr. Stewart. A seasonal couple had a trailer around here somewhere. They were in charge of keeping the campground clean. Too much tourist contact for me.

Okay, time to dial. It rang a couple times on the other end.

"This is Stewart," the voice said.

"Hi, I'm Sam Hunter. I was told to call you by..."

"Yes. Thanks for calling. Please tell me what firsthand information you have about the relationship between this Frank Noble and Sally Jordan. Just what you know for sure. Nothing else."

I told him what Sally had told me on the trail and later when I sat by her bed and listened. I told him what the nurse had said to me outside her hospital room.

He asked if there was anything else and I told him things I had noticed before Sally collapsed down at Cleetwood. How she was sick and upset weeks before the miscarriage. And about that strange encounter I had seen between Sally and Frank in the maintenance yard.

"Now, I'm going to ask you a question. I want you to think about it carefully," he said. "Do you think there's any chance Sally misrepresented what happened at Frank Noble's house?"

I had already thought about that. It all came down to this: Sally's word against Frank's.

"No. I don't think she misrepresented what happened."

"Do you think Frank Noble is capable of what she says?" he asked.

"From what I've seen, yes, he is." I quickly asked a question, even though the answer was obvious. "Mr. Stewart, are you going to have to talk with Sally?"

"Maybe. You weren't an eyewitness to any of this?

"No."

"Thank you, Sam. That's all I need right now."

Click.

I felt like I'd been punched in the stomach.

I got back in my car and leaned forward against the steering wheel with my head in my arms. The gray area was closing in around me. Things I was certain about just days ago were not so clear to me now. I had talked on the phone to a man I didn't know. I had made statements about who was guilty and who wasn't, when I wasn't even there. I was playing with people's lives, including Sally's. This was getting to be more than I could handle.

I sure hoped Frank wouldn't visit me today.

But there he was, at 9:30 in the morning—an unusual time. His demeanor was different as he got out of the truck. No sunglasses. His body language didn't shout "watch out." He looked up and down the trench. I kept poking at rocks. What was he doing? He walked up to the end of the trench—maybe ten feet away from me.

"We have to settle this once and for all, Hunter. I'm tired of it."

I looked up at him. "How do we do that, Frank?" I went back to poking at the rocks.

"Man to man. We go somewhere after work and settle it man to man."

"You want to fight, Frank? Best man wins? Is that your plan?"

"It doesn't have to come to that, Hunter. There has to be some way to hammer this out."

That took me completely by surprise. He wanted to make a deal. But what deal could be made? He couldn't give back what was taken. What did he have to offer? Nothing. And I was bluffing, too. I had nothing to offer except to let bygones be bygones, and I hadn't come this far to do that.

"NO, FRANK."

He turned and stomped back to his truck. I sneaked a peek. His body language said rage. He started to turn. I stared back down at the bottom of the trench.

"HUNTER!"

I looked at him.

He snarled, "Then watch your back."

CHAPTER 19

"**H**E SAID 'WATCH YOUR BACK,' HUH?" repeated Dave after I told him what happened. "Well, he's either raising the bet to see if you'll fold, or I guess he means it. But I wouldn't worry. People like him are usually all talk. He's just mad because a kid like you is challenging him. He's supposed to be able to run over people like you. I think everything will be fine."

"How can everything be fine, Dave? That's a little optimistic, isn't it?"

We were sitting in green lawn chairs next to the Weber. Dave was supposed to be watching the coals while Betty and Debbie went up to the Rim Village Store to get paper plates and Dr. Peppers. I had adjusted the lawn chair so I could lie way back. My shoulders and arms were killing me. So were my feet.

"Maybe. But I have the best minds in our nation's capitol working on this problem. I've got seventy-five-thousand-a-year, high-powered, political game players racking their brains to find ways to save your butt."

"You do not."

Dave poked a coal with a stick. "I got a couple guys."

"You know, Dave, you've been awfully tense the last few days. You've avoided me like the plague. And now, all of a sudden, you're downright cheerful. I'm having trouble keeping up."

"Okay, I admit I was a little concerned there for a while. But then I told myself that we're just going against Frank Noble, a dirt-pounding maintenance guy. If we can't outmaneuver him, we ought to go home. Like I've told you before, the people I work with are the toughest hand-to-hand government infighters there are. They fight for millions of dollars in government funding every day. If they have to bludgeon someone to get it, they will."

"Well, if you have a plan you ought to tell me, Dave. I'm thinking I'm about to be fired or worse."

"I don't have a plan. And it may well be that nothing can be done. All I can truthfully say is that I'm trying. I've spent about fifty dollars in change on phone calls. That's all I can tell you. I'm sorry. By the way, how did your call with Stewart go this morning?"

I told Dave what Stewart had asked and how I'd answered. I ended with, "Dave, I think I need to call Sally. I can't just let her get a phone call about this out of the blue."

"I think you're right, Sam. It'll be a pretty miserable call. But she's had a rough enough time. You need to let her know what to expect. Get her number from Chris and call in the morning." He looked at his watch. "With the time difference, it's too late now."

"I got a letter from her yesterday. I have her number."

Dave looked at me and sighed. "This is pretty complicated, isn't it?"

I nodded. "Dave, I don't know exactly what to tell her. I don't understand what's going on."

"I know."

Betty came rumbling up the gravel road in the station wagon. Dave got up and stared at the coals. He bent over and flipped the still-black ones with a stick. He looked at me and mouthed the words, "Hang in there."

✳ ✳ ✳

For the second straight morning I stood outside the Mazama Campground phone booth at dawn. I called Sally at nine her time, figuring she'd be up by then. I was relieved when she picked up the phone herself. I had been dreading trying to explain to her mom or someone else who I was. It went downhill from there. I was too late. She told me coldly that John Coffey, the senator's chief of staff, had called her late yesterday afternoon, asking questions.

I tried to explain, but she wasn't listening.

"I'm sure you have your reasons for telling, Samuel. But they just don't matter to me right now." Then her voice broke and got softer. "I guess I was wrong to trust you."

Then she hung up.

Dave had warned me Sally might react that way, but I wasn't prepared for it. Now I really wanted to go home.

At least there was some good news in the maintenance yard a couple hours later. Frank was gone. Charlie said he was taking off Thursday and Friday. Charlie told me he was sorry, but that didn't get me out of the rock trench. Frank left him specific instructions about that.

"What did you do, Sam?" Charlie whispered. "He hasn't told anybody anything, except he wanted to break in a B & U guy just right. Maybe your initiation will be over this week."

"Hope so, Charlie."

Even the trail crew seemed to think I had had enough rock pile work. I asked Ron if he could hold up for just a second. I needed to deliver a message to Dave. He said, "Okay, but hurry it up." Last week it would have been, "Get in the damn truck."

When I told Dave that Frank was off, he got a puzzled look on his face. He wondered out loud if his friends in high places could have come through already. He also said I shouldn't get my hopes up. I jogged over to the crew cab, thanked Ron and jumped into the back with the tools.

All morning I kept one eye on the road in front of me. Frank was off work, but I didn't know where he was. I imagined a dozen different scenarios where he pulled off a sneak attack and then made a fast getaway in his civilian clothes.

At lunchtime a green truck came around the corner. *Keep calm, Sam, it isn't Frank.* There were five or six of those standard park service maintenance trucks that everyone used. It could be anyone.

As it got closer, I could see it was Dave. This was a first. Maybe that meant the coast was clear. Otherwise, Dave wouldn't be cruising around up here. I could relax for the rest of the day. Do some cartwheels. Give some rim tours. Maybe open a roadside stand and sell Crater Lake rocks.

"Hey, Dave! Welcome to my world," I shouted, as he got out of the truck. "You're just in time for a guided tour of my trench."

"That's great. I thought I'd missed it," he said, surveying the big dig.

"See this twenty-four-inch-long hole? That's what I've accomplished since last week. But now, let me turn your attention to the strategically placed rocks you can see right over there. This is what we call the Dave Fielding trench measurement system. Behold."

He inspected my work critically. "You know, maybe I should measure that again for you."

We joked around a bit more about my absurd task.

"Sam, maybe we should back off Frank. This looks like pretty good duty to me."

Dave abruptly put a halt to our comedy routine and went back to the truck. "I forgot, this is my excuse for coming up here, so I'd better give it to you. I told Charlie you'd forgotten a bottle of cold water and I needed to run it up to you at lunch."

"Why Charlie?" I asked. "He's not your boss."

"Just wanted it to be official. You're not supposed to get visitors, I hear. And there's one other thing. I just happened to be driving past Frank's house. His truck wasn't out front and the curtains were drawn. Of course, his truck could be in the garage, but I think he's a guy with too much on his plate to be worried about parking his truck in the garage."

"Wow, good job on the recon. Every little bit helps to keep my morale up."

"All right then, have a nice day up here in this cream puff job of yours."

The rest of the afternoon went pretty well, considering. I had plenty of tourists wanting to hear my blue lake spiel. Thanks to a weak spot I found in the rock, I actually made some trench progress. And that view was always there, just over my shoulder. During a break, I watched a speck of a boat travel from Wizard Island all the way around, past the small island of lava rocks called Phantom Ship.

For the first time in a couple days, I didn't feel so bad. Impending doom seemed on hold.

Dave waited for me at the maintenance office while I put away my gear. He asked me if I'd called Sally. I told him yes, but I had been too late and she wasn't taking it too well.

"I'm sorry, Sam. Just remember what she's been through. Give her some time. Listen, I want you to come over for supper again. I'll have some more info by then. I have an important phone call at 5:30."

"I've been begging for information for a week. And now you want to give me some the one time I can't be around. I've got the pump house tonight. The six to midnight shift. Why don't you come up after it gets dark and fill me in?"

"Maybe. Or I'll catch you tomorrow after work. No rush with Frank away. How about this? If I've got important news, I'll come up. If not, it can wait till tomorrow."

"You afraid to go out at night, Dave, or what?"

"Why am I even helping you?"

I peeled off to my cabin and he kept walking toward the trailer. Actually, I had to hurry up because I had to eat dinner and pack up everything I needed for the pump house shift. It was going to be a good night because I had a book I'd been wanting to read for awhile; *The Boys of Summer* by Roger Kahn.

✳ ✳ ✳

The pump house sat in the middle of one of the most beautiful national parks in the country. By all rights, it should have had a great view. But it didn't. The spring pops promisingly out of the side of the mountain, but, unfortunately, the road to the rim was built around it. And the pump house ended up in the middle of a switchback. Instead of an awesome view from the front door, all you could see was a bit of road going up or down the mountain, some pine trees, and about twenty feet of Munson Creek before it disappears.

You weren't supposed to be outside gawking, anyway. While it was still light, the Park Service wanted you in the pump house, out of sight.

If you didn't have a book, the stars were a decent alternative. If you could tune out the generator. Outside the pump house, the thump of the generator got annoying. Inside, it was a reassuring late-at-night kind of sound, like a heartbeat.

I spent a few minutes outside watching night fall into place, then went back inside and got my reading bed set up. I propped a sleeping bag and a pillow where all I had to do was look up from my book to see the gauge. I had an alarm clock in case I fell asleep, and a cooler full of cookies and Dr. Pepper. I had become a professional and efficient pump house gauge watcher. Fill out my overtime slip, please. Thank you.

About 9:00 something banged against the door.

"Hey, Dave, is that you?" No sound. *Oh God, not a bear, please.* I quietly got up, took a careful step and peeked around a piece of machinery.

"Surrrrprrrrise."

Frank's hair was plastered down on his head. He had a brown hunting vest on, dirty jeans and boots. He looked drunk.

"Thought it was your good buddy, Dave, huh? He must have driven by my house twelve times today, looking to see if I was home. He must be really worried about you. He should be."

"Why is that, Frank?" My heart was pounding. I wasn't going to let this maniac goad me into an argument. This was way different from our past confrontations. Frank was drunk, so anything could happen. I needed to talk him out of here so there wouldn't be any trouble.

"Because it's time to settle this thing man to man. And I don't think you're much of a man, so that could be a problem for you."

"What do you want, Frank?"

"I want you to drop the bullshit about Sally before somebody gets hurt. And I mean drop it NOW."

Frank took a couple steps toward me. His words weren't slurred, so I didn't know how drunk he really was. He wasn't staggering, but his steps were overly slow and deliberate. That's how he was talking, too.

"Stay back, Frank. Talk to me from there," I said.

"Whatsa matter, college boy, you scared?" He took another step forward.

"What do you want, Frank?"

"I told you. Drop the Sally thing. Everyone will be better off if you just drop it. I don't know why you're doing this."

I just looked at him. I tried to keep my body language non-threatening by standing casually, with my hands in my pocket.

"You're drunk, Frank, and you should go home before you do something that's going to make things worse."

"You're not going to talk your way out of this, you punk. Now I'm telling you to give it up or you're going to wish you had."

I needed to decide—and quickly—if he was really going to attack me. I wasn't sure. His eyes were narrowed and red. His face was one giant sneer. He had his body puffed up, his shoulders raised. He took another step.

"So I'm just supposed to forget what you did, Frank?"

"I didn't do anything, how many times do I have to tell you? She came to my house because she wanted to have sex. So we did. That's it. Why are you making this federal case when nobody else is?"

"Because some people call what you did RAPE."

By mid-sentence, my brain was screaming, *Watch out!* But it didn't do any good. I watched passively as everything shifted into slow motion. I saw Frank pull something from his back pocket. He swung and hit me on the side of my leg. There was nothing slow about his attack, but I don't think it mattered because all I did was watch.

For a split second I didn't feel a thing. But then ALL I could feel was a searing pain that started at my thigh and spread up and down my leg. Before I could yell, he had swung and hit me again in the same place. My brain and body both collapsed. I felt myself falling.

Through the fog in my brain I heard footsteps. Then I felt bodies rolling over me. Something clanged against the floor. I moved my head to the side and tried to focus. I thought I saw two men sliding, one on top of the other. I must have blacked out. The next thing I knew, somebody was in my face asking me if I was all right.

What a stupid question. *Get out of my face,* I yelled inside my head.

"Sam, are you all right?" It was Dave. A few feet away, I could see Ranger Bob with his knee in Frank's back. Ranger Bob yelled something at Frank, but the words sounded like they were coming from underwater. A deep breath didn't help.

"Where's the pain, Sam?"

"My leg, Dave." I looked next to me on the floor. I pointed at what looked like a two-foot steel pipe on the cement about fifteen feet from me. "He hit me with that." Then I closed my eyes.

I heard Ranger Bob say calmly and clearly, "Give me your other hand, Frank. Fighting isn't going to help."

"You're making a big mistake, ranger," Frank yelled. "You need to call the head of maintenance right away or you'll be sorry."

"I'm not calling anyone, Frank." He clicked the handcuffs tight. "Sam, you're going to press charges, right?"

I looked up at the ceiling. What in the hell was going on?

Dave raised his hand. "Just wait a minute, now. Bob, can you bring Frank over here? I've got information you all need to hear. Especially Frank."

Ranger Bob grabbed Frank by his arm and dragged him across the cement floor. It wasn't hard. Frank slid really well after he pulled his head up so it wouldn't drag. When Bob stopped, Frank's face was flat on the cement. Frank could tilt his head and get a good look at Dave with one eye.

"What do you want," growled Frank.

"Shut the hell up, Frank. I'm now the only friend you've got. I'm trying to save your life here. Keep talking and I might change my mind."

Dave's voice was low and menacing. Frank didn't say anything else. Dave pulled a piece of paper from his shirt pocket and then bent down close to Frank's face.

"The first thing you should know, Frank, is you've worked your last day at Crater Lake National Park, no matter what happens. You're done here."

"Go to hell," Frank spat.

"I'm putting a piece of paper in your pocket. It's the number you're going to call tomorrow, to get an appointment to talk with a very important man in Washington D.C. His name is John Coffey. Don't worry, you won't have to wait long for him to get back to you. He's the chief of staff for Senator Robert Mills of Pennsylvania—the minority leader of the Senate. Coffey is the designated hit man for Senator Mills. He goes out and fixes the senator's problems. And right now you're the biggest problem Senator Mills has.

"Don't worry, the senator doesn't know what you did to Sally. If he did, you would already be in jail. Turns out, Sally knows the senator as 'Uncle Bob.' But Coffey's the one that got her the job here at Crater Lake. So Mr. Coffey is very unhappy. He's had a staffer looking into your park service background this week. He knows about your uncle in the Western Regional Office. He knows about your consistently offensive behavior.

"So the only reason you aren't in jail right this minute is Sally's privacy and the tiny bit of gray area that's part of this incident. You're going to be offered a great deal, considering all the circumstances, not to mention what's gone on tonight. You get to be a truck driver for the park service wherever one is needed right now. If you fight it or say anything about this, the full weight of a powerful senator and the Department of the Interior will drop on your head."

Dave paused for a second, staring at Frank.

"Yes, Frank, the Park Service is no longer willing to protect you. If fact, you're now their worst nightmare—someone who is a lightening rod for an important senator. There's nothing a government bureaucrat hates worse. Now, nobody's going to know about this, except for a select group of people in the Park Service, the Department of the Interior, and the senator's chief of staff. But people are going to figure out real quick that you're bad news, so you should be careful not to mess up, Frank. These people have long memories."

Frank started to say something.

"Shut up, Frank. Don't say a thing," yelled Dave. "You're this close to jail. You're getting a great deal, so just shut up. Otherwise a lot of really bad things are going to happen to you."

Frank raised his head so he could turn his face away from us. Ranger Bob looked at Dave, then me. Dave motioned to the ranger to go outside with him. Frank and I were alone again in the pump house. I looked over at his limp body. I couldn't build up any anger. Maybe it was because my leg hurt so bad. He looked toward the pump house wall.

Dave and Ranger Bob came back into the pump house. Bob had a first aid kit. He came over and sat down next to me. He pulled out a cold pack and some aspirin. He didn't have to ask me where I had been hit, because my pant leg was bulging where the swelling had started.

"Sam, is there any ice over in your cooler?" asked Ranger Bob.

I nodded yes.

"Dave, could you bring the cooler over here? If you can figure out a way to get that ice on his leg, I'll take Frank back to his house. Then I'll come back and help you get Sam home. Frank, are you agreeing to what Dave told you?"

There was a muffled yes from Frank. Ranger Bob picked up one end of the pipe and put it into a paper bag. He pulled Frank to his feet, but didn't take the handcuffs off. He told Frank they'd come off at his house. Bob shot us a look of amazement as he led Frank out the door.

"Sam, I know you're hurting, but Bob doesn't think your leg is too bad. He'll get you some stronger painkillers. Other than that, it's ice and more ice and, of course, staying off your feet. Tomorrow, everyone's going to hear about how you pulled your hamstring bad when you fell in the dark during pump house duty. A week or so of lying around your cabin and I'm betting you'll be fine. I'll take the rest of your shift tonight. Bob will take you home when he gets back."

"Dave, did I just get assaulted with a steel pipe and no one's being arrested?"

"C'mon, let's get you set up here on your sleeping bag. Once we get you situated, I can stack all the ice up around your leg and you can start to relax." Dave fussed around for about ten minutes getting ice stacked, getting some food and drink out of the cooler and making sure the pillow was comfortable. Then he sat down on the floor, his back against the rock wall.

"Let's see, you had a question. The answer is yes."

"Okay, thought so. That's perfect. It fits in just right with the rest of my summer."

"Sam, you told a man that you were taking his life away from him and you—a twenty-year-old kid—were doing it right in his face. You were humiliating him. What did you think was going to happen?"

"Dave, you told me to go for it."

"You had already unleashed your 'bolt from heaven' strategy. You couldn't stop then. I was just hoping he wouldn't kill you before I could get Coffey to take my call."

I didn't say anything for a while. I took some deep breaths. The ice was doing a good job of numbing my leg, so it didn't hurt as much. Sometimes my deep breaths were actually sighs. Dave kicked my good leg.

"You did the right thing, Sam, you just don't know what you don't know."

I sighed again and shook my head. "Did you really drive by Frank's house twelve times today?"

"Nah. Maybe six or seven. Who told you that?"

"Frank."

"Oops."

"How did you get Ranger Bob involved?"

"When you dropped that pump house shift news on me walking home, I almost had a coronary. What a perfect time for Frank to make his move. I always figured he'd attack sooner rather than later. He's not the type that could take crap from you for very long.

"I went up to make my phone call at headquarters, taking the chance no one would hear or get what I was talking about. Then I went in and tried to find out where Ranger Bob was. He was scheduled for the graveyard shift tonight, so I figured he was home sleeping. I woke him up and I told him the problem. I'm sorry, Sam, but I had to tell him about Sally. The story doesn't make much sense without that part. Around 8:30, we started driving up and down the road to the rim to see if Frank would show up at the pump house. It didn't take him long."

I told him I didn't even want to know about the senator thing for a while. I was having trouble digesting what I had heard already. I asked him if he wanted a pecan cookie. He said yes and dug a handful out of the bag I tossed over to him.

"Dave, I can't see myself living past the age of twenty-five; I'm just too stupid."

"Well, you're obviously not the sharpest crayon in the box," he said laughing.

"Shut up, I got there. Just the hard way. I may need to get my leg amputated, though." Dave laughed again and just kept munching on the cookies.

As the ice numbed my leg, I got real sleepy. "Hey, Dave," I mumbled, "I may take a little nap here. Would you mind watching the gauge for me? I wouldn't want to get in trouble."

CHAPTER 20

M Y LAST DAYS IN THE PARK ended up being pretty much just like my first days in the park, back in early June when Johnny and I pulled snow poles out of the near-frozen dirt. This time, there were no snowdrifts and I was jamming the tall orange snow poles back in the ground.

We were working in a cloud of cold mist about halfway between park headquarters and Mazama Campground. It was the middle of October and Crater Lake National Park was preparing for another mountain winter of five hundred plus inches of snow.

Billy was my snow pole partner. He was the R & T guy who dismissed me as a political appointee early on and then, later, placed all the blame for the water problems on me and my B & U pals. But now I was his best buddy because, well, there was nobody else. If he wanted to work fast, he needed me.

All the other seasonals were gone. The permanents didn't like to board up cabins and put in snow poles, so they were happy when Billy and I volunteered to stay on an extra month. I wasn't ready to go back to school and this was a good excuse. There would always be next term. My parents weren't crazy about it, but all I had to do was bring up the money to end that argument.

The water crisis was long forgotten. Senator Hatfield had convened a Congressional hearing on the park closing. In a career highlight for the Oregon senator, softball after softball was tossed up for him to hit out of the park. He officially concluded that there had not been a cover-up, as such, by park officials, but rather a series of serious blunders compounded by inexperience, inattention, and the poor training of many of the park and federal health personnel involved in the water crisis. He said there had also been a breakdown in the park chain of command. Confusion resulted from the overlapping jurisdictions and the fact that nobody seemed to be in charge.

In a widely reported sound bite, aimed squarely at the park superintendent, he said, "Rather than trying to save the people who were on fire, you were looking around for what started it."

There were water injury settlements to figure out yet, but that was a way off, as an army of litigators swarmed the federal courthouse in Portland, filing civil actions. I'm sure George Haswell was sharpening his sword and getting ready for a fight. But he was certain to go down with the ship this time.

The park's water now came from Annie Springs. The Munson Springs pump house was scheduled to be torn down, rock by beautiful rock. Ranger Bob told me that the YCC had a new boss—the National Park Service. And a new superintendent started work at Crater Lake the first of October. The chief ranger position was open. The maintenance chief transferred and, of course, Frank was gone.

Frank's sudden disappearance set off a ton of speculation down at the maintenance office. Charlie had taken over as interim leader of R & T and conspiracy theories sparked, then roared out of control. Dan got to tell everyone the official story. I wasn't there, but I heard he delivered the news with a smile. Frank got a job at Grand Tetons, where he was needed immediately, so he had to go without saying goodbye to anyone. A moving company packed up his stuff and now it was like he had never been here.

The seasonals who worked for Frank didn't buy the story for a second. They knew the Prince of Crater Lake wouldn't go without some monstrous beer blowout celebrating the greatness of himself. He'd want to be seen as leading the parade out of town. The seasonals kept asking the permanents what really happened. The permanents kept saying things like, *this goes on all the time with the Park Service. He'll be back to say goodbye. Just you wait and see.* The permanents didn't believe that any more than the seasonals did, but this was one time they enjoyed spouting the company line. They knew something political had gone down, but who cared. It was like Christmas in summer. Frank was gone.

According to Chris, my name often popped up in the Frank conspiracy theories. After my first day back at work, he stopped by for a Dr. Pepper and laid out the rationale.

"Here's the argument for it being about you," he started. "Out of the blue you get pulled into the R & T group, even though everyone knows that's the last thing Frank would ever do unless he was forced to by a big boss. He hates B & U people. So he sticks you in a hole, breaking rocks, as punishment. Now, everyone knows you're a smart-ass."

"What do you mean, a smart-ass?" I interrupted with mock indignation.

"Just shut up and listen to the whole thing," he said. "You get sick of digging the rock pit and you say something to Frank. He says something back. You say something else. It becomes a real pissing contest and you guys decide to discuss it after work. There's a fight. Somehow you survive, but you disappear into your cabin for a few days. And Frank disappears completely. You eventually come back, Frank doesn't. Bottom line, some politician friend of yours jumped in and pulled the plug on Frank."

I shook my head in disbelief. "And you guys laughed at my water cover-up conspiracies." I wouldn't have minded setting the record straight somehow, but I couldn't say anything resembling the truth about Frank because it might lead back to Sally and that just couldn't happen. Tall Paul came running down the stairs from his attic bedroom.

"Hey, Paul," Chris yelled. "Sam doesn't believe me that everyone thinks he got Frank transferred."

Paul had stopped in the bathroom to take a look at himself in the mirror, but we could easily hear his answer.

"It's true, Sam. The R & T boys don't know whether to kick your ass or call you 'sir.'"

"Oh my God," I said. "If only I really had power like that. I wouldn't be living in this dump, that's for sure. I'd be calling up the supe, saying get me a room over in Steel Circle or else."

"So that's all you've got to say, Sam? You're officially denying everything?"

"You stopped by while I was holed up. Did I look like I had been in a fight, Chris? I don't remember any bruises or puffed up lips or black eyes or anything like that."

"You didn't come to work for a week."

"You saw me, I couldn't walk. I pulled my hamstring. A pulled hamstring isn't generally what you get in a fight. Or, if you do, you get a lot of other things with it. C'mon, Chris. You can't really believe that crap, you're an educated man."

Chris put his empty soda bottle on the table, got up and headed for the door. "I think you're a bad liar, Sam."

"Well, make sure you tell the boys I would have loved getting Frank fired for that ugly trench detail he put me on, but I had nothing to do with it. You guys are talking crazy."

Chris grabbed for the door handle. Paul walked across the living room ready to follow him out the door. I asked Chris to hold up for a second and Paul said, see you guys, and maneuvered around him to get out the door. Chris looked back at me.

Chris and I hadn't talked much since that night when he drank the beer and asked me if I loved Sally. We'd joke when the R & T crew ferried me to and from trench duty, but he'd stopped dropping by except for that one time during the week I didn't work. And he kept that visit short and sweet, strictly a courtesy call.

"Have you talked to Sally lately?" I asked.

"Yeah, just yesterday. She sounds good. She told me to say hi."

Chris stood at the door for a few seconds. He looked as if he wanted to say something else.

He looked at me for about twenty seconds. "Goodnight." He walked out the door leaving me with my roomful of silent explanations.

* * *

The day before I was scheduled to leave, Billy and I put on our park service slickers and planted snow poles in a hard rain.

"You guys are working way too fast," groused Wes from the driver seat of the truck. "Why are you working so fast? What's the point?"

"Ask him, Wes," I said, looking at Billy. "You know how he is."

Billy smiled. "What are you complaining about, Wes? You don't have to do anything but sit in the truck."

There was no doubt that Billy was a maniac. He liked to work hard. He ran the road patching crew during the summer and I think he enjoyed making the seasonals assigned to him whine. Billy was only twenty-five, but he acted like an old hardnosed redneck. He was always saying something like, "If I don't work hard, I won't be able to get a good night's sleep."

This hurry-up style of work pissed Wes off because it interfered with his coffee drinking. We'd plant poles and bang on the truck for Wes to move ahead. We were banging on that truck all the time. He didn't like it. Working with Billy reminded me of the part in *Cool Hand Luke* when Paul Newman convinces his road gang to lay asphalt double-time, so they can get the day's job done before noon. Except we did it all day long.

I didn't mind. I spent my last couple days in the park outside in the sweet-smelling forest. No problem. It felt good. And it was easy to get lost in my thoughts with the mindless repetition of the work.

At lunchtime, we stopped at Mazama Campground next to Annie Springs. We had made the turn at the ranger shack and were heading back up the hill planting poles. We backtracked a quarter of a mile so we could take our break in the campground.

"We're taking an hour lunch, goddamn it," snarled Wes, looking squarely at Billy. "I don't care if you don't get your damn beauty sleep. I'm the permanent here, so don't give me any lip."

Billy smiled his serial killer smile and walked off at a quick pace.

"Where's he going?" Wes asked.

"You're asking me? Wherever crazy people go to eat lunch, I guess."

I headed off toward the creek that ran next to the campground, leaving poor Wes to fume. He didn't have a single person to listen to the highlights of his colorful life. Both

Billy and I had heard them already. We'd even politely lis-tened to some repeats, so we felt like we'd earned our lunch-time peace and quiet.

The rain was back to a polite drizzle by the time I got to the spot near the creek where Sally and I had seen a doe ear-lier in the summer. I settled under a tree where it was mostly dry. Seeing that doe with Sally seemed like years ago.

I ate my peanut butter and jelly sandwiches, lost in my thoughts about the summer.

Dave's wife, Betty, had come by every day around noon during the week I spent resting my leg. I guess she was just making sure I was all right. She'd bring some soup or a sandwich and wash whatever dishes had piled up in the sink. She'd leave something easy for dinner in the fridge. We'd chat a little and then she'd head off. The last day of the week she brought me a second letter from Sally. They'd let Dave take it at the post office in the headquarters building. I was propped up in bed and Betty tossed the envelope on my lap, before she went into the kitchen.

Sally didn't sound quite so angry, but she was obvi-ously still hurt. Chris had told her how Frank had disap-peared and she had been able to put two and two together. She said she was glad he was gone. And she apologized for hanging up on me. She said she'd like to know exactly what happened. And that was about it.

Betty handed me a tray with a bowl of chili and shredded cheese and an apple, then sat down. "How's Sally doing?"

"Okay, I guess. She seems to be feeling all right, but it's pretty clear she still hates me. To tell you the truth, I'm sur-prised I got this letter."

Betty ran a hand through her short grey hair, then leaned forward. "Sam, you need to quit beating yourself up about breaking your promise to Sally. I know why you made the promise. At that moment, it was crucial for Sally to be able to trust you. But I think you know now it wasn't a good promise to make." Betty tapped the blue envelope lying on the bedside table with her fingertips. "So I hope you'll write her back. And I hope you'll tell her she needs to talk with someone about what happened to her. And just remember, as much as you think she hates you, right now she hates herself even more." Betty sighed and stood up. "With everything you've been through, I imagine you think it would be easier on both of you if you just disappeared. But, if you do, she'll always wonder if it's because you stopped liking her when you found out what happened."

Then she smiled. "End of lecture, my dear."

* * *

After I went back to work, I spent a lot of evenings at Dave's trailer. It seemed like a sanctuary because Dave and Betty knew what happened. I could talk freely and not worry about letting something slip. And I got to pester Dave for more of his opinions on college students. I got a lot of useful information sitting around that barbecue. But Dave warned me that hardly anyone learns anything important until they actually put their hand in the fire and get burnt.

"Great, Dave," I said. "Can't wait for more of that." Dave laughed. I think he got some pleasure from giving me the hours of advice that he would like to have given his son. I thanked him almost every day for his help with Frank. But, looking back, my real gift was just letting him talk about whatever he wanted.

Dave and his family left for their home in Southern California the first Saturday in September. During one of her lunchtime visits to my cabin, Betty had confided that this would be their last summer at Crater Lake. She told me that they had first started coming after their son had died. "Time can hang heavier in the summer and both of us just needed to get away—be someplace different, where the memories didn't smack you in the face every time you turned around. Especially Dave, I think." But she was happy when he'd recently told her he thought they should plan to stay at home next summer.

When Dave told me the news, he said it was because he was getting too old for honey runs. He also said he'd be happy to write a special letter of recommendation if I wanted to come back next year and take over the honey run job.

We talked briefly about me visiting in L.A. But, being from a military family—always moving away from people—I'd learned not to expect much regarding the future. Better to stick with, we'll see you if we see you.

Dave pulled me aside after Betty announced she was now officially packed and ready for the highway. It was a brisk, clear Saturday morning. Birds were happily yakking away. It was about 7:00, way before my usual start time.

"Sam, there is one thing you can do to thank me," he said.

I didn't say anything. I waited for him to tell me.

He looked down at the dirt, then looked at me for about ten seconds. "Promise me you'll be a more forgiving son." He paused. "Okay?"

Tears welled up in my eyes. It was my turn to look down at the dirt. "I promise, Dave." He shook my hand. They drove off and I was alone again.

The only two people who ever broke through my layers of self-pity had left me. Probably forever. Like leaves that happily spin and circle for a moment in an eddy, people— sooner or later—always move downstream and disappear around the bend.

* * *

"HUNTER, SLEEP TIME IS OVER, LET'S GO," yelled Wes through the trees. I heard the truck start up, so I walked the few feet over to the campground entrance and waited for them to pick me up. Some mindless, sopping, chain gang-like work was what I needed right now.

The wind knocked the rain sideways, just how Billy liked it. He was about twenty-five pounds lighter than me, but eight times stronger. Wiry was the wrong way to describe him, unless you replaced that wire with steel piping. He didn't just carry twenty-foot snow poles from the truck. He jogged with them.

"What's the matter, political appointee, can't you keep up?" That smile again. No, I couldn't jog like him, but I worked nonstop and we made our way quickly up the hill. Another day and we'd be done with this last job.

Mid-afternoon, a green ranger station wagon drove by without even a wave from the driver. That reminded me of

Ranger Bob Roberts, because Bob always waved. But he was gone now, too. He taught fifth graders in Medford when he wasn't a seasonal patrol ranger. I took him out to dinner at Becky's one night, after I got back on my feet, to thank him again for his help.

That night in the pump house, Bob had learned everything that had happened to Sally. But not once had he brought it up or asked any questions. I admired him for that. During the drive to the restaurant, he asked me about Sally and then said he was glad to hear she was doing better.

"Did you ever hear about the day she tried to take my job from me, Sam?" When I shook my head, he continued. "It was over by Vidae Falls. I was making my rounds and saw her truck pulled off the road, so I decided I better check things out. I found her on her hands and knees trying to patch up that wonderful bed of moss that grows at the bottom of the falls. She told me she had come across this family filling one of those round scotch-plaid coolers with chunks of the moss. She said she got so mad she pulled over, marched over to them and said, 'What you're doing is illegal. I don't have the authority to give you a ticket, but I've got a radio in my truck and I can call a ranger who can.' But, Sally, I said to her, you don't have a radio in your truck. And she started laughing. 'I know,' she said. 'I just stood there, glaring at them, scared to death they'd call my bluff.' I'd found her trying to put back the moss those people had dug up.

"From then on," Bob told me, "I'd stop whenever I saw her truck pulled over somewhere. Just in case she was trying to take law enforcement into her own hands again."

Bob and I both laughed at the story. I could imagine Sally standing there, indignant, with her yellow hard hat on her head and her hands on her hips.

While we ate that night, I learned a deep, dark secret about Ranger Bob. His first two summers at the park, he worked maintenance. B & U. OH MY GOD.

"How did you keep that quiet, Bob?"

"There must have been a massive communications breakdown between departments one summer and I sneaked through. I was able to get a job as a naturalist for a few years. Then I took some law enforcement courses at a college and here I am. I don't think there's anybody working here anymore that remembers I worked maintenance."

The thing I liked best about Bob was his love for Crater Lake. It seemed like he had a story about every square inch of this park. Whether it was about a freeloading bear at the rim campground, or an accident on the Pacific Crest Trail out in the middle of nowhere or the year an unexpected wildflower bloomed at Vidae Falls.

He had started coming up here as a kid and he was going to stay as long as the Park Service would let him. If I had a vote, I'd pick someone like Bob to be the park superintendent. He'd take better care of the place than some bureaucrat.

* * *

Billy and I ran out of poles about the time we got across the road from park headquarters. Wes was not going to the shed for any more poles today. That was final. Billy rolled his eyes but offered no resistance. It was about ten past four, so in Wes's book it was way past time to head back to the maintenance office.

I told them I'd walk back. I needed to stop at headquarters and check my mail.

Wes gave me a wave of indifference and started up the truck. I looked both ways and jogged across the wet road to the headquarters parking lot. I flapped my rain gear before walking through the front door. No need to make a mess on the carpet. As I rushed in, I almost knocked over Elizabeth, the office manager.

She said, "Oh, I'm sorry, excuse me."

What? Was this my old friend Liz? She must not have recognized me. The last time I heard her saying anything about me she was calling me one of the dregs of the earth. Of course, that was when I was emptying office trash cans for a living. Now that I was slamming snow poles into the ground, maybe that made me all right in her eyes. Or maybe she was just caught by surprise and didn't know me from Adam.

Oh no, Dan Jenkins was at the mail window. *Prepare to be yelled at one more time, Sam.* Shouldn't be picking up mail on government time.

But when I walked up, Dan had a smile on his face. "How ya doing, Hunter?" He shook my hand. "Thanks for staying and helping with the snow poles. We all appreciate it." I said no problem. I'm not sure, but it looked like he had a bounce in his step as he walked out of the building.

I had mail—another letter from Sally. She must have gotten mine. I'd decided to just come clean about everything. I'd written that breaking my promise was the last thing I wanted to do, but there had been no choice. I was sorry it had hurt her so much. I'd told her how Dave had worked his magic and what had happened at the pump house. I'd said I was always willing to listen if she needed to talk, but I hoped she'd share what happened with someone at home. I told her I missed her and hoped she was well.

The rain had stopped, so I decided to walk back across the highway to where the rim road ends just below park headquarters. Lately my evening walks took me to the Castle Crest Wildflower Garden a hundred yards back up the rim road.

The wildflowers had long since finished blooming for the year. The explosion of purples and yellows and blues was over by the end of August. It was more like a glen than a garden now, and I liked that. A brook noisily skipped back and forth through the half-mile hemlock-lined trail. Tiny springs created miniature bogs and marshes. After the tourist season ended, I had the flower garden all to myself after work.

I'd usually take a stroll around the circular trail, looking at and listening to the water. Then I'd find a place to sit and wait to watch the animals. There were rabbits and squirrels and, occasionally, a marten. I swear I saw a red fox twice, but Ranger Bob, the former naturalist, said I must have been drinking at the time. My favorite was the small deer that would drink water at the far back of the garden, where springs trickled out of the rock slope.

This garden had been the last stop on the Crater Lake tour I'd given my father the week after Dave had left for the summer. Actually, Ranger Bob gave the tour and I tagged along, looking for opportunities to get in the conversation. Begging Bob to come along had been a genius-like move on my part. My dad happily interrogated him all day long and

Bob just as happily spewed out information in response. It was a match made in heaven.

After saying goodbye to Dave that Saturday morning, I had driven home for the rest of the weekend. My dad had tried not to look surprised when I asked him to come up for a day. Mom liked the idea right away and kind of nudged him into saying yes, although I think he would have anyway. I told him I'd even book an expert to join us so he could get the facts right from the source.

My dad arrived at 10:00 and Bob drove us to Rim Drive in his truck. I looked for opportunities to talk in paragraphs rather than in the two-word sentences I usually used with my father. We hit the park highlights—the best views of Wizard Island and the Pumice Desert, then we decided to go down Cleetwood Trail. We didn't have time to take the boat tour, but I thought my dad would like to see the lake up close.

On the hike down, Bob told the story of the Sally rescue. He told it like an old dime western with me in the role of Wild Bill Hickok. Yeah, your son held the litter on his back with one hand and, with the other hand, he dragged six or seven people up the trail behind him. Stuff like that. Bob gave me a wink. Smiling, my dad looked over at me and I just rolled my eyes.

"How is Sally?" Dad asked.

"She's feeling better, according to her boyfriend," I said.

"You haven't been in touch with her?" he asked.

Oh here we go. Our patented conversational style. *Okay, try, Sam.* "I got a letter from her after she got home." It was a pretty feeble effort. The man was a trained investigator. That wasn't what he meant and I knew it. I needed help. *Bob?*

Saint Ranger Bob jumped in and told Dad that Sally was a sweet girl and then recounted the complete Vidae Falls moss story. In the spirit of full disclosure, I had told Bob about the family communication issues while I was begging him to come along on this field trip. He agreed to come anyway.

We reached the boat dock without any other close calls. There wasn't much happening at the ticket shed, as the tourist season was over and they were only going to be open a couple more days. Steve Haswell wasn't there.

I suggested we eat lunch over at my favorite spot—the point where I watched the schools of salmon. We pulled out the sandwiches and drinks we had packed in our jacket pockets.

After we ate, Bob excused himself and headed to the port-o-potty leaving my dad and I to watch the Kokanee by ourselves. We watched a school of the tiny salmon swim by in silence for about a minute.

My dad turned to me. "You know, I wasn't trying to interrogate you back there. I'm just interested in what's going on with you. I'm supposed to be, I'm your father."

"I know, Dad."

He nodded and we both looked out at the water. Those stupid fish just kept swimming by. I told him about the time I watched a school for twenty minutes while I waited for the boat to Wizard Island. I told myself that I had to remember to try harder. I'd promised.

When Bob came back, I told them both about the trout Sally caught on Wizard Island. Things went better after that. Bob and my dad got along great and spent the rest of the day talking with little prompting from me. I finally relaxed. I didn't mind being with them. I didn't feel the pressure to have to talk much. Bob would bring me into the conversation at regular intervals to tell a story about the Crud or spreading lime or the pump house shifts. And Bob knew exactly what not to talk about—digging trenches, hamstring problems, bosses, etc.

We got back to the cabin late in the afternoon. We waved goodbye to Bob. I pointed out the nearby landmarks like the maintenance yard, Castle Crest, Munson Creek, and where a young bear kicked over a garbage can a couple nights in a row, trying to find dinner. Then we both knew it was time for him to go.

He turned to me. "Thanks for inviting me up. I really enjoyed it." He stuck out his hand in the motion a wild west gunfighter makes when he draws his gun. It surprised me. I smiled. "Me too," I said. He got in his yellow Chevy Luv truck, backed up, waved, and drove away.

At twilight in the wildflower garden, the mist turned into snowflakes and began to cover the ground. It had snowed off and on at the park over the last two weeks, but the snow hadn't stuck. Two young deer cautiously stepped out from the trees in the back of the garden. They stopped. Looked around. Hopped across the trail into the marsh, where they stopped again and waited. Listening in the snowfall.

You couldn't see it, but there was a pulsing, pounding feel of something furious coming: winter charging back into the mountains. It made me shiver.

I walked back to my cabin and opened Sally's letter. She said she had talked to her mother about what happened and that had helped. She said she wasn't mad anymore. Just terribly tired. Then came the regular stuff—what classes she was taking, the weather, how she missed the beauty of the park and was sorry she hadn't gotten to see more of the West Coast. But something was different. No mention of the future or phone calls or even Chris.

She ended by saying again that she was really, really sorry and hoped I understood.

A girl had gotten close, maybe it could happen again sometime.

*   *   *

Two days later, the first true storm of the season arrived to escort me out of the park for the last time. As I packed my car, I looked up and watched the angry waterfall of clouds boiling over the cliffs above the maintenance yard. Wind blew hard from behind the hemlocks. Mother Nature was in an impatient mood, anxious to blast away the memory of what had happened in her park during the summer. Heavy driving snow followed me to the entrance.

A tattered autumn still hung around on the other side of Fort Klamath as I drove through the tiny town. No storm clouds, just a light drizzle. The sun was showing through the clouds by the time I reached Klamath Lake. I drove about half the length of the lake, then decided to pull over to the side of the road and park in a gravel turnout. I got out of the car and took off the parka I'd put on for the snowstorm.

Klamath Lake still looked like dishwater. Hard to believe that most of this water had come from the crystal streams where I had spent the summer. I looked back up the lake toward the mountains, to where I thought the rim might be. I couldn't see anything through the cloud walls. I kept staring like I could.

Cars and trucks whizzed by on Highway 97. It was about sixty degrees and the sun was taking command in the Klamath Basin. I got back in my car and started the engine. I sat there waiting for a string of tractor trailers loaded with hulking logs to pass. Funny how, down here, it was a perfect fall day, but forty minutes away at Crater Lake, a blizzard was on a rampage. *Watch out for those trucks, Sam. Don't want to be a newspaper headline*: Heroic Crater Lake Ditch Digger Killed By 10-Ton Log On Way Home, Park Service Mourns. I gunned my tiny Volkswagen. *Wait, Sam. Don't be in a rush. It's not like you know where you're going next.*